Praise for Jennifer Snow

"Readers will enjoy the mix of sexy love scenes, tense missions, and amiable banter. This entertaining introduction to Wild River will encourage fans of small-town contemporaries to follow the series."
—*Publishers Weekly* on *An Alaskan Christmas*

"*An Alaskan Christmas* is heartwarming, romantic, and utterly enjoyable."
—Melissa Foster, *New York Times* bestselling author

"Prepare to have your heartstrings tugged! Pure Christmas delight."
—Lori Wilde, *New York Times* bestselling author, on *An Alaskan Christmas*

"An exciting contemporary series debut with a wildly unique Alaskan setting."
—*Kirkus Reviews* on *An Alaskan Christmas*

"Jennifer Snow is one clever writer."
—*RT Book Reviews*

"Never too late to join the growing ranks of Jennifer Snow fans."
—*Fresh Fiction*

Four Brides

mira

mira™

Recycling programs
for this product may
not exist in your area.

ISBN-13: 978-0-7783-6943-1

Four Brides

Mira
22 Adelaide St. West, 40th Floor
Toronto, Ontario M5H 4E3, Canada
www.Harlequin.com

Printed in U.S.A.

CONTENTS

Also available from Debbie Macomber and MIRA

Midnight Sons

THREE BRIDES,
NO GROOM

Debbie Macomber

In memory of my mother, Connie Adler,
who gave me life, love and taught me to laugh,
and Marie Macomber, who shared her wisdom
and her son.

Prologue

The fountain located in the center of Queen Anne University in Seattle was thought to be the very heart of the private college. It was here, in the dead of night, where young lovers with pounding eager hearts rendezvoused. It was here that words of love were whispered between urgent kisses, where promises were made and, sadly, promises were broken. Its shadow had entertained laughter and joy, sorrow and tears.

The fountain had borne witness to it all.

It was to this fountain that three women came that summer afternoon, each arriving from a different direction, each burdened with memories from fifteen years past.

The first to arrive was Gretchen Wise. Miss Popularity, the class president, beautiful and smart, too. Unfortunately not smart enough to recognize the kind of man Roger Lockheart was before she accepted his engagement ring.

The second was Carol Furness, the head cheer-leader, filled with energy, enthusiasm, joy and pur-pose. She'd built her future around a football hero, only to learn Eddie Shapiro was anything but.

And lastly Maddie Coolidge, the class "bad girl," who'd played a tricky game of looking for love and, like so many before her, searched in all the wrong places. Who would have believed that math profes-sor John Theda would steal far more than her heart?

The fountain welcomed them all.

Gretchen Wise walked slowly toward the old ce-ment fountain and smiled as the memories swirled around her the way water rushed around a rock in a swift stream.

She could almost hear the echo of laughter from those long-ago years. How happy she'd been back then: young, carefree, excited and so very much in love—with the wrong man. Fifteen years earlier she'd barely been able to appreciate her own gradu-ation, not with her head full of wedding plans and Roger.

Roger Lockheart, the love of her life. The man of her dreams.

The rat.

She thought about him now and again, fleetingly and with a twinge of sadness. Sometimes she enter-tained thoughts of all the might-have-beens. Only natural, she concluded.

How handsome her old college sweetheart had been, how confident, his future on a fast track to success. He'd been scheduled to take his bar exam two weeks before their society wedding, and had been guaranteed a position in his father's high-powered law firm.

The day Roger had presented her with an engagement ring had been one of the happiest in her young life, the day she'd removed it from her finger one of the saddest.

Many an afternoon had been spent soaking up the sunshine at the beautiful old fountain. Students had cooled off in the cold spray or splashed barefoot in the ankle-deep water. The fountain was as old as the university itself. Every brochure the college had produced in its distinguished one-hundred-year history had pictured students gathered around the fountain socializing and studying.

Sitting on the cold concrete rim now, Gretchen swung her gaze to the nearby law school. The two-story redbrick building with the wide flight of stairs leading up to the double doors remained much the same. The ivy had been clipped back, and the lawn on the side of the building had been replaced with a concrete patio.

She had spent many an idle afternoon sitting in this very spot, anticipating Roger's arrival, never guessing where he'd actually been.

It had been a warm afternoon like this one when she'd first talked to Josh Morrow. Heedless of rules, Josh had ridden his Harley-Davidson motorcycle down the narrow pathway and attempted to pick her up. The man lacked nothing if not audacity. It was one of the rare times she'd seen him without some blond bimbo sitting behind him, clinging to his waist. More often than not it had been Didi Wilson. When Roger had seen Josh flirting with Gretchen, he'd been livid. As if she'd ever given Roger reason to be jealous! Maybe she should have.

Gretchen nearly laughed out loud at the memory. Josh Morrow had enjoyed life on the edge. He drank, swore and gambled on a conservative college campus that frowned upon all three. He was said to live on beer and cigarettes. He challenged every teacher unfortunate enough to have him in class, fought the establishment and generally raised cain. Josh had grabbed life by the throat and courted danger, and he'd fascinated her.

Everything was different, and yet nothing had changed. Carol Furness strolled across the lush green grass toward the fountain. Oh, my, had it really been fifteen years? It didn't seem possible, and in many ways it felt like yesterday.

Carol had been the envy of every girl in class. Shortly after Christmas her senior year, she'd become engaged to Eddie Shapiro. Eddie was now a football legend at Queen Anne. A legend in Carol's mind, too, but for other reasons. Their romance was a classic: the football hero and the head cheerleader. Fifteen years ago she had been athletic, bright and talented. She liked to believe she still was.

No thanks to Eddie. The worm.

And yet she had much to thank Eddie for. If he

hadn't dumped her, she might never have gotten to know Clark Rusbach. The class brain, a wizard with computers, a genius. Clark was technically too cute to be classified as a geek, although Eddie had often referred to him as one. In retrospect it was easy to recognize that Eddie had been jealous of Clark.

Clark knew a lot about computers, but next to nothing about women. Carol had admired him from afar, had gone out of her way to be friendly in the few classes they'd shared, and tried to tell him, without upsetting Eddie, that she admired him.

The dividends of her kindness had been rich indeed, if only she'd been smart enough to recognize what she'd had.

Maddie Coolidge wondered if anyone would recognize her as she sauntered across the campus in the direction of the fountain. She'd changed. The outlandish attention-seeking bad girl of her youth was no more. The girl she'd been had died a painful death, the victim of a costly, but worthwhile, lesson.

With the fountain in sight, her steps slowed. It had been at this fountain fifteen years earlier that she'd last seen John Theda.

The cheat.

A number of other choice descriptions filled her mind, but she pushed them aside, refusing to dwell on her former mathematics professor. He'd courted her, wooed her with words and deeds—all on the sly, of course, lest word escape that he'd fallen for a student. John had pledged his love and asked her to be his wife. She had accepted, her joy exploding. What fun it had been to pretend with him, to act as if there was nothing romantic between them.

While she might have fooled everyone else, Brent Holliday had known. Who or what had allowed her secret to escape, Maddie never learned. The preacher's son seemed to think a few well-chosen words would set her on the straight and narrow path, but he had been wrong. But then, she'd had a few difficult lessons to learn in those days. Lessons that hadn't come easy.

"Gretchen?"

At the sound of her name, Gretchen turned and was greeted by a familiar face. Someone from her graduating class. She struggled to dredge up a name to go with the face.

"It's Carol. Carol Furness."

"Carol." Gretchen couldn't believe she'd stumbled on a sorority sister here at the fountain an hour before the formal reunion festivities were scheduled to start. They hugged each other fiercely.

"I wondered if that was you," Carol said, sitting down next to Gretchen on the edge of the fountain.

"Have I changed so much?" Gretchen asked. "Lie, if you have to."

Carol responded with a good-natured laugh, her blue eyes twinkling. "Not at all. You look the same as you did the day we graduated. I would have known you anywhere. The years have been good to you."

"Ditto for you, Carol." Gretchen smiled. "I couldn't resist coming down and walking around the campus."

"Me either," Carol admitted as she scanned the grounds. "I haven't been back in all these years."

"Nor have I." But Gretchen doubted that the reasons for her absence were the same as her old sorority sister's.

"Are you attending the dinner and the dance later?"

The day of the reunion was here, and Gretchen had yet to make up her mind. "The dinner definitely, but I don't know if I can drag my husband to the dance."

"The same with me," Carol said. "My husband's a wonderful dancer, but he refuses to believe it."

"Gretchen? Carol?" The voice belonged to a tall striking auburn-haired woman approaching from the left.

Gretchen hadn't a clue who it was, and she looked at Carol for help. Carol just shook her head.

The redhead grinned. "Not more than two minutes ago I wondered if anyone would recognize me. I've changed, I know. It's me, Maddie Coolidge."

"Maddie?" Gretchen couldn't believe it. The Maddie Coolidge she remembered was nothing like the well-groomed woman who stood before her now. Maddie had been outlandish in appearance, as well as in word and deed. Stubborn and defiant, a nonconformist. Yet beneath all the bravado Maddie had a heart of gold.

Gretchen recalled that Maddie had struck up a

close "friendship" with John Theda, a math professor. It was supposed to have been a secret, but everyone knew the two were secretly engaged. The romance had caused quite a stir about campus, but then "controversy" was Maddie's middle name.

"You look wonderful," Carol said, standing up and hugging Maddie. Gretchen did likewise, and then all three sat down, with Gretchen in the middle.

"I'm pleased someone else thought to stop off at the fountain," Maddie said.

"It brings back memories, doesn't it?" Carol murmured thoughtfully.

The three were silent for several moments. Caught up in the wonder of years past, Gretchen suspected.

"I was hoping to get a chance to talk to you, Carol," Maddie said excitedly. "I bet you've had a fabulous fifteen years. I don't pay much attention to professional sports, but whenever I hear anything about football, I keep my ear open for news of Eddie."

"Eddie Shapiro?" Carol asked on a disdainful note. "The guy's a worm."

Maddie looked shocked. "You were engaged to him, weren't you?"

"Yeah, but he dropped me like a hot potato once he was picked up by the pros." Carol folded her arms and crossed her legs. Her foot swayed so hard she created a draft. "Let's change the subject, shall we?"

"Of course," Maddie said apologetically.

A short awkward silence followed while Gretchen absorbed the information. Like Maddie, she'd assumed Carol and Eddie had married. "What about you, Maddie? Being a professor's wife certainly appears to agree with you."

Instant hot color blazed in Maddie's cheeks, and her eyes snapped with fire. "I never married John Theda. The man's a cheat."

"Weren't you two engaged?"

"Oh, yes, until John got what he wanted, and it's not what you think. I suspect it was one of the shortest engagements on record."

"What about you, Gretchen?" Carol asked, quickly changing the subject once again. "How many children do you and Roger have?"

"Roger Lockheart?" Gretchen said. "I haven't seen that rat in years."

Gretchen watched as her two college friends exchanged glances. It seemed they were as shocked by her news as she was by theirs.

"Well, it appears we have a lot more to discuss than we realized," Gretchen said. And to think she'd worried herself sick about this silly reunion. She leaned back on her hands and smiled softly. "If I'm hearing you correctly, you were both engaged and then dumped."

They nodded.

"Me too," Gretchen confessed. "So there we were—three brides and no groom. Who would've believed it?"

"I can't believe you didn't marry Roger," Maddie whispered, apparently having trouble taking it all in. "He was always so...so perfect."

"I used to think he was wonderful," Carol added.

"At one time I thought so, too," Gretchen admitted.

"What happened?" Carol asked. "From what I remember, you and Roger were less than a month away from your wedding."

"Yup."

"If you tell your story, I'll tell you what happened with John," Maddie promised. "I'd like you to know."

Carol grinned. "And I'll spill my guts about Eddie Shapiro."

Gretchen laughed. "Hell hath no fury like a woman scorned."

"You don't know the half of it," Carol said.

"I do—" Maddie smoothed her hand down her skirt "—and you'll get the whole story from me. It's time someone knew exactly what kind of person John really is." She glanced at Gretchen. "You go first, then Carol and then me. I can't think of a better way to spend the afternoon."

Gretchen's Story

One

This was supposed to be one of the happiest days of Gretchen's life. The day was memorable, all right, but it would be forever marked as a day of pain and betrayal. Emotion clawed at her throat, and she battled tears. She wanted her mother, but her parents had already left the campus. They'd driven up to Seattle from San Francisco to attend her college graduation and were taking a few extra days to visit Victoria, British Columbia, before returning home and making the final arrangements for her wedding to Roger, and she didn't want to bother them on their brief vacation.

Except Gretchen was beginning to doubt that there would be a wedding.

She stood at the far end of the sweeping veranda of her sorority house, out of view of her friends. Most were excitedly loading up their cars with another year's accumulation of treasures. She could hear their tearful farewells, their promises to keep in touch.

Promises.

She held her stomach and raised her chin in an effort to forestall the brewing emotion. Her long blond hair cascaded down the middle of her back. Roger loved her hair long, enjoyed playing with it, brushing it, burying his face in it.

"Sweetpea?" The sound of Roger's contrite voice came from behind her.

She'd always hated his pet name for her, but no amount of protest could persuade him to come up with another.

Standing directly behind her, he cupped her shoulders and nuzzled her neck. "Let's talk about this, all right?"

"Talk?" Gretchen asked with a short abrupt laugh. As far as she was concerned they had nothing to discuss.

"You've got to know Didi doesn't mean anything to me." Now his hands were in her hair, lifting the thick tresses to his face. He wove his fingers into it and brushed his lips across her crown.

Gretchen's eyes slammed shut at the sharp pain.

"It was stupid," Roger continued. "I want to throw up every time I think about how incredibly stupid I was. My only excuse is that I was drunk."

"You cheated on me with another woman, and I'm supposed to forget it ever happened because you were drunk?"

His hands returned to her shoulders and squeezed. "Didi's always had the hots for me. You said so yourself, remember? I...I wasn't thinking straight.

I was with the guys, celebrating, drinking, and the next thing I knew, Didi was coming on to me. She wouldn't take no for an answer. Ask anyone. She was all over me and...you know how those fraternity parties can get."

Gretchen's stomach clenched. "Don't tell me any more. I don't want to hear it."

"But I have to tell you. I need to. This is going to stand between us unless you know it all. You've got to believe me, Gretchen, I'm as sick about what happened as you are."

She said nothing, too numb to argue.

"Didi knows we're engaged, but that didn't stop her. I told her again and again that it was you I loved, but she wouldn't listen. The next thing I knew she'd stuck her hands inside my clothes."

"In front of everyone?" Gretchen cried in disbelief.

He hesitated, and when he spoke, his voice was barely audible. "We...we were in a closet."

"A closet?" Gretchen nearly choked on the word.

"She was feeling me up, and, Sweetpea, I'm so very sorry, but I'm only human. I was...excited, and then she had her mouth on me and was saying things like she bet my uptown girl never did anything like this for me and—"

"I don't want to hear any more," Gretchen said again, more forcefully this time.

"But it's true," Roger whispered. "You insisted on waiting until we were married to make love, and

I've respected your wishes. But I don't think you appreciate what sexual frustration can do to a guy."

"In other words this is all my fault."

"No, no. If anyone's to blame, it's Didi. When I woke up this morning, I was sick to my stomach, knowing what I'd done. I couldn't be sorrier. Say you'll forgive me. I'm begging you, Sweetpea. We can't let someone like Didi come between us. If you do something foolish, you'll be doing exactly what she wants. The only reason she came on to me was to hurt you."

"And you let her."

He paused. "Let's put this behind us, all right? Mom's looking forward to you spending the next few days with her. All she can talk about is the wedding plans, and that's exactly what you need to help take your mind off my unfortunate slip."

So that was how he thought of infidelity, as an unfortunate slip.

"What do you say, Sweetpea?"

She pressed her fingertips to her temple. "I need time to think."

"What's there to think about? I told you everything. This isn't easy for me, you know. I just bet Didi took delight in letting you know what happened. She's just being nasty, looking to ruin both our lives. You're not going to let her, are you?" The soft pleading quality was back, the desperation to make matters right, as if that were possible now.

"What did you expect would happen when you

went into a closet with Didi Wilson?" she demanded, whirling to face him.

His bloodshot eyes revealed his shock at being confronted. "I...I was drunk."

"Not too drunk apparently." If he expected her to sweep his indiscretion under the proverbial carpet, she couldn't do it, *wouldn't* do it. Not without giving the matter a great deal of thought.

"The wedding's less than a month away," he protested.

He didn't need to tell her the date of her own wedding. "Are you saying it's too late to change our plans?"

"You wouldn't! Baby, please, don't do anything stupid."

"Like you did?"

He let her words soak in before saying, "Two stupid acts don't make a right."

It amazed Gretchen how desperately she wanted to forget what Didi had taken such pleasure in telling her. The other woman's timing didn't escape Gretchen's notice, either. While she'd been escorting her parents around Seattle's tourist attractions, her fiancé had been doing who knew what with another woman.

As if that wasn't bad enough, Didi had hit her with the ugly details shortly after the graduation ceremony. Instead of getting to enjoy the sense of exhilaration and accomplishment she'd felt on receiving her diploma, Gretchen had seen her world fall apart when Didi cornered her on the front steps of the sorority house shortly after her parents had left for Canada and delivered her news.

"Mom's waiting," Roger pressed now, breaking into her thoughts.

"Then she'll just have to wait. I told you, I need time to sort everything out." Gretchen knew that his mother was not the patient sort. Stella Lockheart was a forceful woman who generally got what she wanted. Both Roger and his father catered to her wishes rather than risk dealing with one of her explosive outbursts.

Gretchen could tell by the way Roger's breathing altered that he wasn't pleased with her decision. He'd been calm and in control, at his persuasive best. Now he was impatient and frustrated. Fine, so be it. She wasn't going to let him pressure her, nor would she be rushed because he was afraid of a confrontation with his mother. This was *her* life, and she was determined to take a long hard look before making a decision about the future.

"OK, if that's what you want," Roger said shortly. "I'll tell Mom to go on ahead without you."

She nodded.

He lingered a moment longer, his gaze boring into hers. "There isn't any reason to tell Mom about what happened, is there?"

Gretchen almost felt sorry for him. "Why would I want to humiliate myself even further?" she asked.

He was visibly relieved as he turned and hurried toward the parking lot. As Gretchen watched him go, the knot in the pit of her stomach tightened. Needing to do something, anything other than stand there on the veranda, she moved down the steps and began walking. She soon found herself by the fountain, and with a heavy heart, she lowered herself onto the concrete rim. The urge to bury her face in her hands and weep was nearly overwhelming, but she had too much pride to publicly display her pain.

Most of the activity around the school had stopped. Graduation was over, and the majority of students had already left the campus. She was grateful for the quiet, a rarity at the university. She needed to mull over what she'd learned, to assimilate what Didi had told her, followed by Roger's weak justifications.

Every time she tried to make sense of the cold ugly facts of his infidelity, distance herself from them, she stumbled over the pain.

Again and again, Roger had told her how much he loved her, how she would be the perfect wife for him. His insistence caused her to wonder if he was mouthing his mother's sentiments, not his own. A man who truly loved her wouldn't step into a closet with Didi Wilson. But at the same time, Roger was full of regret. Despite her own pain, she could sense his. He was genuinely sorry. She wanted, *needed,* to believe that.

One thing he'd said rang true. Didi had never made a secret of how attractive she found Roger. Nor had she bothered to disguise her dislike for Gretchen. It was probably that dislike that had prompted Didi to confront her.

Didi's neck had been covered with hickeys so livid that no amount of makeup could fully hide them. She'd boldly walked up to Gretchen, looked her in the eyes, smiled and then casually asked her if she knew what Roger had been doing the night before. At Gretchen's stunned silence, Didi had crudely asked Gretchen if she thought she was woman enough to satisfy Roger's healthy sexual appetite. The question insinuated that she wasn't and never would be.

The roar of an engine shattered the peace. Gretchen glanced up to see Josh Morrow speed across the campus parking lot on his Harley, a plume of dark exhaust in his wake. He'd been cited by campus security a dozen times, she'd heard, for driving above the speed limit, but it hadn't fazed him.

Josh was a loner, a known troublemaker, a rebel. She'd spoken to him once months earlier, and Roger had been furious with her. In the weeks since, she'd avoided Josh, but that hadn't stopped her from noticing him. He stood apart from everyone, watching, studying. The outsider, looking in. He hadn't sought her out again, and she was grateful. She supposed it was natural to feel a certain attraction toward Josh. She suspected a lot of the women at Queen Anne did. Maybe it was the black leather and the motorcycle, the sense that the love of a good woman would tame him.

Now her gaze must have lingered on him a second longer than was prudent, for he eased his huge bike to a stop, placed his feet on the road to maintain his balance and stared at her. After what seemed an eternity, he revved the engine, then roared over the cement curb and onto the narrow walkway, directly toward her.

Gretchen stood, her heart in her throat. The last thing she wanted was company.

He pulled to a stop right in front of her. Lifting the helmet from his head, he studied her for a moment and then asked with surprising gentleness, "Gretchen, what happened?"

She stiffened, shocked that he had read her so easily. "Nothing."

His smile was decidedly off center. "You should never lie, not when you do such a poor job of it."

She lowered her gaze and rubbed her palms together. "It's something I'd rather not discuss."

He stepped off the Harley and lowered the kickstand. "Fair enough."

His size was intimidating. He was at least six-two, maybe even six-three, almost dwarfing her five foot eight. She crossed her arms over her chest, wondering at his intentions. As if he didn't have a care in the world, he leaned over the fountain, scooped up a handful of water and drenched his face.

He glanced toward her and chuckled, the sound low and teasing. "Don't worry, I won't bite."

"I'm not worried," she lied.

His soft snicker told her she hadn't convinced him. "I don't sacrifice virgins, either."

"I suggest you don't start now. I'd crawl off the altar."

He laughed, but this time the sound was rich and

deep. Ignoring her, he turned his face toward the sky, and his features glistened as the water dripped from his face. "Where's lover boy this afternoon?" he asked.

His question caught her off guard. From his tone, it was clear that Josh knew about Roger and Didi. How many others did? Her face filled with a rush of hot embarrassed color.

"Who told you?" she asked, her voice low and trembling despite her effort to remain cool and calm. Between Didi and Roger's so-called friends, the news must be everywhere by now.

"Is it important?" he asked. His words were soft, quiet, as if he feared saying them would increase her pain.

"No, I guess it isn't." Some students thought of Gretchen as privileged. While it was true her family had considerable wealth, when serving as the student-body president she'd crossed swords with any number who willingly tossed her background in her face. Her hard work as a communicator and volunteer, and her fervor for honesty and justice, often won them over. Until recently she preferred to think of her friends as many and her enemies as few. Now she wasn't so sure.

Josh's gaze turned narrow and assessing, which increased her embarrassment tenfold. She inhaled a quivering breath.

"Roger's a first-class fool," Josh said at last. "He deserves to have his teeth kicked in."

While in theory she agreed with him—she wanted

to see Roger suffer for what he'd done—her sensibilities didn't lean toward violence. Roger had allowed the blame to ricochet from Didi to Gretchen and then back to Didi. Gretchen wanted to scream and demand that Roger accept responsibility for his own actions. To own up to what he'd done, instead of listing excuses meant to absolve him of any guilt.

"Gretchen!"

As if her thoughts had conjured him up, Roger was striding across the lawn toward the fountain. "What the hell are you doing here, Morrow?" he asked, arriving breathless, his chest heaving.

When Josh didn't immediately answer, Roger faced Gretchen. "Is he pestering you?"

"Of course not," she replied, angered by both the question and the insinuation.

"I told you to stay away from Gretchen," Roger snarled at Josh. As though she needed his protection, he reached out and grabbed hold of her arm.

"I suggest you let go of her," Josh said, his voice deceptively calm.

Roger ignored him. "Come on, Gretchen, let's get out of here."

She jerked her arm free of his grasp and met his look squarely. "I haven't finished thinking about you and me yet."

Anger flared in Roger's dark eyes. "What's Morrow doing here?"

"What do you care?" Josh asked, his words a challenge.

Roger glared at Josh and seemed to be weighing the odds of engaging in a fistfight, then decided against it. Wisely, she thought.

"Gretchen, I think you'd better come with me," he said, calmer this time.

"I'm not ready to leave yet." She wasn't looking to defy Roger, but she needed time to deal with a multitude of pressing questions. Decisions had to be made, the consequences of which she would have to live with for the rest of her life.

Again Roger's eyes flared with anger.

"You heard the lady," Josh inserted smoothly, with that cocky grin of his.

Gretchen whirled on him. "I can do my own talking, thank you."

"Fine." Josh raised his right hand in a mocking gesture of peace.

Tight-lipped, Roger said, "Either you get out of here, Morrow, or I'm calling security. Your kind isn't welcome around here. Why don't you go visit your daddy in prison? Have a good look around, since that's where you're headed yourself."

Josh looked unconcerned, which only served to anger Roger more. But Gretchen noticed the vein in Josh's temple throb and knew Roger's words had affected him.

"You should have been expelled long ago," Roger added, then doubled up his fist and took a wild swing at Josh, who didn't so much as blink when the punch went wide.

"Maybe Dean Williams is looking for a valid excuse to be rid of me," Josh suggested casually. "What he really needs is a charge that'll stick. How about assault?" As he spoke, his fist shot out and exploded against Roger's nose.

Stunned, Roger stumbled backward. His hand flew to his face, and blood oozed between his fingers. "I'm bleeding!" he cried in horror. "Now you've done it, Morrow," he threatened. "You're finished at this school. I'll make sure of that."

"I can't tell you how worried I am." Josh reached for his helmet and climbed aboard his motorcycle. He started the engine and then, as though in afterthought, he turned and looked at Gretchen. His eyes locked with hers as he slowly extended his arm to her.

She hesitated, unsure what to do.

"Go with him and the engagement is off," Roger threatened.

It was all the incentive she needed. She slipped the diamond ring off her finger and tossed it to Roger, then leaped onto the motorcycle behind Josh.

He revved the engine, spewing exhaust at Roger, then raced off in the direction of the sun.

Two

Gretchen had never ridden on a motorcycle before. She wrapped her arms tightly around Josh's waist as they headed down the narrow asphalt pathway. When he changed gears, she could hear Roger shouting curses after them. Closing her eyes, she savored the look of shock and dismay on Roger's face when she'd returned his ring and leaped onto the back of the Harley with Josh. In retrospect, her actions had been foolhardy, but also purely instinctual. As the wind whipped her hair around her face, she smiled. This one small act of rebellion had cheered her considerably.

They sped across the school parking lot toward the busy four-lane street that bordered the university. Gretchen didn't have a clue where Josh was taking her, and at the moment she didn't care. She angled her face into the wind, letting it dry the tears from her cheeks. For the first time since Didi had confronted her, the oppressive tightness surrounding her heart lessened.

Josh eased to a stop in a restaurant parking lot several blocks from the university. He twisted in the seat to look at her, keeping the huge bike balanced between his legs.

"Where do you want me to take you?" he asked.

"Where?" she repeated, not knowing how to answer him. It would have suited her to ride off into the sunset and forget everything. Forget Didi. Forget Roger and the ugly scene by the fountain. Forget that she had less than fifty dollars cash on her and nowhere to go.

"To the airport?" Josh suggested.

"I… Roger's mother has my ticket. I'd originally planned to spend a week with her putting the finishing touches on our wedding plans."

Josh glared at her. "You're not going to ask for that creep's ring back, are you?"

"No." And she meant it. Despite all the time and energy—and emotion—that had gone into the wedding plans, she could not accept what he'd done. One part of her had wanted to look past his infidelity and pretend everything would eventually be all right. But the other part knew their relationship would never be the same again. If Roger was unfaithful before they were married, she could never trust him after the wedding. He was nowhere near ready to be a husband.

"Good," Josh said. "You deserve better."

"Could you take me to Mary Ann Seawright's?" she asked. Mary Ann was a friend who lived nearby. Gretchen could stay there until her parents returned from British Columbia. Of course, she could always contact Mrs. Lockheart about her airline ticket, but she preferred not to. She feared Roger's mother would attempt to change her mind, and Gretchen lacked the emotional energy to lock horns with the woman. If anyone was forced to deal with her, it should be Roger. Gretchen preferred to sever all ties.

"Does Roger know Mary Ann?" Josh asked.

"Yes. She goes out with his friend Bill Beckett. The four of us often double-dated." Of course, she realized, that meant Roger would soon know exactly where she'd gone.

"Where's home?" Josh asked next.

She bit her lower lip. Home had never seemed so far away. "San Francisco, but my parents are on vacation. They won't be back for several days." Not until then did she realize she had no means of getting home, anyway. Unlike so many other parents, hers had never chosen to give her an all-purpose credit card, and she had run her bank balance down to nearly nothing in preparation for setting up a new joint account with Roger.

That cocky half grin of Josh's slid into place. "As it happens, I'm headed in that direction. You can ride along with me, if you want. I'll drop you off in Frisco and continue on my way." He paused as if to read her reaction to his offer. "Fact is, I'd welcome the company."

Gretchen wasn't sure how to answer. While it was true that he was offering her a way out of a tricky situation, she didn't really know Josh Morrow. His reputation would be enough to turn her mother's hair prematurely white.

His eyes glinted with challenge, and it seemed he was waiting for her to reject his generosity.

"I appreciate it, but…" She stalled, unsure and a little afraid.

"But?"

"I don't have much cash with me. Fifty dollars at the most, although I do have a gasoline credit card."

"Hey, we're in fat city," Josh teased. "I've only got a little more than a hundred bucks myself."

She grinned. "OK, I accept." She'd never done anything more impulsive in her life. She might not know Josh very well, but she trusted him. Of course, she'd also trusted Roger. But she was her own woman, and despite the bad-boy tag Josh wore like a badge of honor, she would rather ride home with him on the back of a Harley than deal with Roger, or his family, ever again.

"I'm sure my father would be more than happy to reimburse you for any expenses," she said.

"We'll discuss that later. What will you need to take with you?"

"Not much," she promised, knowing he wouldn't have room for more than the essentials.

Once he checked to be sure Roger was nowhere in sight, Josh dropped her off at the sorority house with a promise to return within the hour.

Mrs. Vance, the housemother, regarded her anxiously when Gretchen walked in the front door.

"Thank goodness you're back," the middle-aged

woman said with a heavy sigh. "Roger Lockheart was here no more than five minutes ago, looking for you. He's such a nice young man, and he's worried sick about you taking off with Josh Morrow that way. I never did trust a man on a motorcycle."

Gretchen bit her tongue to keep from saying that she trusted Josh far more than she did Roger. It wouldn't do any good to argue, and she didn't have time to waste.

"Give Roger a call, why don't you?" Mrs. Vance called as Gretchen raced up the stairs. "I'm sure it's nothing more than a lovers' spat."

Ignoring the suggestion, Gretchen hurried to her room, where her two large suitcases rested undisturbed. She quickly sorted through what she'd packed, scooped up what she truly needed and stuffed it into a small tote bag. Then she sat on the edge of the bed, went through her purse and counted her cash. Fifty-five dollars. Afraid that if she lingered much longer Roger would return, she raced down the stairs, pulling out her cell phone on the way.

Luckily Mary Ann was home. "I need you to do something for me," Gretchen said without preamble.

Her longtime friend must have heard the urgency in her voice. "Of course. What do you need?"

"I'm leaving my suitcases with Mrs. Vance. Could you come and get them for me?"

"Uh, sure, but why in heaven's name do you need me to—"

"I don't have time to explain now," Gretchen broke in. "I've broken my engagement to Roger."

Mary Ann gasped. "Gretchen, for the love of heaven, what happened?"

"I'll call and tell you everything once I'm home."

"Home? But how are you going to get to San Francisco?"

Gretchen heard the unmistakable roar of Josh's Harley outside. "I can't tell you now. I'll phone soon, I promise."

"But…but…"

Gretchen severed the connection. She reached for her purse and the tote bag, and discovered Mrs. Vance standing in front of the living-room window. The woman was holding the curtain to one side and glaring, her mouth twisted in disapproval.

"I wonder what that Morrow boy is doing here?" she muttered.

"He's here for me," Gretchen announced, enjoying the pure shock value of the statement.

The housemother gasped and swiveled to stare at her. "But you—"

Gretchen interrupted her. "I'm going with him." Until that moment, she hadn't realized how much she longed for her home and her family. "Goodbye, Mrs. Vance."

"Gretchen… Gretchen, I must insist—"

"I'll be fine, don't worry." She raced out the front door and bounded down the steps. Josh handed her a second helmet, and while she placed it on her head and fastened the strap, he tucked the tote bag into one of the leather bags draped over the back of the bike. He climbed on, and she positioned herself behind him.

Before they roared away, Gretchen turned back to find Mrs. Vance standing on the porch, her fingertips to her mouth as if she wasn't sure what she should do.

Gretchen, however, had never been more confident. Only a few hours earlier her heart had been breaking. Now, on the back of Josh Morrow's Harley, with the wind in her face and her arms securely wrapped around his muscular torso, she was free. Truly free.

Unfortunately, the feeling didn't last. Before long, questions and doubts were buzzing through her head like mosquitoes over a stagnant pond. The wedding invitations had been engraved, and her wedding dress ordered from an exclusive boutique. Her parents had booked the ballroom of a five-star hotel for the reception. All that money and effort, all the planning and dreaming, had been wasted. Her face burned with humiliation, knowing she was the one who would have to deal with the cancellations. But what was the use in dwelling on the negative? The only important thing was that she couldn't marry Roger.

After some time on the road, the deafening sound of the Harley vibrating in her ears, she shifted on the seat, both physically and mentally miserable. What had seemed daring and exciting a few hours earlier appeared exceedingly foolish now. Her back ached from holding herself upright and not leaning against Josh. Her legs felt as if they were locked into position, and she was certain her calves would soon cramp up on her. To top everything off, Josh apparently had the bladder of a camel.

When at last he did stop, she was afraid he would need to pry her off the bike with a crowbar. She looked around and realized they were at the ocean. Huge rolling waves crashed against the shore, then lovingly stroked a frothy trail across the sand. Large gray-and-white gulls circled overhead, and the scent of the sea lingered in the moist air. The sun was a brilliant orange disk on the horizon, ready to slip out of sight. Already dusk was settling in.

"Where are we?" she asked, easing first one leg and then the other away from the motorcycle. Josh lent her a hand, which she gratefully accepted.

"Cannon Beach, Oregon," he replied.

Vaguely she recalled crossing the Columbia River at Astoria. She'd actually kept her eyes closed most of the time, needing to think. At this rate, she should be home within two days, three at the most.

With his hands braced on his hips, Josh surveyed the sky. "I don't think it'll rain." He left her and walked toward the beach. She looked longingly at the public rest room but followed him, wanting to know where he intended to spend the night. It went without saying that they wouldn't be sharing a room.

Her shoes quickly filled with sand, and she found keeping pace with him difficult.

"We'll bed down here for the night," he announced.

"Here?" she asked, looking around. All she saw was barren sand. "The beach?"

"Do you have any better ideas?"

She glanced over her shoulder at the long row of oceanfront hotels.

"For seventy-five bucks you'll get a room the size of a refrigerator," he said, his gaze trained on the ocean.

She squared her shoulders. "Well, then, the beach it is."

He grinned as if to say he admired her adventurous spirit. "There's a shower in the public rest room, if you want to take one."

Gretchen did. She was afraid to look in a mirror, certain there must be bugs glued to her teeth. Her clothes felt plastered to her body.

She took what she needed from the saddlebag—a towel, washcloth and her cosmetic case—and headed for the rest room. It smelled of urine and ocean, but looked clean enough. The shower stall, minus the curtain, was in one corner. She stripped off her clothes and stood under the spray. Despite the lukewarm temperature, it felt luxurious.

As she turned her face into the water, the ache returned to the pit of her stomach. She leaned against the back of the open stall and cradled her middle. That morning she'd awakened thinking all was right with the world. She had her business degree and within weeks would be wed to Roger. And now, in the space of a few hours, her reality had changed completely.

When the water turned from lukewarm to chilly, she reached for the towel. Once she was dressed, she felt better. It was when she combed out her long blond hair in front of the metal mirror that she made the decision. She stared at her distorted reflection, the comb halfway down the side of her head.

She had only herself to please now, not Roger. Her fingers trembled as she dug through her cosmetic bag until she found a small pair of scissors. Seizing the pale tresses, she snipped at the sides with erratic, disjointed motions. She hacked and cut until the long strands of hair lay at her feet like discarded remnants of spun gold. Despite the distorted reflection, she knew she'd brutalized her once lovely hair. Breathing hard, she waited several minutes before she gathered up the courage to go back outside.

By the time she left the rest room, the sun had completely set. A full moon cast a golden glow across the beach. Josh had spread out a blanket and lit a small driftwood fire, and was now working his pocket knife against a stick, whittling it to a point. He glanced up as she approached. He said nothing about her mutilated hair.

"There's a grocery store not far from here," he said. "I got us wieners and buns."

Gretchen nodded, then self-consciously sat down on the end of a log and started to shake. Exhaling harshly, she raised her fingers to her head to investigate the damage. It wouldn't have hurt to wait, she realized. In a couple of days she would be home, and a trained professional could have cut it. She could only guess how horrible she looked. Tears stung the back of her eyes.

"Give me the scissors," Josh said gently.

She still had them clenched in her fist. He took

them from her and sighed as he ran his fingers through the uneven tresses, his touch strangely intimate.

She swallowed tightly. "Roger insisted I keep it long," she whispered. Cutting it had been an act of defiance, a way of casting her former fiancé from her life, but in doing so she'd only hurt herself.

Josh took his time clipping away here and there. At last he stood back to admire his handiwork. "Not bad," he said with a slow smile. "Even if I do say so myself."

Gretchen reached for her compact and flipped it open. With the light from the fire and the moon, she could see that his touch had been masterful. She barely recognized herself. She now wore a short pixielike cut that flattered her cheekbones and deep blue eyes.

Her gaze returned to Josh. "You're a man of many talents. Thank you," she murmured.

Her words appeared to please him. He reached for his knife and the stick he'd been sharpening earlier. "I don't know about you, but I'm starved."

Gretchen couldn't have eaten if her life depended on it. She sat with her chin resting on her knees and studied the fire. "You go ahead. I'm not hungry."

They sat side by side, surrounded by the sound of the ocean and the crackle of the fire as he cooked himself a wiener.

"Is it true what Roger said?" she wondered aloud. "About your father being in prison?" She wasn't sure what had prompted the question. Probably she should never have asked.

Josh stilled. "Yes." But he didn't elaborate, and she didn't question him further. Although he claimed to be hungry, he didn't eat more than one hot dog. For a long time afterward he sat cross-legged on the blanket he'd brought, staring into the flames as though hypnotized.

"Josh," she whispered, after the uncomfortable silence grew too long to bear. He didn't look at her right away. She waited until he grudgingly gave her his attention. "I'm sorry. I had no business asking you about your father."

Without acknowledging her apology, he rose to his feet and disappeared into the darkness. She watched him go, resisting the urge to go after him and apologize again. Angry with herself, she pressed her forehead against her knees and wondered how she could have been so insensitive to a man who'd been nothing but kind and helpful.

After the tumultuous events of the day, she was convinced she would never be able to sleep. She stretched out on the blanket, covered herself with a thick sweater and tucked her head against her bent arm. She was asleep almost immediately, only to jerk awake a moment later. That happened several more times before the physical demands of her body won out over the emotional trauma of the day.

Gretchen wasn't sure at what point during the night Josh joined her. Her eyes fluttered open to see that the fire had died down to glimmering coals. She was on her back, and all she could see was the dense spattering of stars above. She rolled her head to one side and found Josh asleep on the other side of the blanket. Relieved that he was back, she rolled onto her side and tucked her sweater more closely about her shoulders.

The next thing she was aware of was the loud discordant cry of a seagull. She opened her eyes to gray light. To her surprise, she felt warm and cozy, although the fire had long since died out. She soon realized the source of her comfort. Josh had placed his leather jacket over her shoulders. He sat nearby, his hair apparently wet from a shower.

"What time is it?" she asked, lazily stretching her arms above her head and yawning.

He grinned. "Morning."

"That much I guessed." Raising herself on one elbow, she strained to see her watch.

"About five-thirty or six, I'd guess," he said, looking toward the water.

She sat up and rubbed the sleep from her eyes, then realized she was famished. Her stomach growled loudly. "Oh, dear," she said, and flattened her hand against her abdomen.

"Looks like we'd best scrounge up something to eat," he said. He stood and extended his hand to her. It took them a while to pack up everything. While he loaded up the Harley, she brushed her teeth in the rest room, put on some lip gloss and combed her hair, amazed again at the transformation the haircut made in her appearance. She doubted that Roger would even recognize her now.

When they rode into town and parked the Harley

at a curb, another question came to mind, one she had a feeling Josh could answer. Needing someone to hold on to, she slipped her hand into his.

"How well do you know Didi Wilson?" she asked. She'd often seen Didi with Josh. She knew it was none of her concern. Nevertheless she needed to know.

His gaze narrowed, and his steps slowed. "How much did Didi tell you about her and Roger?"

She frowned, her hand still in his. "Just that…that she was at the fraternity party with him."

Josh's fingers tightened around hers.

"I don't hate Didi," she said, although it was difficult to regard the other woman with kindness. In many ways Didi had done her a favor, though it was difficult to think of it in those terms at that moment.

Josh heaved a deep sigh, and his hand tightened around hers. "Didi's pregnant."

"How can she know so soon?" Gretchen asked indignantly, and then it hit her. Hard. Square between the eyes. Roger hadn't been with Didi Wilson just that one time but several. She closed her eyes and swayed with both shock and anger.

"How long have they been lovers?" she demanded. When he hesitated, she asked again, steeling herself for the answer. "Tell me, Josh. I have a right to know."

"Six months, maybe more."

She grimaced and clenched her free hand into a fist at her side. The entire time she'd been engaged to Roger, he'd been physically involved with Didi.

It was enough to make her ill. She recalled all those afternoons he'd been late to meet her. It got to be a big joke between them. All the nights when he'd claimed he was studying. She should have known, should have realized. What about her friends? Her face burned with the realization that others must have known and yet no one had bothered to tell her.

As if reading her thoughts, Josh said, "Roger kept it quiet. I doubt anyone else knew."

"*You* did," she said.

"Didi's my friend."

But she noted he didn't say how good a friend the woman was.

"Does Roger know about the baby?" she asked, once she found her voice.

"No." Josh shook his head.

"Is Didi going to tell him?"

Again Josh paused. "I don't know. That decision is hers."

She studied him, and wondered if he had been Didi's lover, too. If so, she didn't want to know about it.

His grip on her hand relaxed. "Come on, you look like you could use a cup of coffee." He led her to a café on the main street and held the door for her. Although it was still early, the place was busy. With a majority of the tables occupied, Josh opted to sit at the counter. Once they were settled, he handed Gretchen a menu.

The harried waitress cast them an apologetic smile as she raced by, her arms loaded down with plates. "I'll be with you folks as soon as I can."

"We're in no hurry," Josh assured her.

The woman returned a few minutes later with the coffeepot. "The other waitress called in sick at the last minute, along with the dishwasher. Mighty convenient case of the flu, if you ask me," she said as she filled their cups.

The cook slapped the bell and set two more plates on the shelf. The waitress glanced over her shoulder and grumbled under her breath. "I'll be back to take your order in a minute. I don't want those breakfasts to get cold."

"No problem," Gretchen said.

Josh helped himself to a couple of doughnuts from a plate beneath a plastic dome. He handed one to Gretchen.

As the waitress moved past, Josh said to her, "Listen, if you're shorthanded, I can wash dishes."

The waitress hesitated.

"All I want in exchange is a decent breakfast for me and my friend."

"Harry," the waitress called into the kitchen. "We got ourselves a volunteer. The guy claims he can wash dishes." She looked at Gretchen. "What about you, honey? Did you ever wait tables?"

Gretchen could see that Josh was about to answer for her. "Sure," she said quickly, although it was a bald-faced lie. She brushed the doughnut crumbs from her hands and slipped off the stool.

"There's an apron and an order pad behind the counter."

"Great," Gretchen said. She wasn't at all sure

she would be able to pull it off, but she was willing to try. She tossed Josh a saucy grin as she tied the apron around her waist. Then he disappeared into the kitchen.

"If you'd do the coffee refills, I'd appreciate it," the waitress said, swishing past her. "Those tables need to be cleaned, too." She pointed at two that had just emptied. "By the way, my name's Marge."

"I'm Gretchen." She reached for the glass coffeepot. It didn't demand a lot of skill to refill coffee cups around the room. Once she'd finished that, she found a large square tub and hauled it over to the vacated tables, then dumped the dirty dishes inside. After she wiped the surface clean and handed Marge her tip money, she turned to discover the tables had already filled up with new customers.

By the time the breakfast crowd had thinned out, it was midmorning. Gretchen sat down and counted her tips. She had collected close to twenty bucks.

"Sure do appreciate the help," Marge said, sitting down next to her at the counter.

"Glad I could do it."

Josh appeared from the kitchen, drying his hands on a dish towel.

"I'm so hungry I could eat a cow," Gretchen said.

Marge winked at Josh, then looked toward the kitchen. "Harry, cook me up a couple of our best steaks, and don't be frying up any of those skinny breakfast ones, either. These kids deserve T-bones."

Three

Gretchen couldn't remember when she'd enjoyed a meal more, although she felt like a fraud accepting it. Her waitressing skills left a lot to be desired, and by the end of three hours her feet hurt, her back ached, and she had a new appreciation of the skills required to wait tables.

It was almost noon by the time they were back on the road. Unlike the previous day, when they'd ridden hour upon hour without a break, Josh stopped every ten or fifteen miles, wherever there was a scenic overlook. Gretchen had traveled down the Oregon coast any number of times and found the scenery breathtaking. But nothing compared to viewing the magnificence on a bright sunny day in June from the back of Josh's Harley. It went a long way, in fact, to assuaging the ache in her heart.

She didn't want to think about Roger or the wedding, and yet they filled every corner of her mind. She didn't mention his name, not once, during any of their stops, but she talked about everything else without pausing for breath. Josh's patience was nothing short of miraculous. She couldn't remember ever being so talkative. She told him story upon story of growing up in San Francisco. She endlessly bragged about her older brother, and dragged out four or five pictures of her eighteen-month-old niece.

At each stop Josh would sit on the rock-wall railing with his back to the ocean and listen as if he'd never heard anything more fascinating. Gretchen wished she'd paid more attention in psychology class so she could appreciate what was happening to her. Could analyze it and stop this infernal chattering.

He rarely commented, just sat and listened, nodding and smiling now and again. Their last stop to view the scenery was Rockaway Beach. While standing in the glorious sunshine, looking out over the relentless surf, she started laughing as she told a story about her niece. She'd asked Jazmine to get her a pair of shoes, and the toddler had promptly delivered every pair Gretchen owned.

As she neared the end of the tale, her laughter altered and unexpected tears flooded into her eyes. "I…I don't know why I'm going on like this," she said when she found it impossible to hide what was happening.

"I know why." He stood and gently placed his hands on her shoulders. Then, with a tenderness that made her want to weep even more, he pulled her close and wrapped his arms around her. "It's all right,

Gretchen. Go ahead and cry. You're hurting. The man you loved isn't the person you thought he was."

Like water through a burst dam, her sobs broke free. They seemed to surge upward from the deepest part of her, until it wasn't only her shoulders that shook but her entire body. She tried to break away from Josh, but he wouldn't allow it. He pressed her closer, murmuring words of comfort all the while.

She clung to him, burying her head against his shoulder, letting him absorb her anger and hurt. The roar of the ocean slamming against the rocks seemed to echo her pain.

Once her energy was spent and her sobs turned to sniffles, she eased away, keeping her head lowered in embarrassment. He would have none of it. He tucked his index finger beneath her chin, raised her head and met her eyes.

"It's all right," he said.

A slight smile trembled at the corners of her mouth, and she nodded.

"I give up." The words were half whisper and half groan. As soon as he said them, he lowered his mouth to hers. The kiss was slow and deep, so deep she felt it all the way to her toes. Intense, yet incredibly tender.

After a moment Josh slid his fingers into her short hair, cupping the sides of her head as he angled his mouth over hers, urging her lips apart with the tip of his tongue. He sighed when, in a daze, she accepted his invitation and opened for him. Shyly her tongue met his, but gradually she gained confidence as the kissing continued. What had begun as a slow easy exercise quickly became demanding and urgent.

She wasn't sure what would have happened if a car hadn't pulled off the highway just then. Hearing the sound of wheels grinding against the gravel, Josh broke off contact. He studied her for a moment.

"You OK?" he asked, touching his forehead to hers while holding her face between his hands.

She nodded, not knowing how else to answer him. But she *wasn't* OK. She'd been weeping for one man and kissing another. And liking it so much she hadn't wanted to stop. She glared at the new arrivals, wishing they would leave, then realized how ridiculous she was being.

"We better get back on the road," Josh said, steering her toward the Harley.

Although she followed him silently, her mind brewed with half-formed questions. First and foremost she wanted to know what had prompted him to kiss her. She didn't want his pity, but at the same time, she knew she would be a fool to believe any part of that soul-stirring kiss had been because he felt sorry for her.

Once she was safely tucked behind him on the Harley, he started the bike and steered them back onto the road. The wind whipped against her face, and she closed her eyes. Josh was dangerous—that was what she'd always heard. Now she knew why. The danger wasn't his arrogance, the way he challenged authority or defied danger. It was the effortless way he could make a woman feel desirable.

They didn't stop again for what seemed like hours. The day before she had held herself away from Josh, her spine rigid, determined to minimize any physical contact. Not so now. Her grip around his waist was tight; she craved the physical reassurance of his solid body.

Josh stopped in Tillamook when they hit a red light. "You hungry?" he asked.

She realized, somewhat to her surprise, that she was. "Yeah, I guess I am." Then, knowing their finances were limited, she asked, "What can we afford?"

"Cheese."

"Cheese?" While she knew neither one of them had a lot of cash, she didn't think they were in dire straits.

"Some of the best in the country. I'll show you."

Tillamook was home to a huge dairy-products factory. She smiled and flattened her cheek against his back, grateful to have him for a friend. It felt good and right to be this close to him. Her entire four years of college, she'd barely talked to him. By any reasonable measure they were little more than strangers, yet she felt closer to him after these two days together than she did to some of her sorority sisters with whom she'd lived for years.

Josh turned left at the next light and then pulled into a large bustling parking lot. The building was enormous, complete with gift shop, touring areas, and plenty of free samples of a surprisingly large selection of cheeses and ice cream. He purchased a box of crackers, some cheese and a bottle of red wine.

"For a picnic," he explained, as they headed back

to the bike. He smiled, and it was such a rare thing it caught her unawares.

"You should do that more often," she said, as she fastened the strap of her helmet. At the question in his eyes, she said, "Smile."

His response was to frown, drawing his thick eyebrows together and darkening his face. Not for the first time, she was struck by what an attractive man he was. She wasn't alone, either. In the cheese factory, she had noticed a number of women openly assessing him. Apparently they liked what they saw. For his part, he appeared oblivious to the attention his looks generated.

Seeing him now, wearing that well-practiced scowl, she couldn't help it, she laughed outright. It was all for show. Beneath that dark brooding exterior lay a man with a kind and generous heart. A man she was only beginning to know, yet already liked immensely.

"What?" he demanded.

"You. Let's get moving, pal. I'm hungry."

He grumbled something she couldn't hear under his breath and climbed on the Harley. Without hesitation, she positioned herself behind him and automatically locked her arms around his middle. It felt so right and natural to be close to him. Less than twenty-four hours earlier she'd made the most daring move of her life by trusting him to deliver her home safely. And trust him she did, more with each passing hour.

Josh found them a quiet corner on a secluded section of beach. The afternoon was glorious. The ocean breeze was blessedly cool, and a thicket of tall grass rustled softly behind them.

They sat on the blanket, nibbling the cheese and crackers, and sipping the wine from plastic glasses. After a while, replete, Gretchen lay on her back and gazed at the sky. She was amazed by how tranquil, how at peace, she felt. Stretching her arms above her, she smiled lazily. All she could hear were the waves pounding the shore and the frantic cries of gulls.

The wine seemed to have loosened her inhibitions—at least that was what she blamed for the path her thoughts were traveling.

"Josh, can I ask you something?" she said.

An uncomfortable silence followed. Uncomfortable enough to cause her to turn her head and look at him. He was sitting with his arms braced behind him. "You don't want me to ask you anything?" Surely he would want to know the question and *then* decide if he would answer it.

His frown was back, darker and more intimidating than ever. "Are you looking for me to apologize for kissing you?"

"No!" If he did, she would be offended. Her response to his kiss had been relegated to the far reaches of her mind. She needed time to analyze what had prompted her heady reaction, but she wasn't up to a lengthy examination just yet.

"What, then?" He crossed his arms.

She closed her eyes and angled her face toward

the sun rather than look at him. "Never mind," she said, silently laughing at him. "It wasn't important."

"Ask me," he barked.

She rolled onto her stomach and trained her gaze on the ocean. "It has to do with Didi Wilson."

"What about her?"

Gretchen paused, unsure now that she wanted to proceed, but the need burned within her, and she knew she wouldn't be completely at peace until she discovered the answer. Besides, at this point she couldn't walk away from the subject gracefully. She inhaled and held her breath momentarily. "I realize it's none of my business…"

"Listen, if it has to do with Didi and Roger, I'd rather not—"

"No," she said, interrupting him. "Not them. This has to do with Didi and *you*." Her words were like a hatchet coming down on a chopping block.

His gaze pinned her. She exhaled sharply and blurted, "Have you…did you and Didi…you know… do that?" She couldn't make herself say the words. *Make love. Did you make love to Didi?* Her heart was laid open, exposed, revealing everything. Over the past six months she'd frequently seen Didi riding through the campus on the back of Josh's Harley. Her arms had squeezed him, her ample assets pressed against his back.

Now she knew that Josh hadn't been Didi's only love interest. With a shock, she realized that while the news of Didi and Roger had shattered her world, if she learned that Josh had been Didi's lover, as well, she would be devastated. She should have known better than to ask a question when she was afraid of the answer.

"I've changed my mind. I don't want to know," she said hurriedly, then leaped to her feet, kicked off her shoes and raced toward the surf. Her face burned with humiliation, but she had no one to blame but herself. She raced into the ocean, gasping at how cold it was. The surf surged against her thighs before she stopped running. Her pulse pounded in her temple.

"Gretchen!"

She heard Josh call, but she ignored him. The lunch that had made her feel so pleasantly replete now felt like a rock-hard lump in the pit of her stomach.

"Come on, Gretchen, would you listen to me?" He stood at the water's edge, glaring at her.

"I shouldn't have asked," she said. "It was none of my business. Please, I don't want to talk about it anymore." She pranced about in the shallows, trying to make him think she was having the time of her life.

"Stop that right now." It was the same tone of voice her father used to employ with her when she was a child and misbehaving. A tone full of authority she didn't challenge.

She stopped playing in the surf and faced him.

"Didi's my friend," he said. "Nothing more. Never has been and never will be. Understand?"

She nodded miserably.

Josh extended his hand to her in much the same way he had the day before, when he'd invited her to climb onto the back of his motorcycle. "Come here before you're completely drenched."

The water was so cold her feet had gone numb. Mustering every shred of dignity she possessed, she remained where she was, her chin angled high and proud. How desperately she longed to believe him!

"Don't make me come in after you."

"Would you?"

He didn't hesitate. "Yes, but trust me, you'd regret it."

The threat was as bold as the man himself. "Really?" She reached down and with feigned nonchalance dangled her fingers in the water.

The challenge was there, bold as ever. The confidence he'd exuded didn't waver as he lowered himself onto the hot sand and removed his boots one at a time. Then he stood and unfastened his belt.

"Josh." She watched, fascinated.

"I'm not getting these jeans wet. It's uncomfortable riding in wet pants." He peeled down the zipper and hooked his thumbs through the belt loops, clearly prepared to remove both his jeans and his underwear.

"Okay, okay. You win." She raced out of the surf and onto the beach, heading for the blanket. She heard him chuckle and call her a coward as she passed him.

His taunts evolved into a sexy smile as he followed her back to the blanket. It had been a childish thing to do, she thought, challenging him that way. Especially when the outcome had already been decided. Josh would win because he always won.

Soon they were back on the road again, breezing down the highway, soaking up the sunshine and scenery. And she realized he was right. It *was* uncomfortable riding in wet jeans.

The sun was just beginning to set by the time they reached Newport. Dozens of mammoth kites of various colors and designs battled the wind, rising and plummeting on the fickle fancy of the currents. Campfires flickered here and there along the beach, competing in color with the setting sun.

Gretchen was tired, more tired than she wanted to admit, even to herself. They hadn't traveled nearly as far as Josh had hoped they would, but then, they'd gotten a late start and taken two hours out for a picnic lunch.

Josh parked the Harley and reached for her hand once they'd stored the helmets. "Let's get you a hotel room tonight."

She didn't miss the implication. While she was nestled up warm in a bed, he would be sleeping on the beach. Alone and cold.

"Hey, I go where you go," she said.

His eyebrows shot up. "Is that an invitation to your bed?"

She blushed. "No."

"Pity." He grinned at her.

Josh teasing? Josh joking? His brief smile went a long way toward lightening her spirits. "You're nothing but a big phony," she declared.

His gaze narrowed. "What do you mean?"

"Beneath that he-man exterior, you're a pussycat."

He shook his head. "I wouldn't count on it, if I were you."

"But I already am."

Once again she found Josh grinning as he located a quiet spot on the beach, one protected from the elements as well as the curious stares of others. Soon they had a fire of their own blazing away. While he unpacked their things, Gretchen smoothed an area of sand and spread the blanket over it. Silently they worked together as a team, then sat down in front of the fire.

"Why'd you want to get me a hotel room?" she asked. They had a wonderful spot on the beach, she realized. The weather was great, and she was as comfortable here as she would be on any bed.

He didn't answer, and Gretchen, puzzled, glanced at him. "You assumed I need to be pampered, right?" It irked her that he would think that, and her tone told him as much. People often assumed that, because her family was wealthy, she'd been spoiled and coddled her whole life. Certainly she'd been given opportunities that weren't available to most people her age, but her parents had never overindulged her.

Josh shook his head. "When I first met you, I assumed you'd be another one of those spoiled rich kids, but you've proved otherwise."

She was pleased. Pleased enough to forget her inhibitions, lean over and kiss him. The action had been purely instinctive, without forethought.

He leaned back in surprise. "What was that for?"

"To thank you for the compliment."

"I complimented you?"

Willing to admit her weariness now, she let her body rest against his, her head on his shoulder. After a time he put his arm around her, and she smiled, utterly content.

"Tell me about your family," she said lazily. If she hadn't been propped against him, she might not have felt the tension shoot through him. His back went rigid, and his arms stiffened slightly. She'd done it again. Just when it seemed they were comfortable with each other she'd said something to upset the delicate balance. She couldn't believe she'd forgotten that his father was in prison and he didn't want to talk about it. "Josh, I'm sorry, I didn't mean to pry. It's just that my own family is so much a part of me."

He didn't respond for what seemed like an eternity, and when he did speak, his voice was gruff with emotion. "My mother died when I was sixteen." His hand stroked her upper arm, as if he needed the reassurance of human contact.

Gretchen placed a hand over his. "I'm sorry," she whispered.

"It happens. My dad was never the same. It was as if he couldn't bear the agony of losing her, so he chose to self-destruct. He's serving time, as you know." He didn't elaborate, and she didn't ask. Instead, she brought his hand to her face and gently laid her cheek against it.

"A lot of people wonder how I landed at Queen Anne," he continued, his voice close to her ear. "My grandfather left me money in the form of a trust, the condition being that, if I wanted a college education, I attend his alma mater."

"Do you want a college education?"

His short laugh was without humor. "I went, didn't I?"

All evidence she'd seen to this point said he wanted anything but what Queen Anne had to offer. Josh constantly challenged authority. He appeared to go out of his way to cause trouble. Why, only the day before he had given Roger the incentive and opportunity to end his college career right as he was about to graduate. And it would be just like Roger to make whatever trouble he could for Josh and delight in it.

"Why'd you do it?" she asked, changing the subject. "Why'd you slug Roger? He'll go out of his way to use it against you."

"Let him," Josh answered. "I can deal with it."

"But—"

"The bastard deserved it."

That much Gretchen agreed with. It had been all she could do not to cheer when she saw Roger's bloody nose. Especially after he'd attempted to sucker-punch Josh.

Before she allowed herself to think what she was doing, she broke away from him, shifted position and knelt in front of him. His questioning gaze met hers in the dim light afforded by the fire. Smiling, she placed a hand on either side of his face and leaned forward to kiss him.

The surge of desire she experienced when their lips met was enough to make her bold. She wrapped her arms around his neck as their mouths worked together in a frenzy of tongues, lips and unmistakable desire. She offered and he took, greedily.

Abruptly Josh jerked his mouth away from hers. He sat back, panting, his shoulders heaving. "What was that for?" he demanded.

Gretchen's eyes remained closed. "Don't ask. Just kiss me like that again."

"No."

"No?" Disappointed, she opened her eyes. "Why not?"

"Because you don't have a clue what you're doing." He stood, and she was pleased to note that he didn't look very steady. She felt decidedly off balance herself, but somehow it was a good feeling.

"Wipe that silly grin off your face," he muttered.

If she hadn't been so happy she would have been downright insulted. He'd kissed her and it had been the most wonderful experience of her life. Now he didn't seem able to hold still. He circumnavigated the blanket three times. She was getting dizzy watching him.

Suddenly it dawned on her, and it was all she could do to keep from giggling. "Joshua Morrow, I tempt you, don't I?"

He started to deny it and then appeared to think better of it. "I'm getting you that hotel room, and I don't want any arguments, understand?" His voice was hard and unfriendly. "You'll sleep alone, too." She wasn't sure if he was saying that for her benefit or his.

Gretchen covered her mouth in an effort to contain a brewing fit of laughter.

"Stop looking at me like that," he demanded.

"Like what?"

"Like…that." He shrugged as if at a complete loss for words.

She had never seen Josh unnerved, had never suspected she would be one to shatter his cool. It told her that their kisses had affected him as much as they had her. She felt almost giddy with a sense of wonder and power.

"Come on," he ordered brusquely.

"Where are we going?"

"I told you. I'm getting you a motel room for the night."

"Josh—"

"Don't argue with me." From the tight set of his mouth and his combative stance, she wasn't inclined to do so.

"Oh, all right, but you're being ridiculous."

She rolled her eyes, and then, feeling happier than she had all day, she gathered up her personal items and obediently followed him to the bike. They set off and didn't find a vacancy until their third stop. Although she was the one who registered, the man at the desk handed the room key to Josh. He hesitated before accepting it; he obviously didn't want the man to think he would be spending the night with her. Finally his hand closed over the key, and he escorted her outside.

The room was small, the furniture cheap, but

overall the place looked clean, despite the faint stale scent hanging in the air. Gretchen set the tote bag holding her belongings on top of the bed.

Josh stood outside the room, his arms crossed in a defensive way that defied her to even try to talk to him. She'd seen him assume that same stance at college a hundred times. The hard-edged look that said he didn't give a rip about anything or anyone, so you had better keep your distance.

"This OK?" he asked.

"It's fine," she assured him.

"Good. I'll be going, then."

"You won't leave me, will you?" she blurted without pausing to think he might take her question differently than she intended. "In the morning," she clarified. "You'll still be here, won't you?" The thought of not seeing him again hit her with a pain she hadn't anticipated.

His features softened fractionally before he spoke. "I'd never do that. I said I'd deliver you to your family, and I will."

"Promise?"

"Promise."

Out of gratitude, or perhaps relief, she walked across the room and hugged him. He returned the gesture with what felt like reluctance. Once she was in his embrace, she closed her eyes, savoring the closeness.

"Good night," he whispered, and kissed the top of her head.

"Good night," she returned, stopping herself from

asking a series of unnecessary questions, which she knew would only have been an excuse to delay him. She didn't want to think of him out there alone on the beach, but she couldn't stop him from going, either.

After what seemed like an inordinate amount of time, they dropped their arms and stepped away from each other. "I'll shower here in the morning, if you don't mind," he said.

She nodded and clenched her hands, already missing him—and he hadn't even left.

He hesitated for a moment, then was gone.

Alone in her room, Gretchen was certain he'd wanted to tell her something. She'd recognized the look in his eyes. But whatever it was he'd decided to keep it to himself.

She showered, enjoying the glorious sensation of standing under the spray and letting it splash over her face. She slipped into her pajamas and used a sweater for extra warmth. Then, sitting on the bed, she watched TV and brushed her hair, or what there was of it. She wondered how long it would take her to get used to its being this short. Josh had worked miracles with the hack job she'd done. She sighed. For two days they'd spent nearly every minute together, and without him there to share these quiet moments, it felt as if a part of her was missing.

The program ended, and she was about to turn off the television and go to sleep when a loud knock sounded against her door.

She scrambled off the bed, wondering who on earth could be coming to her room this late. "Who is it?" she called, making her voice sound strong and confident.

No response.

"I'm not opening this door until I know who's there."

Another moment passed before the answer came. "Josh."

Four

"Josh!" Gretchen undid the locks and threw open the door. Why was he here, especially after acting as if he couldn't be rid of her fast enough?

"Hi." He stood on the other side of the door, looking decidedly uncomfortable, as though *he* wasn't entirely sure himself why he was there, either.

"Come in." She stepped aside to let him pass, yet he made no move to venture farther than the doorway.

"I can't," he muttered. He rubbed his hand down his face and shook his head, as if to clear his thoughts.

"You wanted something?" she asked. She drew the sweater more tightly about her and was glad she'd thought to wear socks. Frowning, she thought she smelled beer on him.

He seemed to read her thoughts. "I figured it'd take a little fortification to say what needs to be said."

"It's that bad?"

"It's about what happened," he said.

"What happened?" She wasn't playing dumb. She honestly didn't know what he meant.

"Us, you know?"

"About us…kissing, you mean?"

"Yeah." He buried his hands in his jeans pockets, and his gaze stubbornly refused to meet hers.

Gretchen had never seen Josh look so self-conscious or tense. She waited, deciding to let him speak without further coaxing from her. The seconds ticked by, and still he remained silent.

At last he met her gaze and said, "Don't put any stock in those kisses, all right?" His words were stark and half-angry.

At first she didn't respond, but then she couldn't keep from asking, "Why not?"

"Because," he said forcefully, "girls like you don't get involved with guys like me, understand?"

"Josh—"

He raised a hand, stopping her. "Let me speak. You've had a miserable couple of days, and—"

"But I haven't, not really, I—" His gaze narrowed at her interruption and she shut up.

"You're no longer engaged to Junior Warbucks. You're separated from your family at a time when you need their love and support most. It's only natural for you to turn to me for comfort—natural, but not advisable."

"You're making me sound like a child."

"Whatever," he announced crisply. "Listen, Gretchen, don't set your sights on me. I'm not your type."

She opened her mouth to argue that he was quite possibly *exactly* the type of man she could love, but he stopped her once again, yanking the rug out from under her feet.

"And you're not my type, either," he growled. "I can't say it any plainer than that, can I?"

His words smarted, and she instinctively jerked back, as if she'd taken a punch in the solar plexus. Every breath brought her pain.

"I don't mean to hurt your feelings," he said. "You're a sweet kid, but it's best to get this out in the open before you end up getting hurt."

He thought of her as a kid! Worse, a sweet kid! He made it sound like she was in pigtails, skipping down the beach licking a rainbow lollipop.

"I don't want there to be any misunderstanding between us," he continued. "I'll deliver you to your family, and that'll be the end of it. So don't be putting any weight on that kiss. It should never have happened—but I blame myself. Rest assured, nothing like that will happen again."

"That was what you wanted to say?" she asked, as though exceedingly bored. She wrapped her dignity about her as tightly as she had the sweater.

His eyes registered his surprise at her easy acceptance. "Yeah."

"Fine, then, you've said it."

He blinked once. No doubt he'd anticipated an argument. Well, she wasn't about to give him one. If that was the way he felt, she wasn't going to force herself on him. After all, she still had a thin layer of pride, which was about all she'd managed to salvage after Roger. And what little remained she was determined to guard very carefully.

"If you don't have anything more to say, I'd like to go to bed." She forced a loud yawn. She would go to bed, all right, but she knew it would be one hell of a long time before she slept.

Josh turned abruptly and walked away.

Gretchen shut the door, closed her eyes and pressed her forehead against the cool wood. Her heart was heavy. Practically speaking, she had no choice but to accept him at his word. But he hadn't fooled her. He was interested in her. Very interested.

Her fingers investigated her short hair as she climbed into bed. She lay there a good long time before she reached for the nightstand and turned out the light.

In the morning they were overly polite with each other, behaving like awkward strangers with nothing in common and little to say. They got an early start, hitting the road shortly after seven, fortified only with coffee. Neither was hungry. If they rode hard, didn't stop often or for long, they would reach San Francisco by evening, Josh told her. The minute they were on the highway, Gretchen could see that he was determined to be rid of her that day. He set a killing pace.

She sat stiffly behind him as they roared down the highway, doing her best to avoid touching him. He, too, was avoiding her. Unlike the previous day, when he'd stopped every few miles to admire the view and to give her the opportunity to talk, he pressed on with punishing determination.

When he did finally pull off the highway, it was to gas up. Although she didn't complain, Gretchen's entire body ached, especially her back.

He climbed off the Harley while she slowly eased herself from the seat and headed into the small mom-and-pop grocery for something to drink.

"Do you want anything?" she asked, making sure she sounded friendly yet reserved.

"Nothing." Then, as if in afterthought, he added, "Thanks."

She walked into the store. After checking to be sure he couldn't see her, she rubbed some of the soreness from her buttocks and the small of her back. She stopped when she discovered the elderly male clerk eyeing her with appreciative interest. He had the good grace to look embarrassed when she glared back at him.

Doing her best to walk normally, she made her way to the rest room. Afterwards she stopped at the refrigeration unit and reached for a bottle of spring water. Her mouth was dry, her body sore and miserable, and her heart was heavy. Not a good way to start the day.

As she stood in line to pay for her purchase, she noted the flashing red and blue lights of a police cruiser.

"What's going on?" she asked the man at the counter.

The clerk craned his neck to see out the grimy

window. "Looks like they're arresting some young fellow. He better pay for his gas before they haul him away. Otherwise I'm gonna confiscate his Harley."

"His Harley?" Gretchen repeated. Her heart, which had felt sluggish and lackadaisical only seconds earlier, shot into overdrive. The police were arresting Josh! Leaving her purchase on the counter, she raced out the door half a second in front of the clerk.

It was worse than she'd feared. Josh had his arms handcuffed behind his back and was being pushed toward the cruiser. Even from a distance of ten feet she could feel the anger emanating from him. His eyes were wild and his jaw so tight his face had gone white.

"What's going on here?" she demanded, outraged on his behalf and not afraid to let it show.

The officer barely glanced her way. "Do you know this man?"

"I most certainly do." Her hands flew to her hips and she braced her feet, prepared to do battle. "Why is he handcuffed?"

The officer spoke without emotion. "He matches the description of a robbery suspect—age, height, clothes. Motorcycle. All adds up to probable cause." The officer met her eyes, silently daring her to challenge him.

She didn't doubt the patrolman would welcome an excuse to haul her away, too, but she refused to give him one. Josh needed her free.

The officer resumed shoving Josh toward the patrol car.

"What about his rights?" she cried, desperately trying to find an excuse to delay him.

"I read him his rights."

"Gretchen." Josh furiously whispered her name under his breath in warning.

"He has a right to an attorney." She looked to the clerk for confirmation.

"He owes me eight bucks for gas," the man said.

"I'll pay for the stupid gas!" Her heart hammered as she paced in front of the police officer. Josh was now sitting in the patrol car, his eyes closed as if he was mentally removing himself from the ugly scene.

"Do you have a license to drive that bike?" the patrolman asked her.

She glanced over her shoulder at the Harley. Josh's pride and joy. The symbol of his rebellion. "Yes, I've got a license," she lied, knowing that if she didn't, the police would impound the bike. Heaven only knew how long it would be before Josh got it back, and she couldn't risk that.

"You'll take care of it, then?"

Although she knew it was pointless to protest, she did anyway. "Look. Josh didn't commit a robbery. He was with me all morning. We left Newport Beach at seven. You can call the motel and they'll verify..." She trailed off, remembering that she was the one who'd registered for the room, not Josh. He hadn't spent the night with her. She couldn't account for his whereabouts every minute of the night. But in her heart, she knew he would never rob anyone.

"Leave it," Josh said, his voice low and tight, sharp with frustration.

Gretchen clenched her hands into fists, finding it impossible to stand by and do nothing. She was the only one who appreciated how humiliating this was for him. How difficult. The pain in his eyes when he'd told her about his father being in prison haunted her. Now to face jail himself for something he couldn't have done, wouldn't have done...

"Please," she whispered, feeling helpless and small. She wasn't even sure who she was asking for help.

"We were in Newport Beach last night," she said, so fast the words ran together. She was willing to say anything, do anything, that would convince the officer he had the wrong man.

A sly smile lit the patrolman's face. "Yes, I know."

She clamped her mouth shut, determined not to offer any more unsolicited information. She wanted to help, not hurt, Josh's cause. Her chest tightened painfully, and she found it impossible to stand still.

The patrolman opened the driver's door and climbed into the vehicle. She planted her palms against the passenger window. "Josh!" she cried, wanting somehow to reassure him.

He turned his head toward her. Afraid she was about to erupt into sobs, she covered her mouth with her hand. Josh's eyes steadily held hers, and then he smiled. Through his anger, frustration and humiliation, he reached out to her. *He* was the one reassuring *her*.

Gretchen bit her lower lip so hard she tasted blood.

"Miss, miss." The clerk took hold of her shoulders and pulled her away from the cruiser. She stood back helplessly as Josh was driven away, her gaze following the car until it was no longer in sight.

The clerk waited an impatient moment while she composed herself, then asked, "You going to pay for that gas or not?"

"Yes," she murmured, and stepped back into the store.

When she was back outside, she crossed to the Harley, donned Josh's leather jacket, dark glasses and helmet, and swung one leg over the seat, pretending she knew what she was doing. Not only did she not have a motorcycle license, she hadn't so much as twisted the key in the ignition before. She felt like weeping.

Dragging in a deep breath, she squared her shoulders and decided then and there that she would find a way not only to start the bike, but ride it. She had to do it for Josh.

He'd been there for her when she'd needed him, hadn't he? He'd taught her so much about herself in the past couple of days. She'd felt helpless and lost when they'd started out together. But he'd believed in her, restored her faith in herself. She wasn't going to let him down.

The bike felt enormous between her legs, a monster ready to overpower her. Her grip tightened on the handlebars. She refused to give in to anxiety. Refused to be intimidated.

It shouldn't be that difficult, she realized, forcing herself to think positively. After all, she'd watched him start the thing any number of times.

She twisted the key.

The engine didn't catch.

She tried a second and a third time with the same result.

Breathing hard, she closed her eyes and reminded herself of everything that was at stake. One more time, she decided, and this time, by heaven, the bike would start.

She turned the key. When the engine roared, the Harley vibrated with such force it nearly toppled her.

Releasing a shout of triumph, Gretchen thrust her arms into the air, feeling like an Olympic champion. She glanced over her shoulder to be sure the road was clear, then managed to head down the highway and into town.

Her speed increasing, it surprised her how easily she managed to drive the Harley. Anyone looking at her dressed as she was would assume she was a motorcycle mama. Let them! One thing was certain: she wasn't about to let anyone or anything intimidate her again.

For another, her father and brother were going to hear about this. Two of San Francisco's finest attorneys, they would make mincemeat of the charge against Josh. By the time the dust had settled, Josh Morrow would own this two-bit town.

Rejuvenated, fire in her blood, Gretchen parked the Harley in the county courthouse lot. Head high and shoulders squared, she was determined to make an entrance that rivaled John Wayne in his finest.

"I'd like to see Judge Joseph Logan," she announced to the receptionist. She didn't have a clue who Judge Logan was, but if he insisted on having his name listed in the front of the courthouse, then he should expect to take appointments.

"I'm sorry, but Judge Logan died fifty years ago," the receptionist replied in a polished tone without cracking a smile. "We named the courthouse after him."

"Oh. Then who else is there?" Gretchen demanded, although much of her bravado had evaporated.

The woman looked sympathetic. "No one, I'm afraid."

"OK. I guess what I really need is a good attorney."

The receptionist's face brightened. "I can help you with that. Janet Mercer's office is across the street. You tell her Maggie sent you, OK? Whatever the problem is, Janet can help you."

Gretchen was so grateful she could have hugged the receptionist. "Thank you," she said.

"No problem. Listen, I hope everything works out."

Heeding the woman's advice, Gretchen hurried across the street and found Janet Mercer's name listed, along with three others, on the door outside a small brick office complex.

Apparently Janet didn't have a large enough clientele to warrant a secretary. Her office was simply a single room, with a desk, computer and one guest chair. A woman who didn't look much older than Gretchen herself glanced up when she entered the room.

"Hello," she greeted cheerfully. "I'm Janet Mercer. Can I help you?"

"Yes." Without waiting for an invitation, Gretchen lowered herself into the guest chair. She spoke nonstop for five minutes, hardly pausing long enough to breathe as she told Janet everything.

"They took him to the jail?" Janet asked.

"That's right," Gretchen said.

"Well, in that case, I better get over there." Janet stood and reached for her purse.

The attorney led the way to the jail, asking a question now and then as they moved along the flower-lined sidewalk. Gretchen found the woman so warm and personable, she wondered if the receptionist had steered her wrong. What she needed was a legal warrior who would fight for Josh, not Mother Teresa!

Janet soon proved she was everything Josh needed. The mild-mannered attorney turned into a tigress the moment they entered the jailhouse. She announced herself as Josh Morrow's attorney, and as for Officer O'Malley's "probable cause," she laughed in the man's face.

Gretchen attempted to follow Janet into the interview room where Josh was being questioned, but she was barred. With nothing else to do, she sat with her hands tucked under her thighs in a small waiting area, while Janet did battle alone.

A couple of times Gretchen thought she heard

raised voices, but she wasn't able to make out the words or even figure out who was speaking. About ten minutes later the door opened and Josh walked out of the room, freed from the handcuffs and rubbing his wrists.

Gretchen leaped to her feet, restraining herself from rushing forward.

Josh stopped when he saw her. And grinned. It was the biggest, most beautiful smile she'd ever seen. She felt her own mouth relax into a matching smile, and the next thing she knew they were rushing toward each other.

She closed her eyes as he swept her into his arms. His hug was fierce. Speechless, they clung to each other as if they never intended to let go.

"Okay, you lovebirds," someone said gruffly from behind Josh. "Move it outside, will ya? The last thing anyone wants to see around here is a little happiness. We don't know how to handle it." The officer chuckled.

Reluctantly, Josh released her. She lowered her feet to the floor and smiled up at him, battling back emotion.

"Where's the Harley?" he asked, looping his arm around her shoulders.

"Right where I parked it," she told him with more than a hint of pride.

"You rode it into town?"

"Yup. Ten miles over the speed limit, too. I was in a hurry."

He stared down at her. "I don't believe it."

"Believe it."

"All by yourself?"

"Yup."

"Clearly I underestimated you."

She grinned. "It would seem so."

Janet appeared. "You're free to go," she announced.

"He is?" Gretchen couldn't keep the delight out of her voice.

Janet nodded and strutted across the room like a peacock with its feathers on full display. She was obviously very pleased with herself. "This calls for a celebration," she said. "I don't suppose you two have had lunch yet, have you?"

Josh looked at Gretchen. "As a matter of fact, we haven't had breakfast."

"Great. Then you'll be good and hungry. Lunch is on me."

Josh started to protest, but Janet stopped him, chuckling softly. "Don't worry about it. I'll just add it to your bill."

Gretchen wasn't sure where they were headed, but they laughed and joked like old friends as Janet led them to an outdoor barbecue place two blocks away. The aroma of pungent sauce, alder smoke and sizzling meat made Gretchen's empty stomach growl. She planted her hand over it, hoping to still the rumbling.

Josh glanced down at her and reached for her hand, lacing their fingers together. "I'm sorry," he said as they stood in front of the large printed menu posted on one side of the red building. Picnic tables in bright primary colors dotted the grassy area.

"For what?" she asked.

"Last night," he answered, keeping his gaze trained on the menu.

"Oh." Why he'd chosen now, of all times, to tell her, she would never know. Then again, maybe she did. Since he was apologizing within Janet's hearing, she herself couldn't very well question what had prompted his visit last night. Or why he'd lied. And she knew he had, because the way he'd held her when he'd been released from custody, the way he'd pressed her close to his heart, contradicted everything he'd said.

They all ordered the barbecued-pork sandwich, with baked beans and corn bread. "This isn't the fanciest place in town," Janet said, "but I have my reasons for choosing it."

"What are they?" Gretchen asked.

"You'll see soon enough."

She was right. Halfway through their lunch, several patrol cars arrived.

"I'd say those reasons are here," Josh said, then licked his fingers clean of barbecue sauce.

The attorney chuckled again. "Okay, so I like to gloat now and again. It serves old O'Malley right. He hauled Josh in just so he could look good for Chief Davidson. I know his tricks, and I consider it my duty to make sure everyone else knows them, too."

"You enjoy living on the edge, do you?" Josh teased.

"Wouldn't have it any other way."

Gretchen noticed how Janet's gaze zeroed in on one particular officer. She recognized the longing in the other woman's expression; she'd felt the same thing herself in the past couple of days. Janet dragged her eyes back to her lunch with a resignation Gretchen could almost feel. The young attorney had been happy and animated moments earlier, but she grew suspiciously quiet now.

"Someone you know?" Gretchen asked, motioning with her head toward the tall athletic-looking officer.

"Yeah, I know him." Janet pushed aside what was left of her lunch. "His name's Gary Foreman. Unfortunately we don't see eye to eye on a number of important issues and—"

"You like him, though, don't you?" Gretchen asked.

"Does it show that much?"

"Yeah, it does."

"Oh, dear." Janet lowered her gaze. "We're constantly at odds with each other. At one time…well, never mind, it isn't important now. He's very good at his job, and unfortunately, so am I."

Gretchen stood, then reached for her empty paper plate and Janet's almost full one. She walked over to the Dumpster and deposited them both there. On the return trip, she routed herself past the table where Gary sat alone, his back to Janet. She would say one thing for the attorney—she had excellent taste. Gary Foreman was exceptionally good-looking.

"Hello," she said, boldly meeting his eyes.

"Hi." He sounded hesitant, suspicious.

"Why don't you come over and join us? My friend and I are having lunch with Janet Mercer. I think you know her, and since you're eating alone…"

Gary frowned, his thick dark brows drawing together. "Who on earth are you?" he asked, instead of replying.

She had his attention, she noted. "Gretchen Wise. Janet's wonderful. She just got my friend released after he was arrested. It was a case of mistaken identity."

His frown deepened, and he stared at her as if he thought she might be crazy. Then he suddenly got up, picked up his lunch and gestured for her to lead the way.

"What were you two talking about?" Josh demanded as she and Gary reached the table.

"Nothing important," she said, and winked at Janet, who was staring in shock at Gary.

As soon as he sat down, Gretchen turned to Josh and said, "I think it's time we left."

"I think so, too," he quickly agreed.

They thanked Janet, ignoring her wide-eyed insistence that they stay, and Josh wrote down an address where she could send him a bill. As they walked away, he started hammering Gretchen with questions. "What the hell prompted you to do that?" he demanded. "You don't even know the guy."

"Shh." She walked across the street and pulled him behind a huge fir tree. "Tell me what's happening back there."

He rolled his eyes.

"Josh, I'm serious. Are they talking?"

"It looks that way."

"Cool!" She'd never done anything as bold or as crazy in all her twenty-two years.

"Well, I'll be," he muttered.

"What? Tell me!" She didn't dare look herself, because she didn't want either of them to know she was watching.

"Janet just tossed my address in the garbage."

So Janet appreciated her little conversation with Officer Foreman. "Good. Now let's get out of here before someone else finds an excuse to arrest you."

"My sentiments exactly," he said. "Now, where did you say my bike was?"

"I parked it in front of the courthouse," she told him.

"I can't get over you driving the Harley," he said, and linked his fingers with hers.

"I couldn't very well leave it at the gas station, could I?" She reached into her jeans pocket and retrieved the key.

Josh walked across the street and stroked the motorcycle the way a man might touch the woman he loves and hasn't seen in far too long. He stowed her purse for her, then eased himself onto the seat, inserted the key into the ignition and gave it a twist.

Nothing. Not even a cough.

He glared at Gretchen. "What on earth did you do?"

Five

Josh was furious. He seemed to be accusing her of some unspeakable crime against his beloved Harley. "This is a delicate machine."

"What did I do?" she repeated with dead calm. "Let me see," she said, playing dumb and striking a thoughtful pose. She tapped her index finger against her cheek as she mulled over what terrible abuse she might have inadvertently heaped on his most cherished possession.

"You must have done something!"

That did it. Her temper had never been explosive, but she'd had it. His accusation detonated her anger to such a degree that she could feel her pulse pound in her temples like a hammer against an anvil. Her hands knotted into tight balls at her sides.

"Sure I did!" she shouted. "First of all I saved your precious Harley from being impounded. Then I made a raging idiot of myself in the courthouse, demanding to see a judge who's spent the past fifty years pushing up marigolds." She pointed at the building, in case he didn't appreciate her sacrifice, which clearly he didn't. "Then I found you the best attorney in three counties to get your sorry butt out of jail. And that's just for starters."

He tried to speak, but she wouldn't let him.

"Tell me, Josh, what have I gotten in exchange?"

"You shouldn't have done it."

"What? Ride your precious bike?"

"No, gotten involved."

"You honestly think I should have left you there?" He was being ridiculous.

He didn't hesitate. "Yeah, that's what I think. I told you before, and I meant it."

"I heard you the first time—I'm not your type." He was purposely picking a fight with her, and she couldn't understand it. Minutes earlier they'd been joking and having fun. He'd hugged her as if she held the key to his sanity.

"The last thing I need is some society girl fawning all over me," he grumbled.

His words stung. "OK," she said. "If that's the way you feel, then I think it would be best if we each went our separate ways. I'll find my own way home from here." She whirled around and started walking.

She was half a block away when he called after her, "I promised I'd get you to San Francisco, and I don't make promises lightly."

Nonchalantly turning around, she waved an imaginary magic wand. "I hereby absolve you of your promise. You're free to go."

"I won't chase after you, Gretchen." His eyes were hard, his jaw tight and stubborn, and she couldn't doubt he meant what he said.

"I wouldn't want you to." With her back to him once again, she continued walking as if she were strolling through a meadow filled with wildflowers and hadn't a care in the world. Her pride got her as far as the city park, all of five blocks from the courthouse. By that time the sick feeling in the pit of her stomach had overtaken her. The knot in her throat had grown so tight it was all she could do to keep from weeping.

She found a picnic table and sat on the top with her feet resting on the bench. She reviewed her options. Normally, in volatile situations she was the one with a cool head. Her ability to remain calm in difficult situations had been one of her strengths as student-body president. This simply wasn't like her.

She drew in a ragged breath and attempted to clear her mind. With her cell in her purse back on the Harley, a pay phone near the refreshment stand in the center of the park appeared to be her only option. Her parents were due back in San Francisco that day, though she didn't know what time their flight arrived. If she called them collect, they could wire her the funds to see her home. But worrying them was the last thing she wanted to do. The minute they learned of her plight, her mother was sure to panic, and her father wouldn't be much better.

Three days after her college graduation and she was on the street, no better off than a bag lady. No, worse than a bag lady. Everything she'd brought with her was packed on Josh's Harley. She didn't even have her identification with her.

She covered her face with both hands, questioning how she could have done anything as stupid as walk away from her purse, all her funds and clothes, and any chance she had of helping herself.

Janet Mercer would help her, Gretchen realized, but she would feel foolish asking, after rushing in and extolling Josh's virtues to the attorney earlier. Well, she had no one to blame but herself. She'd gotten herself into this ridiculous mess, and by heaven, she would get herself out—one way or another.

The thought had no more filtered through her mind when she heard the distinctive sound of a motorcycle. Her heart reacted with a wild surge of hope, but that quickly died. Josh had made a point of telling her that he wouldn't chase after her, and she didn't doubt for an instant that he'd meant it.

Nevertheless, it was Josh who slowly cruised past the park, his eyes searching the grounds. The temptation to raise her arm and wave him over was strong, but pride dictated that she do nothing. If he was really searching for her, he would see her. Still, she had to practically sit on her hands to keep from flagging him down.

Josh saw her, Gretchen was certain, and she tilted her head away, hoping to give the impression of royalty assessing her surroundings. But he didn't stop. Instead, he drove on past.

Perhaps he was expecting her to come rushing

after him and beg him to take her home. Squeezing her eyes closed, she swallowed her disappointment. Josh Morrow's pride was legendary; he'd stood up to Dean Williams and hadn't flinched. He would have no problem walking away from her.

Just when she was ready to swallow her dignity and go to Janet for help, she heard the motorcycle a second time. Her heart raced as she watched Josh approach. Straightening her spine, she sat up, refusing to allow him to see how distressed she actually was.

He pulled into an empty parking slot at the tree-lined curb and turned off the engine. He took his own sweet time removing his helmet and climbing off the bike. Fascinated, she watched how every movement he made seemed to be in slow motion. Not until he opened a saddlebag did she realize the reason he'd come back. At least he had the decency to return her belongings.

He approached her with all the enthusiasm of a man walking toward the electric chair. He could have been a robot for all the emotion he expressed. His gaze was as hard and unreadable as when she'd left him in front of the courthouse. Wordlessly, he set the tote bag on the picnic table beside her.

"Thank you," she mumbled. She bit her lower lip to keep from saying more.

"It was the electrical connector," Josh told her. "It'd vibrated loose."

She wanted to ask him if she'd somehow been responsible for that, but resisted. Most likely he would be quick to blame her if she was and reluctant to admit otherwise if not. His hesitation told her everything she wanted to know.

The words hung between them like a thick London fog.

He glanced over his shoulder at the Harley, as if eager to depart. Then he studied her for a moment. Was he assessing the damage his carelessly flung accusations had done? At last he said, "I meant what I said. I won't beg you to come with me."

"I know."

He cracked a smile, not of amusement, but tempered with chagrin. "You can be stubborn."

He hadn't seen the half of it.

He continued to study her; then his eyes softened. "Goodbye, Gretchen."

He started back to his Harley, and she wound the straps of the tote bag around her hand. "Josh!" she cried, leaping off the table.

He turned back to face her.

She wasn't sure what she wanted to say. Even if she *had* known, she wasn't sure she could have squeezed the words past the thickness in her throat. Earlier he'd clung to her, and now he was walking away from her and showing no regret. Worse, she was letting him.

"Yes?" he said.

She bit her lip and shook her head. "Nothing."

His shoulders momentarily stiffened and then just as quickly sagged in defeat. "Gretchen, listen—"

"I'm not a society girl." Of all the ridiculous things he'd said to her, that one hurt the most. She shook her head and then said what was on her mind. "Why do you want to argue with me? Do I scare you that much?" Her gaze didn't budge from his. They'd come this far, and she wasn't about to lose him now. Her heartbeat felt like a crash of cymbals inside her chest. She read the confusion in his eyes, the restraint.

"Yeah, I guess you do," he admitted reluctantly. Then he held out his hand to her. "Come on, it's time we got back on the road."

"You're sure you want my company?"

He stepped forward and tenderly cupped her cheek. When he spoke again, his voice was low and gravelly. "Yeah, I'm sure."

She rewarded his honesty with a fierce hug. She was giddy with happiness.

When she climbed onto the Harley behind him and wrapped her arms around his middle, he placed his palm over her fingers and squeezed them.

When he turned the key in the ignition, the bike quickly roared to life.

As they pulled back onto the highway, she tried to analyze what had just happened.

With the wind pummeling her from all sides, and the sun beating down on her head, she kept her eyes trained on the passing scenery and her thoughts focused on the events of the past several days. Josh cared about her. He didn't like it, but he cared. She cared about him, too. So much that it sometimes hurt. After all, she'd cared about Roger, too.

It troubled her that she hadn't recognized the kind

of man Roger was sooner. The signs had been there. His lack of attention. His unexplained absences. The careless, almost lackadaisical attitude toward their meeting times. His frequent excuses.

She'd been blind to it all. Often she'd even been grateful when he arrived late, because she herself had been so busy. Her duties on the student council had demanded a great deal of time and effort, never mind her studies.

Then there was the matter of their parents. Roger's mother, in particular. Stella Lockheart had done everything she could to encourage the romance, done everything she could to make matters easy for the two of them. Gretchen's parents had met Roger's, and the two couples had gotten along famously.

Another thing, Gretchen realized with new insight, was her complete unwillingness to become physically involved with Roger before they'd spoken their vows. While she believed strongly in the importance of waiting until after the wedding, it shouldn't have been that easy. They were two healthy young adults who were supposed to have been deeply in love.

If she'd been engaged to Josh, the physical temptations would have been far more difficult to withstand. She sighed at the thought.

Josh slowed the Harley, and she realized they were stopping at the border between Oregon and California. The uniformed officer at the checkpoint asked them a few simple questions about transporting fruit before waving them through.

California. She smiled, knowing she was close to home. But she felt sad, too, because her wild adventure with Josh would soon be over.

At six they stopped for dinner, splurging on seafood at a casual restaurant overlooking the Pacific. Although the view was breathtaking, Gretchen found her attention focused on Josh. She saw him in a fresh light. Not as the rebellious bad boy who went out of his way to challenge authority, but as a man who welcomed the chance to prove himself. A man filled with potential and intelligence, fighting his past, struggling to discover who he was and forge a promising future.

"Have you decided what you'd like to order?" he asked as he set aside the menu.

"Yes." She smiled at him.

The waitress appeared, and Josh ordered the blackened salmon while she opted for crab Louie. Neither of them seemed to have much to say, but she was deeply aware of how involved with him she already felt.

He held her hand, lacing their fingers together in the middle of the table, until their dinners arrived. Although it had been hours since lunch, neither of them was particularly hungry. Gretchen managed to finish the crab and the hard-boiled egg, but the lettuce and olives remained untouched.

"Too bad they don't need a dishwasher," she said, reminding him of yesterday morning in Cannon Beach.

He grinned. "Or a waitress."

"Oh, I think they'd be grateful I'm not waiting tables."

Their eyes met as they smiled.

"I suppose we should get back on the road," he said.

She wished they could have lingered but knew it was best they press on. Unless they had to stop for gas, their next stop would be San Francisco and her family home. She nearly laughed aloud at the thought of introducing Josh to her family. Her parents wouldn't know what to think when they met him, with his Harley and that chip on his shoulder. The last time she'd talked to her parents, she'd still been engaged to Roger.

When at last they rolled into the City by the Bay, it was after ten o'clock. Night had settled long ago, and the stars twinkled like fairy dust against the black velvet sky. It took another forty-five minutes to reach Daley City and her family home. As he parked the Harley by the curb, she removed her helmet and glanced toward the wide front porch of the three-story structure. Her parents had had the turn-of-the-century house extensively remodeled several years back by one of the city's most renowned architects. The renovation had enhanced the beauty, grace and style of a bygone era.

"Nice place," Josh said.

"I've always loved it."

"How long have you lived here?" He glanced around the upscale neighborhood.

"How long?" she asked, surprised by his question. "All my life."

He glanced at her and announced, in an aloof tone, "In my entire life, I've never lived anywhere longer than twelve months. I wouldn't know what to call home."

"It's where your heart is, Josh," she told him, repeating the old adage.

He dismounted and opened one saddlebag, then handed her the tote bag. It took her a moment to realize he had no intention of going inside with her and meeting her parents.

"Josh, what are you doing?" she asked. "You have to come in!"

He shook his head. "I don't think that's such a good idea."

"But my parents are going to want to thank you for helping me." She touched his arm. "I insist."

"Your parents will take one look at me and call the cops. And I've had all I can handle with law enforcement for one day."

"Don't be ridiculous. Mom will want you to spend the night. You can have your choice of bedrooms."

"Yeah, right, Gretchen. You don't seriously believe your family's going to throw open their arms and welcome me, do you? That'll be the day."

"Would you stop? You're going to meet my parents, and that's all there is to it."

Any further argument he might have offered was cut short when the front door swung open and her father appeared on the front porch.

"Daddy!" Gretchen cried, and raced toward him. Her mother wasn't far behind.

"Gretchen Marie, where in the love of heaven have you been?" Her mother all but broke into sobs of relief. Her recovery was quick, however, when she got close enough to get a good look at Gretchen. She gasped and covered her mouth. "Oh, my, your beautiful hair. What have you done to it?"

Gretchen had more things to concern herself with than her hair. She broke out of her parents' embrace and raced back out to the curb to grab Josh's hand. She hauled him up to the front door. "Mom and Dad, this is Josh Morrow."

"Josh." Her father hesitated and then extended his hand. The two men shook.

"Mrs. Wise," Josh said, nodding stiffly to her mother. He stepped back a pace, indicating his desire to leave.

"I think it might be best if we talked inside, don't you, Mom? Dad?" Gretchen said.

"Of course," her father replied, eyeing Josh. "There appear to be a number of questions that need to be answered, and I don't think the front steps are the place to do it."

Josh didn't show any enthusiasm for going inside, but he complied.

Gretchen watched his face when he walked through the front door and was greeted by polished woodwork created by some of the finest craftsmen at the turn of the century. The oak walls were adorned with family portraits and valuable artwork her mother had collected from around the globe. The stairway curved gracefully up to the second floor.

"Perhaps we'd best talk in the kitchen," Joan Wise said, leading the way through the oak archway. "I'll put on a pot of coffee and we can discuss this like four reasonable adults."

"Mother?" Gretchen asked, wondering what had prompted such a strange statement.

"You've given your mother and me quite a scare, young lady," her father said sternly.

Instinctively Gretchen moved closer to Josh—not because she feared her parents' wrath, but because it appeared they intended to heap blame on his shoulders. She wouldn't allow it.

Before she could respond, Josh said, "Mr. and Mrs. Wise, Gretchen has done nothing wrong."

"We'd like to hear what she has to say for herself before we make any judgments." Her father, the attorney, was at his legal best.

"Who have you been talking to?" Gretchen demanded while her mother fussed with the coffeepot, spilling grounds across the counter because her hand was shaking so badly. Something was very wrong.

The four sat at the round table in an alcove off the kitchen. Gretchen reached for Josh's hand, making sure her parents realized she was allied with him. She wished now that they'd stopped and freshened up before pressing on to her family home. The day on the road had been brutal, and they were both badly in need of a shower and rest.

"Stella Lockheart phoned…."

Ah. Roger's mother. "I can just imagine what she had to say," Gretchen said indignantly.

"Only the truth, Gretchen," her father said. "You ran off with another man." His gaze rested pointedly on Josh.

"Dad!"

Josh said nothing, but a shutter seemed to fall over his eyes.

"Stella said she felt Roger had no choice but to call off the wedding, and frankly, Gretchen, I couldn't agree more," her mother said, her voice quivering. "How could you have done that to such a fine young man? From what his mother said, he's fit to be tied. Hasn't eaten in days and blames himself."

As well he should!

"His father told us he's going to have to send Roger to a counselor." This came from her father.

How eager her parents seemed to blame her! She didn't think she'd ever felt so disappointed.

"Do you have anything to say for yourself?" her father demanded.

"You bet I do!" she cried, so angry she couldn't sit still any longer. "Counseling is exactly what Roger needs. I can't believe that the Lockhearts told you such a ridiculous story. I find it unbelievably insulting that you'd believe them."

Raising her voice was out of character, enough to garner her parents' full attention. "What you heard doesn't even faintly resemble the truth."

"Tell us your version, then," her mother suggested, calmer now.

"*My version?* What I'm going to tell you is the truth." Gretchen didn't leave room for any misunderstanding. "You're both looking at Josh and me as if we did something terrible. I'll have you know, if it hadn't been for Josh, I don't know what I would have done. I owe him more than I can ever possibly repay."

"What about the money we've sunk into this wedding, young lady?" her father asked.

"While I realize you've gone to considerable expense, I'm not willing to throw away my life and marry the wrong man. If that concerns you so much, Dad, I'll repay you myself."

"George, please," her mother said softly, and pressed her hand over her husband's. "Let Gretchen finish. I'm sure there's a logical explanation for everything."

"I don't suppose Mrs. Lockheart told you that Roger was with…that Roger slept with another woman the night before our graduation?"

Her mother gasped, and her father frowned.

"That wasn't the first time it'd happened, either," Gretchen added. "It had been going on for six months."

"Who told you this?" her father wanted to know.

"The other woman," Gretchen said. "And when I confronted Roger, he admitted it. Later I learned that she's pregnant."

"I thought there must be something more to this than what Stella Lockheart told us," Gretchen's mother said, sounding mollified. She tapped her index finger against the table, keeping time with the grandfather clock in the formal living room.

"Why didn't you *fly* home?" George Wise asked. He glanced toward Josh, and while he didn't say anything, his look indicated his disapproval.

"Because Roger's mother had my airline ticket."

"She wouldn't let you have it?"

Gretchen hesitated. "I…I didn't ask."

"Why in heaven's name not?" her father barked. "Instead you impulsively took off with a member of the Hell's Angels, and worried your mother and me half to death."

"I won't have you talk about Josh that way," Gretchen said angrily. She knew that her parents discounted Josh only because they didn't like the way he looked and the fact that he rode a motorcycle. "I don't know what I would have done without him."

Josh glanced at Gretchen and smiled apologetically, then scooted back his chair and stood. "Mr. and Mrs. Wise, it was a pleasure to meet you, but I don't believe my presence here is necessary, nor am I particularly welcome."

For one wild moment Gretchen was struck dumb. "No!" she cried when she found her voice. "I won't let you leave."

His eyes met hers. In that brief moment she realized that nothing she could say or do would change his mind. He'd seen and heard all he needed to be convinced he didn't belong in her world and never would.

"Mr. and Mrs. Wise," he said, "forgive me. I don't

mean any disrespect." Then he reached for Gretchen, catching her around the waist and hauling her into his arms. His kiss was almost primitive. "Goodbye, Gretchen," he whispered when he'd finished.

Her mother gasped, and her father's mouth fell open in shock.

Gretchen was left speechless, stunned when Josh hastily broke away and headed for the front door.

"You aren't going to let him walk out of here, are you?" Gretchen said to her parents, pointing at Josh's retreating back.

Looking uncomfortable, her father cleared his throat. "Frankly, yes, I think his decision to leave is very perceptive of him."

Gretchen stared at her father and said, "Then I'm leaving with him."

"Gretchen!" The panic in her mother's voice almost stopped her.

She placed her hand over her heart as she said the words aloud for the first time. "I love him."

Her mother gasped.

"Gretchen, I forbid it," her father said.

"Oh, Daddy, I'm not a child. Please, trust my judgment. I know what I'm doing. I'm following my heart." She offered them both a quick apologetic smile. "I'll call you, I promise." And with that she raced out the door.

She heard her parents call after her, but she paid them no heed. She saw Josh already astride his Harley. She dashed down the steps and across the lawn to the curb.

Josh scowled when she reached him. "What are you doing here?"

She refused to be put off. "I'm coming with you."

His scowl deepened. "I don't think so."

"Listen here, Josh Morrow. I'm tired of playing games, of pretending. You pay attention now, because I'm only going to say this once. You love me."

"I beg your pardon?" He made it sound as if it was all he could do to keep from laughing outright.

"You heard me," she returned sternly. "Furthermore, I love you. If you think I'm going to let you ride off into the sunset without me, you've got another think coming! We're in this together."

"Hold on." He held up his hand. "Don't you think you're taking a lot for granted?"

"Not in the least. You're going to marry me. My dad paid a fortune for that country-club membership, and we've already got the date reserved. I don't believe anyone will mind that the groom has a different last name than the man I originally planned to marry."

Josh didn't laugh at her joke. "Gretchen, there isn't going to be a wedding. At least not between you and me."

She blinked, uncomfortable with the alternative. "You want to live in sin?"

Pain flickered in his eyes. "I'd never do that to you."

Her relief was substantial. "Oh, good. I didn't think you would."

"I'm going to do you a bigger favor. I'm going to

get out of your life before I screw it up along with
my own."

"Oh, no, you don't," she said. "I've already cast
my lot with you."

"Goodbye, Gretchen." He revved the engine.

Where she found the nerve to leap in front of the
Harley, she didn't know.

He looked stunned.

"I have one more thing to say, and you'd better
listen." She'd never been more serious in her life.

He turned off the ignition. Now he looked uncomfortable. "All right, say it, but I haven't got all night."

"You've got the rest of your life. *Our* lives. It's
plain as day that you and I should be together."

"No, baby, we shouldn't."

"Be quiet," she said, her voice trembling. "I love
you, and there's never going to be anyone I'll love
more. If you leave without me, you're going to regret
it the rest of your life. You'll look back to this time,
this place, and wonder what would have happened
if you'd let me come with you."

"You win some, you lose some," he returned flip-
pantly.

"Don't you dare talk to me like that. Don't you
dare treat my love as if it's something you can toss
away without a care. You aren't fooling me. I know
you. Do you think I could spend all this time with
you and not know your heart?"

"Are you finished?" he asked grimly.

"No."

"Just how much longer is this going to take?"

"Not long." She swallowed tightly and began again. "You told me earlier today that you wouldn't chase after me. Well, *I* won't chase after *you,* either."

"Good. That relieves my mind."

She could see there was no cracking his stubborn pride. She stepped aside and watched helplessly as he restarted the engine.

Her hand covered her mouth to hold back the words to beg him not to leave her. With tears streaming down her face, she watched Josh ride off into the night.

Six

"That's not the end of the story, is it?" Carol Furness leaned back, bracing her palms against the concrete rim of the fountain, her eyes wide with dismay. A soft breeze rustled the leaves of the trees, and sunlight cut a pathway through the shade, splashing across the lush green lawn.

"He left you and rode off just like that?" This time the question came from Maddie Coolidge.

"Yes, just like that," Gretchen whispered in a futile attempt to keep the pain out of her voice. Even after fifteen years, she continued to feel that same crushing sense of defeat. On a starlit night one June fifteen years ago, Josh Morrow had left her standing alone at the curb, the sound of his retreating Harley drowning out her sobs.

Eventually her mother had come out of the house and joined her, gently placing her arms around her shoulders.

"He didn't come back?" Carol asked, breaking into the flood of disturbing memories.

"No," Gretchen replied, staring unseeingly across the deserted campus. "He didn't come back."

"But that's terrible," Maddie said.

Gretchen was aware that she was sitting in the very spot where her heartbreaking adventure had begun. Now Maddie's words brought her forward in time, and she turned to her two friends. "I loved Josh Morrow more after traveling with him for three days than I ever loved Roger Lockheart."

"Perhaps it was for the best," Carol suggested, squeezing Gretchen's hand. "Josh always did have a chip on his shoulder."

"One about the size of Alaska," Gretchen said wryly.

"What happened next?" Maddie asked.

"Next?" Gretchen murmured, pulling herself away from her memories. "Well," she said, unsure where to start, "when it became clear I wasn't going to get over Josh as easily as my parents had hoped, my mother took me to Europe."

"Do you ever wonder what happened to Josh?" Maddie wanted to know.

"Of course," Gretchen answered.

"And what about Roger?" Carol asked.

Gretchen leaned back on her hands. "I imagine the reunion will answer that question. I saw his name on the list of attendees."

"Did you see Eddie Shapiro's name on that list?" Carol asked tightly.

"As a matter of fact, I did."

"That's right," Maddie said, straightening enough to meet Carol's look. "You were engaged to Eddie."

Anger flashed in Carol's eyes. "I was. He got rid of me soon enough."

"I've told you what happened to me with Roger," Gretchen reminded her former sorority sister. "Now it's your turn."

Carol laughed ruefully. "If you think Roger was a jerk, just wait until you hear what Eddie did to me."

"I'm all ears," Gretchen said.

"I've got the afternoon to kill," Maddie seconded.

Carol's Story

One

Carol Furness fell in love with Eddie Shapiro the first time she saw him throw a football. It had been September of her freshman year at Queen Anne University. Standing on the sidelines of the football field, she'd watched the pigskin ball sail effortlessly and gracefully thirty yards into the arms of the tight end. Eddie had made it look easy, his timing perfect, his throw masterful. In that moment she recognized that, with proper training and guidance, he was headed for the pros.

And she'd been right.

Growing up the youngest child and only daughter in a family of five, with two older athletic brothers, she knew more about football than some coaches' wives. She'd started cheerleading in junior high and had set her sights on making the cheerleading squad at Queen Anne the minute she was accepted.

That first day on campus she'd set two goals for herself. Being head cheerleader by the time she graduated—and marrying Eddie Shapiro.

She took over the head cheerleading position her junior year and accepted Eddie's engagement ring the Christmas they were both seniors. They planned a July wedding, and while she was occupied with finishing the last of her credits for her education degree, something wonderful happened.

Eddie was drafted by the pros, chosen in the thirteenth round by the Denver Broncos.

"I never doubted," she reminded him as they hugged each other wildly and danced around the room. "Not once."

Little did she realize that was the beginning of the end.

"What do you mean, you want to delay the wedding?" Carol cried, hardly able to believe what she was hearing.

Eddie lowered his gaze to the lawn outside her sorority house. He butted the toe of his shoe against a dandelion, breaking off the bright yellow blossom, crushing it. Crushing *her*. He apparently had nothing more to say.

"The wedding's less than six weeks away." Someone needed to remind him of that. Her parents had already spent a lot of money, not to mention the mental and emotional commitment she herself had made to their plans these past several weeks. Finishing her classes, studying for finals and getting ready for graduation had been more than enough for one person, but she'd taken on organizing their wedding on top of everything else. Now Eddie was telling her he thought they should wait. Carol hadn't slept more than four uninterrupted hours in a row in over two weeks. She was exhausted and cranky, and the last thing she needed was this.

"I can't help it, honey," Eddie said contritely. "I've got to start training early."

"Surely you can take one day for the wedding." She was willing to forgo the honeymoon. And it wasn't as if the wedding date came as any surprise to Eddie. He'd been the one to choose July.

"I wish I could, but coach won't allow it." He sounded flustered and apologetic, but she wasn't buying it. She recognized that hurt-little-boy act of his, the one he used whenever it suited his purpose. He had a way of getting what he wanted by playing the misunderstood and abused hero. She'd seen him do it any number of times, enough to recognize the tactic when he attempted to work it on her. Well, he could manipulate others, but not her.

"Everything's different now," he insisted, his voice gaining strength. He looked up, and Carol watched the resolve strengthen in his face. In that instant she knew the truth. There was more to this announcement than met the eye.

The fact that Eddie had waited until after the graduation ceremony to tell her didn't sit well with her, either. He must have known his practice schedule with the Broncos weeks earlier. His agent had worked out the details of the contract, and although Carol was soon to be his wife, Eddie had kept the particulars to himself.

That wasn't all. She had noticed that he had been less than attentive of late, but she'd attributed that to the commotion of the final weeks of school, exams, graduation, their wedding plans—everything that was happening in both their lives. His schedule was crammed as he prepared for his induction into professional sports. As crammed as her own.

As graduation approached, it had become increasingly difficult to get him to make decisions regarding the wedding. For weeks she'd been offering her mother excuses, and she'd finally been forced to go ahead without his input. She'd wanted his opinion, but it had been impossible to catch him for so much as five minutes. When she did, his mind was on other matters, and so she'd given up.

Her list of excuses regarding Eddie's behavior had begun to sound hollow even to her own ears.

"Is there something you're not telling me?" she asked point-blank. She would rather get things out in the open now and be done with them.

Eddie shifted his weight and avoided eye contact. "No. Mark warned me I was going to be exceptionally busy for the next several months with practice and the games and all."

Carol had never been keen on Eddie's agent, but her fiancé had argued that he was fortunate to have someone like Mark Raferty on his side. He'd continually discounted her objections, and blindly allowed someone else to make business and now personal decisions for him.

"How long?" she asked, keeping her voice firm and strong.

"Long?" Eddie repeated. A confused I'm-not-sure-how-to-tell-you-this gleam was in his eyes.

"Before we can reschedule the wedding?"

He hesitated, and in that millisecond, in that half a heartbeat, the truth reared its ugly head like a sea monster rising from the waves. All at once what Eddie was saying became clear. As clear as clean glass. Now she understood and wanted to kick herself for being so obtuse, so blind to what should have been obvious all along.

"You want to *call off* the wedding." She said it for him. Without emotion. Without censure. Just hearing the words was a relief in its own right.

"Honey, sweetheart, don't be angry," he pleaded, sounding as if he was about to burst into tears.

Amazingly, Carol wasn't upset. It was almost as if she was standing offstage and watching a scene play out between two strangers. Almost as if she was a nonparticipant. What she should be doing was ranting and raving, giving in to hysteria and dissolving in tears. Instead, a calm settled over her, a sense that this wasn't really happening, that everything would soon be set right. Eddie loved her and needed her. He'd always loved her, as she had loved him.

It took her a moment longer to realize that he was still speaking. "Mark suggested it wasn't a good idea for us to marry now, and I have to say that I agree with him. I'm starting a new life."

She blinked as the words came at her like sharp needle points. "A new life without *me?*"

"There's no need to take it personally. I'm a professional athlete, and I have certain obligations to my career and my team," he said—echoing the words of his agent, Carol was sure. "Certain…sacrifices." He appeared to have trouble remembering the next line of his speech. She strongly suspected he'd memorized and repeated it for Mark before confronting her. That sounded like something Mark would have him do.

Flustered, Eddie shook his head and asked, "Are you OK?"

"Fine. Wonderful." She felt light-headed and realized the color must have drained from her cheeks for him to have noticed. "You'll want this back." She slipped the diamond engagement ring from her finger and handed it to him.

He looked stricken, staring at the diamond in the palm of his hand. "I…I still love you and all, but it's…well, difficult, you see, me going into the pros and all. And…well…"

"It's OK, Eddie." It hurt to listen to him search for reasons to tell her that he didn't want her in his life any longer. He was headed for the big time, and she was just a cheerleader. An ex-cheerleader now. As far as Eddie was concerned, a wife would be an encumbrance in his new life.

"OK? Really? You're not mad, sweetheart?" How relieved he sounded!

"Mad?" she repeated, as if surprised he would

ask such a thing. "Not in the least." She brushed his cheek with her lips. "Good luck," she said brightly.

Her response appeared to stun him. She suspected he'd been anticipating a knock-down-drag-out confrontation, even though he'd opted to tell her in a public place.

Apparently Mark had prepared Eddie to expect yelling, cursing, hysteria and tears. To be fair, her complete lack of emotion came as a shock to her as much as it did to Eddie.

"Mark thinks I have a good chance of making second-string quarterback," he explained hurriedly, looking to her for encouragement and approval, the way he always had.

"I hope you do." She realized she actually meant it.

Suddenly he looked uncertain. "We can still be friends, can't we? I'd like to call you now and again, if that'd be all right."

"Friends," she repeated, and laughed softly. Right. Eddie would do as Mark dictated and break the engagement, but he would still look to her for emotional support. Because what Mark didn't understand was the vital role she played in Eddie's life. Eddie needed her.

In time Mark would know how much Eddie relied on her, and then Eddie would be back with his tail between his legs. It was only a matter of time, but until then she wouldn't make it easy for him.

"No, Eddie, I don't think it would be a good idea if you phoned. If you want to break the engagement, then whatever we shared is over. Completely. Now, if you'll excuse me, I'd better call my parents and do what I can to cancel the wedding."

The least of Eddie's crimes was that he'd put her family through needless expense, allowing them to plan and pay for a wedding he fully intended to cancel. Right then and there, she decided she would pay them back every penny, even if it took her the rest of her life.

"Listen," he said, taking a step toward her. "I realize your family's sunk a lot of money into this wedding—I know I should have told you sooner. It's only fair that your father send me the bills. I'll make sure they get paid."

"All right. I'll make sure Dad forwards them to you." She turned and walked away. Pride was the glue that kept her from breaking into a thousand pieces.

When she got back to the sorority house, the place was buzzing with activity. Excited talk and laughter swirled around her like dust devils as her friends raced up and down the stairs, emptying their rooms. Boxes and suitcases littered the hallways. Silently she walked past her friends, up the staircase and into her room. Sitting on the edge of the mattress, she reviewed her options.

To save money for the wedding, her parents had opted not to fly out from the East Coast to attend her graduation ceremony. By waiting until after graduation to break the engagement, Eddie had not only destroyed her plans for the future, but he'd cheated her out of sharing this special day with the people who loved her and supported her dreams.

Meanwhile, though she had her teaching degree, she was without a job. She hadn't applied for a position here in Washington, believing she would be living with Eddie in Denver in a few weeks. And she'd decided to wait until after the wedding to apply for a Colorado teaching certificate. Eddie hadn't encouraged her to apply for work, but then, he hadn't offered much in the way of advice for several weeks.

Not only had he pulled the proverbial rug out from under her feet, he'd single-handedly destroyed any chance she had of finding a full-time teaching position come autumn. Every teaching job would already have been filled by this late date.

She could always fly home and live with her parents, but she had too much pride for that. Her family had helped her with her college expenses as much as possible, had sacrificed in order for her to attend Queen Anne University. She wasn't going to take advantage of their generosity any longer. As an adult, she would find a means of supporting herself. While she might not be able to find a full-time teaching job, she could always do substitute work.

Despite what he'd done, she still loved Eddie. She'd always loved him, even knowing he was weak. Even knowing how easily he could be swayed by others.

She held her breath and waited for the constriction in her throat to ease. The one thing that gave her hope was that she knew Eddie better than he knew himself. It wouldn't be long before he realized how much he missed her, how much he needed her. Within a month, maybe two, he would be back, pleading with her to marry him.

She could wait that long.

Three weeks later Carol found herself a studio apartment north of the downtown Seattle area. It was small but comfortable, and all she could afford.

Since graduation, she'd been busy submitting teaching applications to seven different school districts. Again and again she was told that the hiring process was complete, but that human resources would keep her name on file.

She made calls every day, and it wasn't long before her persistence paid off. She was asked to substitute for a physical-education teacher during summer school. A paying job, even if it was only for a week, was a start. A job was a job, and she was elated.

Summer classes weren't known for attracting the best and the brightest high-school students, but she didn't let that dim her enthusiasm. Dressed in gym shorts, a whistle looped around her neck, she led a group of fourteen physically unfit students onto the Ballard High School football field. They whined all the way, but she pretended not to hear.

As there were only a few years' difference between her students' ages and her own, she resembled a high schooler herself. Luckily she was tall, five-nine, with rich chestnut-colored hair that bounced against her shoulders.

"We're going to do a mile," she announced.

A chorus of unharmonious gripes followed. One overweight boy fell to the ground and played dead.

"Hey, guys. This isn't a time test. Run, walk, crawl, I don't care," she said, laughing at their complete lack of enthusiasm. "All I'm asking is for each of you to complete a mile."

"You actually want us to crawl?"

"Whatever it takes, but the sooner everyone's finished, the sooner we can shower and go home for the day."

The words "go home for the day" captured the class's attention.

"The other teacher didn't say anything about making us do this," someone complained.

"Really?" Carol flipped back the papers on her clipboard. "Hey, you're right," she said, holding her index finger in place. "It says five miles here."

A short shocked silence was followed by a chorus of disbelief.

The boy who'd played dead miraculously recovered. He sat up and said, "No, it doesn't."

She thrust her right arm into the air. "How many of you would prefer five miles?"

Not a hand went up.

"One mile?"

Every hand went up.

"Then get to it."

With a dismal lack of enthusiasm, the teenagers started jogging toward the track. Being in top physical condition herself, she didn't understand their aversion to exercise. She was sure that by the time they finished the mile—four laps around the track—each and every one of them would experience a surge of well-being.

She was wrong. When all fourteen had completed the required number of laps, they acted as if they'd completed World War Two's Bataan Death March.

Six of the boys had attempted to cheat by only finishing three laps, but she had kept careful count. Amid protests and threats, she'd sent each one back and penalized him an additional lap. It might not have won her an award for popularity, but she doubted anyone else would pull that trick.

To her surprise one of the girls jogged up to her on the way to the locker room. "Thanks," she said, grinning.

"For what?" Carol asked.

"For making Eddie, Jim and Charles do the whole mile. The other teacher probably wouldn't have noticed, and then they'd think they'd gotten away with something."

"They're only cheating themselves."

"I know," the girl said, her blond hair bouncing. "But they haven't figured it out yet."

It hadn't escaped Carol's notice that one of the boys was named Eddie. Like this high schooler, her Eddie hadn't yet discovered that by canceling their wedding, he was cheating himself, too.

Sooner or later he would want her back. Now that she wasn't with him, wasn't there to listen to his tales of triumph on the playing field or have her rub the soreness from his shoulder, no doubt he was already missing her. Sure to be thinking about her.

When he did phone—and he would, she was convinced of that—she would make him suffer, but for only a little while. He had plenty of lessons to learn, and she was the woman to teach them. Her pride had taken a tremendous beating, and he needed to understand that she wouldn't allow him to treat her that way ever again.

At the end of the day, she walked down the high school corridor, the soles of her running shoes squeaking slightly against the floor. Her heart felt lighter than at any time since graduation. Substitute teaching helped keep her mind off Eddie and the fact that she didn't have a full-time job.

She strolled past a line of classrooms and noticed another teacher writing on the blackboard at the front of one of them. Three rows of tables, topped with computers, stretched from one side of the room to the other. No students.

"Clark?" Carol did a double take.

Was Clark Rusbach really here at Ballard High School? Clark was Queen Anne's resident computer wizard. A man so left-brain he practically walked with a limp. Throughout her college career, she had secretly admired his genius.

He was tall, on the lean side, and fiercely intense. His thick dark hair, which needed to be cut, fell awkwardly over his forehead. Although it was a warm July day, he wore slacks and a sweater more suitable for autumn. But then, he never had been one to follow convention. In fact, what had always intrigued her about him was his complete lack of any need to conform. A true individualist, he lived and breathed in a world foreign to her own.

She had hated the way Eddie always made fun of Clark, calling him a nerd and making him the brunt of tasteless jokes. Clark had never reacted to Eddie's crude comments, which had earned him her respect. It couldn't have been easy, but if Clark was bothered by any of it, he didn't allow it to show. His world consisted of bytes, bits and chips, and they appeared to understand and appreciate him far better than his fellow humans did.

"Carol?" He'd turned to stare at the doorway. "Is that you? What are you doing here?"

She stepped into the room and said, "I was about to ask you the same thing." Shortly before graduation, rumors had abounded that Clark had been wooed by Softline, a big Seattle-based software conglomerate. She had heard that the company's young ultrarich owner had personally courted Clark and offered him an employment package with a salary said to be in the mid six figures.

"I'm here as part of a community-service project for Softline. They said it's supposed to help us understand the frustrations of students trying to learn new and advanced programs." Absently he brushed the hair from his forehead. "I don't know about the kids' frustrations," he muttered, "but I experienced a few of my own. Were we this dense?"

She laughed. "I suspect so. At least I was." Although they'd taken a number of classes together, she and Clark had rarely exchanged more than a casual greeting.

He hesitated and then said, "I thought you'd be married to Eddie and living in Denver by now."

Embarrassed, she lowered her gaze, not wanting to talk about Eddie. However, it was only natural that Clark was curious. "I guess you didn't hear. Eddie broke off the engagement. He didn't think this was a good time to marry, what with him signing with the pros and all."

Clark's thick dark eyebrows bunched together. "He broke off the engagement?" he asked, sounding incredulous, as if her former fiancé had made the biggest mistake of his life. "Eddie might have a good throwing arm, but I never *was* overly impressed with his brains. I don't see you two as a couple, really."

His words soothed her battered ego, and she smiled to show him she appreciated his kindness.

"Why are you still in Seattle? I thought your family came from the East Coast," he asked.

"They do…but I like living in the Pacific Northwest and was hoping to get a full-time teaching job." Which was not the entire truth, she realized.

While she put on a cheerful facade, the past few weeks hadn't been easy. Talking about Eddie was like tearing away a half-healed scab. She discovered that tears were close to the surface.

"So how's the job hunt going?" he asked.

Her only answer was a shrug.

"I take it that means not good?"

She tried to put on a happy face and failed. "Not the best, but I'll be fine." An awkward silence followed. "Well, it was nice seeing you again," she said, eager to escape before she made a fool of herself by breaking into sobs.

"I don't know if it'd be much help," he said, stopping her, "but I understand Softline's hiring. It wouldn't hurt to put in an application there."

At this point she wasn't picky. *Have rent payment, will work,* was her motto. "Thanks. I'll give them a try."

A week and a half later, Carol was called in for an interview with a Softline human-resources manager.

"I'm afraid all we have at present are several temporary positions," the woman said, scanning her files. "I notice here that you've got a friend at the company."

Carol could feel the color creep up her neck. "A friend?"

"Yes, one of our up-and-comers put in a good word for you. That helps."

"Well, I'm a hard worker."

"I'm sure you are. What I'd like to do is start out by having you fill in for some of the support personnel when they go out on vacations. I notice your secretarial skills are excellent."

"Thank you."

"Could you start first thing Monday morning?"

"That would be great." Carol didn't bother to disguise her eagerness. Now she could pay the rent and meet her other expenses until school started up in the fall and she could—fingers crossed—substitute on a regular basis.

The woman punched a few keys on her computer keyboard and waited for the printout. "You'll start by replacing one of our executive secretaries." She handed the printout to Carol.

Not until she left the building did Carol read the name of the person she would be working with.

Clark Rusbach.

Two

Bright and early Monday morning, fifteen minutes ahead of schedule, Carol located Clark's office at Softline. Finding his name etched in gold on the door, she experienced a surge of pride that this incredibly brilliant man was her friend.

Knowing Clark, he hadn't anticipated that the woman who'd interviewed her would mention his recommendation. Her guess was that he wouldn't want her to know what he'd done. Nevertheless, it was sweet of him.

She traced her index finger over the incised letters of his name and smiled to herself. Just a month out of college and already Clark Rusbach had made his presence felt in the business world. And yet he also managed to be incredibly thoughtful. Eddie could take a few lessons from Clark. When the time came, she would be sure her former fiancé learned how good Clark had been to her.

Stepping into Clark's office, she paused and

glanced around, soaking in the ambiance. Her smile widened. The one thing you could expect from Clark was the unexpected. While the outer office consisted of a desk, chair, filing cabinet and other secretarial paraphernalia, he worked in what might be best described as a research lab. Well, sort of. The large room held several tables and chairs, multiple desks and no less than six computers. On the walls were diagrams that resembled road maps of China and three calendars, all with Monday the fifteenth—which was a week away—circled in red.

By the time Clark arrived, Carol had coffee brewing and was humming softly to herself. She'd sorted through the regular mail and placed it in a neat stack on his desk. One of his desks. He had five.

"Good morning," she said, feeling slightly awkward. Always before they'd been on equal footing, but now Clark was her boss.

"Mornin'."

"I'm taking Mrs. Derby's place while she's away," she explained unnecessarily,

"So I see." He shed his jacket and hung it in the closet next to her own cardigan sweater. "Do you have any questions?"

"Yes…several." She hesitated, not sure how to begin. "Do you want me to call you Mr. Rusbach? Would you prefer I pretend I don't know you?"

He chuckled. "Clark will do. Relax, we're friends. It was just the luck of the draw that you happened to be assigned to me right off."

"We *are* friends, aren't we?" Until her interview she'd considered Clark to be more of an acquaintance. "Thanks for putting in a good word for me," she said, forgetting that she'd decided not to mention what he'd done.

His shook his head as though to dismiss her appreciation and headed toward his own office.

"How do you like your coffee?" she called after him.

He reached for his mail and glanced toward her. She was standing in the doorway between the two rooms, rubbing her palms together, awaiting his response.

"Hot."

"You got it." She poured him a mug, and then carried it into his office and set it down on the desk with the mail. She started to return to her own room, changed her mind and abruptly turned around. "Clark?"

He glanced up, his gaze expectant.

She hesitated, then said, "I'd like to ask you something…personal."

"Okay."

She hadn't intended to do this, but nothing ventured, nothing gained. "I signed up for ballroom dancing classes at the community center for Monday, Wednesday and Friday nights, and I was wondering…" She trailed off, wondering if it was wise to put him on the spot.

"You need to leave the office a few minutes early those days? Sure."

"No," she said, surprised that he didn't understand what she wanted. "I'd like it if you'd come with me— that is, if you want to." It would be a lot more fun if she had a partner, although the instructor had said she was welcome to attend without one.

"I'm not really the dancing type," he replied.

Carol thought she heard a bit of regret in his voice, as if he was halfway tempted. "But you could learn, and it would be fun."

For a month she'd done nothing but sit in her tiny apartment night after night and feel sorry for herself. The dance classes offered a welcome respite from what was fast becoming monotony.

"Yes, but—"

"You could do it," she coaxed, giving him a warm smile. "No one's going to laugh at you."

"Why me?" he asked.

"Well, because first off, I like you, and there isn't any chance of anything romantic developing between us. I mean…well, you know."

"No. I don't know."

"Because of Eddie."

"What about him?"

"Anytime now Eddie's going to want me back and the two of us will get married," she said.

"You mean to say you'd actually marry him after what he did to you?" Clark looked shocked.

She realized it probably sounded as though she had no self-esteem if she would willingly forgive Eddie when he'd treated her so badly. While she had every intention of marrying him—eventually—she would demand he pay a hefty penance first.

"Eddie can be shallow," she said, hoping Clark understood. "I know that about him, and I know how easily led he sometimes is. I'll make the decision about my future with him when the time comes."

She could see that her response didn't please him. He said, "In other words, you're inviting me to these dance classes of yours because you consider yourself safe in my company because I'm a geek."

She didn't know how to answer.

"I see," he told her when she reminded silent. "Well, in that case, perhaps you should ask someone else." He turned back to his mail, effectively dismissing her.

Carol felt terrible. Obviously he'd taken her silence as confirmation of his statement. She'd been looking to thank him for being her friend and had ended up insulting him. Worse, she'd managed to start off the week on the wrong foot. Depressed beyond words, she slowly returned to her office and propped her forehead on the heel of her hand.

Before Eddie canceled the wedding, she'd been a confident and composed woman. Now, it seemed, words twisted themselves around her tongue, and she possessed all the poise of a four-year-old on roller skates.

That morning set the tone. She and Clark barely exchanged a word over the next four days. At first she assumed she'd insulted him so thoroughly he'd simply chosen to avoid her. Only later did she real-

ize he was working hard. Every now and again he
came into her office needing one thing or another. If
she wasn't available, he left instructions on her desk.
He arrived early and left after she'd gone home. If it
hadn't been for the other secretaries in the department, she would have felt as though she'd been set
adrift on an iceberg.

Mrs. Derby had thoughtfully prepared a list of instructions for her replacement, and Carol followed
them religiously. The other secretaries told her that
Clark was deeply involved in developing a revolu-
tionary software program, a project he'd first envi-
sioned while still in college. On Monday the fifteenth
he was scheduled to give a demonstration of the program's capabilities to the company's board of directors.

That explained why he had basically ignored her
all week.

Friday afternoon at closing time, she cleaned off
her desk and was ready to leave when he appeared
and glanced around.

"Carol, could you—" He stopped abruptly when
he saw her standing with her purse draped over her
shoulder. He seemed surprised, until he glanced at
the wall clock and noted the time. "I didn't realize
it was so late."

"Do you need me?"

He hesitated and then shook his head. "It's fine.
You can go."

"Clark, please, I'd like to help if I can. If it wasn't
for you, I probably wouldn't even have this job."

"What about your dance class?"

"Oh. I decided to postpone it."

"Because you needed a partner?"

"No, not really. It just didn't turn out the way I wanted it to."

He ran his fingers through his hair. "I'll make a deal with you. If you can stay late and help me out here, I'd be willing to take those classes with you."

As far as Carol was concerned, that was the deal of the century. "You're on!"

"You're sure you don't have a date?"

She shook her head. She was reluctant to admit that she still had faith that in time Eddie would come to his senses. She didn't want Clark to remind her that such thinking was dangerous. She knew it was. Yet, hard as she tried, she couldn't make herself believe it was really over with Eddie.

She'd dated him for almost four years. She knew him better than anyone—faults, foibles and flaws. They'd been a team, a couple, two of the most popular personalities on campus. Their love had been a storybook romance. The head cheerleader and the football hero. Their looks had complemented each other, too. She was tall and slim, with rich chestnut-colored hair and deep blue eyes. Eddie was blond and built and gorgeous. A hunk.

Clark was nothing like Eddie. He was more the kind of hero you would find in a spy thriller. At first glance his features were completely nondescript. Not one characteristic about him stood out, and he blended into the crowd.

But once she'd really paid attention to his appearance, she'd realized how attractive his eyes were. They were a soft brown, a shade darker than his hair. He was an inch or so taller than she was, and while she wouldn't describe him as muscular, he looked as if he kept physically fit. Perhaps he jogged or enjoyed hiking.

"So you've decided against dating anyone at the moment?" he asked.

"For now," she said. "It's too soon after Eddie." That was true. She missed her former fiancé too much to think about dating anyone else. "Anyway, I'd like to stay and help," she offered. "And really, you don't need to volunteer for the dance classes unless you really want to take them."

"You're sure?"

"Positive. I don't have any plans other than to veg out in front of the television." That was what she did most nights. She slept poorly, awoke at odd hours. In the long frustrating weeks since graduation she'd become personally acquainted with every late-night show on TV.

"I guess I should warn you," Clark said. "I've had an irrepressible urge to take up ballroom dancing." His face relaxed into a rare smile. The transformation in his looks was amazing. His eyes changed to a warm shade of amber, and a dimple appeared in each cheek. She was mesmerized. It demanded every ounce of control she possessed not to ask him to smile once more just so she could see those dimples again.

Clark needed her to transcribe his notes and then format them for his presentation. It amazed her that someone so familiar with computers didn't like to use one himself. He'd even asked her to print out his e-mails for him.

It took her a couple of hours, and when she'd finished, her stomach was growling. It had been a long time since lunch, and she was starved. Planting her hand on her stomach, she waited for the growling to subside.

"Do you like Chinese food?" Clark asked unexpectedly.

Carol looked over at him. "Chinese? Adore it. Why?"

"I'm ordering dinner. You interested?"

She nodded, returning her gaze to his meticulous notes. "Sure."

"Any preferences?"

"Hot, spicy and lots of it," she answered.

A moment later she heard him reach for the phone behind her. His conversation was followed by a call to alert security that their dinner would be delivered in half an hour.

By the time the food arrived, she had completed formatting the presentation. He proofread the printout while she opened up the numerous white cardboard boxes and dug through the paper bag for napkins and eating utensils. The smell of chili peppers, ginger and vegetables made her mouth water. Sitting on the edge of the desk, she plucked a fat shrimp from a box and brought it, dripping hot chili sauce, to her mouth. Some of the juice rolled down her chin, and she only saved it from staining her blouse in the nick of time. As she set the napkin aside, she noted that Clark's gaze had left the typed presentation and he was studying her.

She froze. "Did I do something wrong?" Perhaps he'd ordered the shrimp for himself and hadn't intended on sharing. Feeling guilty, she lowered the box back to the desk top.

"No, no, you're fine."

Nevertheless, she waited until he'd finished reading before she ate any more. Luckily it didn't take him long. He opted to sit in her chair, leaning it back as far as it would go and propping his feet on the corner of the desk. Both of them worked the chopsticks, too hungry to carry on a conversation.

Once the edge was off her hunger, she glanced at him. "If Mrs. Derby could see us now…" Although Carol had never met the woman, it hadn't taken her long to know that Clark's secretary was a neatness junkie, one who would never risk tainting her workplace with soy-sauce stains.

Clark chuckled.

The chopsticks poised in front of her mouth, she said, "Do that again." At his puzzled look, she said, "I want you to laugh again." She waved him on with her chopsticks.

He frowned, but even that wasn't able to destroy the effect the short burst of laughter had had on him. His eyes had warmed, and he appeared more approachable, more human.

Four days earlier she had thought of him as nondescript. While she admired his genius, she'd viewed him as dull. But having dinner together, sharing Mongolian beef, Szechuan shrimp and Chinese noodles, had been the final step in altering her opinion. While he wasn't the type to call attention to himself, and in fact he avoided it, that didn't mean he was boring. Like her peers at Queen Anne University, she'd been blind to the warm generous man behind the brains.

"Carol?"

She lowered her gaze when she realized she was staring. "Your face changes when you smile," she said.

"It does?"

"Yeah." How unnerving that Clark should have this effect on her! "Are you anxious about the presentation on Monday?" she asked as a means of changing the subject. The transition wasn't smooth, but he was kind enough not to mention it.

"Nervous? No, I can't say that I am."

Again he surprised her. She would have been a wreck.

"I know this program. Door Handle is my baby. All I have to do is let it do the talking for me. If I had any doubts about its performance, any qualms about its effectiveness, I'd be worried. But I have absolute faith in her."

"Her?"

"I think of Door Handle as female. At first she was temperamental and unreasonable, but after a while we adjusted to each other, and now we get along great."

"You think women are temperamental and unreasonable?" she asked, planting one hand on her hip and pretending to be offended.

"Not always," he said, grinning, "but on occasion." He went on to explain a number of bugs he'd fixed as he'd worked on the program, and as he spoke, he became more animated, more excited. Clark excited? This was a side of him she'd never seen. Much of what he said, she'd read as she'd transcribed his presentation. The words had seemed routine on the page, but when he spoke them, she could actually feel his energy and enthusiasm.

She couldn't help being impressed. Clark was nothing like Eddie, who was fond of boasting about his athletic skills, bragging about his accomplishments. Clark mentioned his own talents only in passing. It was the program he was promoting, not himself.

Their conversation evolved slowly between bites of food, and she found herself laughing again and again at his dry wit. When she was certain she would burst if she ate a single morsel more, she set her chopsticks aside and gave a satisfied sigh. "Thank you for dinner. I can't remember the last time I enjoyed myself so much."

"I'm the one who's grateful. I appreciate your staying late," he said as he dumped the empty containers into the wastebasket.

"I was happy to do it." Now was the time to apologize. It was either take advantage of the opportunity now or regret it later. "There's something you should know," she said, capturing his attention. "On Monday I let you think that I'd consider myself safe with you at the dance classes because I saw you as a geek. But I didn't—don't—see you that way, Clark. I see you as a gentleman—that's why I'd feel safe. I think you're...wonderful."

He appeared confused, as if he'd put the matter out of his mind. "Uh...don't worry about it."

"I can't help it. Sometimes I do incredibly stupid things."

For reasons she was hard-pressed to explain, she had the sudden urge to cry. And then she understood.

Just before graduation she'd been sitting on top of the world, and then, in a single afternoon, everything she'd considered important had come crashing down on her shoulders. This was the first time in weeks that she felt like her old self. It was thanks to Clark, and she was incredibly grateful to have him for a friend.

She hid the attack of emotions behind busywork. Silently she removed any telltale evidence of their "crime" by wiping off the desk. As she reached for her purse, she glanced at her watch, uncertain of the bus schedule this late in the evening. While it was close to eight o'clock, the sun had yet to set.

She lingered a moment, realizing she'd enjoyed their time so thoroughly that she was reluctant to leave. "Thanks again." She eased her way toward the door.

Clark nodded. "I've got a few things to finish up here, otherwise I'd walk you to your car."

She didn't correct him. "Good night, Clark."

"Good night, Carol."

She left, and the sound of her footsteps echoed in the corridor. Security let her out of the building. As luck would have it, she'd just missed the bus and was doomed to wait an hour for the next. Dusk was settling over the Puget Sound area, and a breeze rustled through the trees, the wind weaving through the thick green branches, whispering secrets.

Twenty minutes later a red Mustang passed the bus stop, then stopped abruptly, tires squealing. Slowly the car backed up toward her. The passenger window lowered, and she recognized Clark.

"You're taking the bus?" he asked, frowning. "Why didn't you tell me?"

"I was supposed to?"

"No...yes. Hop in and I'll give you a ride home." He leaned across the passenger seat, unlatched the door and pushed it open.

"Thanks," she answered, smiling to herself. After climbing in and giving him her address, she snapped the seat belt into place. When he merged with the freeway traffic, she leaned her head back and closed her eyes, lulled by the country music coming from the CD player. This man was full of surprises. She would have assumed he was more of a classical-music fan. Russian or Italian composers whose names all begin with *P*. Prokofiev or Puccini. Men who'd suffered for their art. Her mental picture of him didn't include Carrie or Keith.

In her relaxed state, with her eyes closed, she grew brave. "I want to ask you something, all right?"

"Ask away."

"I want to know about the comment you made last week about not seeing Eddie and me as a couple."

"It's true. I never did," he returned promptly.

"Why not?" She'd always viewed them as perfect together. But she respected Clark and was eager to hear his reasoning.

This time her question gave him pause. "Eddie was never right for you. He doesn't deserve you."

While that might be true, she loved Eddie. Even now, she found it hard to be angry with him. It wasn't really Eddie who'd broken the engagement but his agent. Mark was the one who'd talked Eddie into canceling the wedding, and once Eddie came to his senses, he would be back.

"You're wrong, you know," she felt compelled to say, irritated with herself now for asking. Perhaps she'd been looking to have Clark reassure her that eventually her world would right itself. That it was only a matter of time before Eddie recognized what he'd lost and wanted her back. She felt lonely and alone, and yes, she missed him. Missed the life they'd dreamed about and planned together. It wasn't supposed to happen like this.

Clark's gaze briefly left the road as he glanced at her. "You asked. If you aren't going to like the answer, then don't ask the question."

"Have you always been like this?" she demanded, gesturing with her hands, which refused to keep still. "Such an expert on everyone else's business?"

Her anger didn't rile him—he didn't even bother to respond—but she was in rare form and wasn't about to end the conversation. Not until she'd gotten him to admit he was wrong. She *needed* him to admit it.

"If you know me so well, then who do you think I *should* marry?" she demanded. There hadn't been a single man on the entire campus she could love more than Eddie. The fact she recognized and accepted Eddie's flaws assured her of that.

The question hung in the air between them like a piece of spoiled meat. "You won't like the answer to that one, either."

"I asked, didn't I?" she insisted. "I'm a big girl. You can say it." She defied him to come up with a suitable candidate. She was meant to be with Eddie. She couldn't stop thinking about him, and she was sure he would come to his senses soon.

When Clark wasn't immediately forthcoming with a response, she asked again, this time with more feeling, more determination, more courage.

"Exactly who do you see me marrying, if not Eddie?"

His fingers tightened on the steering wheel, and she almost cheered. He was squirming in his seat. She loved it. Triumph rose in her. He couldn't come up with anyone better suited to her than Eddie.

Clark glanced at her again. "I could see you married to me," he admitted softly.

She gasped. It was as if someone had sucked out all the oxygen from the car. "You?" she repeated. "You and me? Together?" She hadn't expected him to suggest *that*.

"I warned you that you weren't going to like the answer."

"You aren't serious." This was a joke. She should have known he was just like every other man. His ego demanded he come up with a response, even one so patently nonsensical.

"I'm serious."

"It's your ego, right?" she asked when he exited the freeway. "I realize men have a problem with pride."

"Men aren't alone in that."

"True enough."

Clark and her? She couldn't see it. They were as different as two people could be. Not that there was anything wrong with diversity. But she wasn't right for him. He needed someone who understood him and his high-tech world. Someone really wonderful.

He drove to her apartment building, parked and killed the engine.

Apparently he was waiting for an invitation. "Would you like to come inside?"

"Yes."

"Any particular reason?"

Again he answered with a terse "Yes."

She certainly had no objections to his company,

nor to his seeing her place. The studio apartment was small, but she'd made an effort to decorate it nicely and was pleased with what she'd done. A few stuffed animals sat here and there on the sofa, mostly so she could hold them while she watched television. Her cheerleading pom-poms rested on the fireplace mantel, along with the trophies she'd accumulated during her college years.

Clark stepped inside and glanced around appreciatively. "You've made this homey, Carol."

"Thanks."

She gestured for him to make himself comfortable, and then walked into the kitchen and turned on the faucet.

"What are you doing?" he asked, following her.

"Making coffee."

He frowned. "Why?"

"I thought you'd like a cup...." Now that he'd asked, her making coffee made about as much sense as everything else that had happened that evening.

He moved toward her, his gaze holding hers. His eyes were dark and intense, keen and purpose-filled. He reached out and rested his hands on her shoulders. His touch was light, gentle and, in a small way, comforting. It had been weeks since Eddie had held her, and she'd missed the closeness, the sense of belonging.

"I'd like to prove my point."

"Your point?" She wasn't sure she understood.

With his eyes imprisoning hers, he gently drew

her closer. Apparently he planned to kiss her. Her eyes widened.

He wrapped his arms around her and drew her against the solid length of his body. What she'd suspected earlier proved to be accurate—he was both trim and muscular. Before she knew it, she was wrapped in the warm shelter of his embrace. He smelled of musk and spicy Chinese food, an odd yet pleasing combination.

Her heart pounded so loudly that she was certain he could hear it. She raised her head, anticipating his lips, telling herself that she wanted this over with so she could tell him that while his kiss was very nice, they would never be anything more than friends.

Then it happened. Something she could neither explain nor define. A yearning buried in the deepest part of her being broke free. If anyone had told her such a thing was possible, she never would have believed it. She'd been engaged, involved with one man for years. A man she'd loved—loved still, despite what he'd done.

She'd always been a woman who knew what she wanted and went after it. Never one content to wait patiently on the sidelines, she made a habit of grabbing hold of opportunity with both hands.

That she should experience this…whatever it was, before Clark even lowered his mouth to hers, left her feeling claustrophobic and fearful. Perhaps there was something to what he was saying, although she had trouble comprehending it.

Slowly, with deliberation that bordered on torture,

he pressed his lips to hers. Her heart went into overdrive. She couldn't think to move. In that moment she was his prisoner.

The instant his warm moist lips settled over hers, she was lost. No kiss had ever been more potent. A frightening kind of excitement took hold of her. She stood on tiptoe and slid her hands up his chest to link them behind his neck.

The kiss deepened as she opened to him the way an orchid opens after a rainfall. She wanted more. Her breathing came fast and hard, and she was gratified to realize his breath was ragged, too.

He demanded, and she gave. Freely and without reserve. The heat of their kiss felt hot enough to set off the kitchen smoke alarm as they angled and twisted their mouths, seeking to give more, to take more. To *be* more.

When he eased his mouth from hers, his chest was heaving. Clinging to him, she kept her eyes closed and forced air into her lungs. Even now her heart pounded in her chest like a boxer's fist hammering a punching bag. Never in all her life had she experienced a kiss as profound as this.

She should have known it was too perfect, too beautiful. She should have known it would never last.

It didn't.

Within seconds he ruined the most beautiful kiss of her life.

"I was right, wasn't I?" he said. "You don't know yourself nearly as well as you think you do."

Three

Carol couldn't decide if she was relieved or disappointed when Clark's secretary returned from vacation. Mrs. Derby was exactly as she'd pictured her. Late fifties and meticulously groomed, in a dark business suit with her gray hair primly pulled back in a bun. Punctual, precise and particular. Her personality meshed perfectly with Clark's needs. Everyone said they got along famously.

Carol missed seeing Clark on a daily basis, but at the same time she was grateful they didn't have to spend a lot of time together. Not after what had happened when he kissed her. Especially when she considered her response. She'd gone over that night countless times, but she had yet to make sense of it.

Ego had prompted Clark to kiss her. That part she understood. What she had trouble reconciling was her response. After a while she decided the best thing to do was put it out of her mind, banish that night and the kiss from her thoughts.

Fate seemed to be on her side. Clark didn't have a lot of free time on his hands. Door Handle, his software program, had received a warm reception from Softline's board of directors, and he'd been granted the additional funds he'd requested, along with a handful of staff.

Whenever she saw him, he was surrounded by others, all making demands on his time and expertise. His gaze would follow her, and she made a point of greeting him with a smile or a wave. He had to bow out of the ballroom dancing classes, and while she realized he regretted having to renege on his promise, he had no choice.

Every now and again they would bump into each other in the cafeteria or in the building lobby. He would always stop and ask how she was doing, but she had the feeling the question needed to be rephrased: how are you doing *without Eddie?* Her answer was the same every time. "Good, really good." But the truth was, she'd expected to hear from Eddie long before now.

She didn't need to ask Clark how *he* was doing; the answer was obvious. He worked too many hours, ate poorly and, from the darkening shadows beneath his eyes, she also suspected he wasn't getting enough sleep. While his poise remained unshakable, she instinctively recognized he was frazzled.

As for her, the job with Softline was ideal, because it offered terrific flexibility. She was able to substitute teach as long as the schools let her know in advance. The more time she spent in the classroom, the more she loved teaching. Kids of all ages loved her, and she found herself proving to be a popular teacher. Her performance reviews were full of praise, and she was convinced it was only a matter of time before she was hired permanently.

Teaching had been her dream from the time she was five, when she'd lined up her dolls in front of a small chalkboard. Wearing her mother's high heels and a broad-brim hat her grandmother had given her, along with several long beaded necklaces, she'd lectured her rapt audience on vowel sounds and the importance of not eating glue.

As much as possible, she tried not to think about Eddie. But surely he missed her. Surely he thought about her. Surely he wasn't so busy that everything they'd shared no longer mattered to him. She simply couldn't believe it. After four years of daily contact, she'd simply assumed he would feel as if a part of himself was missing without her at his side.

The waiting was agony. The not knowing. He haunted her dreams, and often she awoke with her heart heavy and her emotions raw. In the beginning it had been much easier. Her anger and frustration had effortlessly carried her through the first few weeks. Later she'd focused her fury on Mark Raferty, Eddie's agent. No one could convince her that Mark wasn't responsible for turning Eddie against her.

As August rolled into September, she began to blame herself for being foolish enough to hold on to any hope of Eddie's wanting her back in his life. Surely he would have contacted her by now if that was the case. Even with Mark's disapproval, he would have found a way to reach her.

He hadn't, and that told her everything.

The first Sunday of September would either break her or make her, she decided. That was the day the Denver Broncos would host the Seattle Seahawks in Mile High Stadium.

She promised herself that she wouldn't so much as turn on the television. It was as simple as that. Why torment herself? Nothing good would come of seeing Eddie suited up in a Bronco uniform. Viewing him, even on television, was sure to make her heartache ten times worse. She would be crazy to make herself miserable on purpose.

It didn't take her long to admit that a promise made was a promise broken. On Sunday morning she dutifully sat in front of the television screen, dressed for the occasion in baggy jeans and a Queen Anne sweatshirt.

The national anthem was playing when her doorbell chimed. She tore her gaze from the screen to run to the door.

"Clark," she breathed, surprised to see him.

"How're you doing?" he asked, and looked past her to the television.

"I assumed you'd be at the office," she said. For a while she'd toyed with the idea of inviting him over just so she wouldn't turn on the football game. But knowing Clark, he would have felt obligated to accept, and she didn't want that. Not when he was so busy with his career.

"I *should* be at the office," he told her, and yawned, stepping into the apartment.

"Then why aren't you?"

His eyes were dark and serious. "You need me."

He removed his jacket and made himself comfortable on the sofa, stretching his arms out along the back. "I know you. Eddie's playing, and you wouldn't be able to resist."

She couldn't very well argue with him.

He patted the space next to him. "Are you going to sit down and watch the game or not?"

"I wasn't going to watch the entire game," she rushed to tell him. "I planned on changing channels just as soon as…" The lie died on her lips when his gaze swung from the television to her with laser accuracy.

"Okay, okay, so I thought I'd check it out. Eddie's the second-string quarterback, so it's highly unlikely he'll even play."

"You're still pining for him, aren't you?"

"Not as much." Embarrassed that what he'd said was true, she downplayed her feelings. She had never thought of herself as weak, but that was the way Eddie made her feel. Years ago, in one of her psychology classes, she remembered the professor explaining that a person's sense of emotional well-being was directly related to the amount of control they had in a situation. Eddie was the one in control of her, and it was time to let go. If only she could!

"Sit down," Clark said again, and again patted the space next to him.

She did as he asked. Leaning against the thick cushions, she pretended to find football and everything that went with it exceedingly boring. It wasn't long, however, before she'd scooted to the edge of her seat, enthralled with the game and clutching her teddy bear to her chest.

"You hungry?" Clark asked.

So intent was she on the action on the football field, she barely heard him. When the Seahawks completed a pass she leaped from the sofa and danced a jig in front of the coffee table. "First down. Did you see that?" she cried, thrusting her arm in the air. At his blank look, she added, "We just completed from third and ten."

"Wonderful. What have you got to eat around here?"

"Not much." She sat back down and pressed her fingers to her lips as a Seattle running back carried the ball five yards, broke free from a tackle and gained three more for a total of eight. It was highly satisfying to envision the Seahawks beating Denver on their own turf. Her heart would ache just a little less if that was the case. It was a matter of honor, of pride, of triumph over a man with a fickle heart.

In three months' time, she had become petty and childish. Too bad. She hadn't felt this good in weeks. Months!

Clark took it upon himself to examine the contents of her kitchen, which in her tiny apartment was directly behind the sofa. She heard him opening and closing cupboards and grumbling under his breath.

"I haven't bought groceries this week," she said over her shoulder. "There's some bread for a sandwich, though." If she remembered correctly.

She heard the bread box open and close, then heard him muttering something about preferring his bread white, not green.

At last she heard a triumphant "Ah!" She couldn't imagine what he'd found, but whatever it was appeared to satisfy him. He set the microwave to humming and soon the apartment with filled with the distinctive sound and mouth-watering aroma of popcorn.

Her stomach growled. She hoped he realized he was a dead man if he didn't intend to share. Her thoughts quickly returned to the football game when Seattle fumbled the ball, setting up the Broncos for an easy score. She fell to her knees and pounded the carpet. "No, no, no."

"Something happen?" Clark asked, sitting back down.

She toyed with the idea of being flippant and decided against it. He might get angry and decide to keep the only edible food in her entire apartment to himself.

"I don't want to talk about it," she said, and sat down next to him, eyeing his bounty.

She generally ate directly from the popcorn bag, but he had emptied the contents into a ceramic bowl. A paper towel protected his knee.

"You're going to share that, aren't you?"

He eyed her skeptically. "Do I have a choice?"

"No."

He chuckled. "That's what I thought."

Old habits being what they were, Carol gave a one-woman cheer, leaping high in the air when, several plays later, Seattle scored their first touchdown of the game.

"You're rooting for Seattle?" Clark asked.

"Of course." His question irritated her. Naturally she would cheer for Seattle. This city was her home, not to mention that her heartless ex-fiancé happened to play for the opposing team. She would love to see the Denver Broncos get their butts kicked purely for having the audacity to draft Queen Anne's star quarterback.

"What about Eddie?" Clark asked next, his words hitting her square in the chest. Too close to her heart for comfort.

"What about him?" How well she could dupe Clark into thinking she didn't care about Eddie remained to be seen. "Football's been a part of my life for as long as I can remember. You think I'm only pretending to root for Seattle just to spite Eddie?" She made the question sound as ludicrous as possible to hide the fact that in fact that was exactly what she was doing. "You're probably unaware that both my brothers played high-school and college football. It's in our family's blood. It's only natural I should love the sport." Too late, she realized she'd given far more of an explanation than necessary. Clark *knew,* and nothing she said would convince him otherwise.

Turning back to face the television, her eyes fell

on the screen at the precise moment the camera focused on Eddie Shapiro. He was standing on the sidelines, looking fit and muscular, and so handsome that merely seeing him produced a sharp unexpected jab of pain.

Pleased with the media attention, he smiled into the camera. And it wasn't just any smile, either. It was a special smile that held deep meaning for her. It was the smile he'd always directed at her after he'd completed a touchdown pass. The smile that reminded her of his love, and the promise that they were a team and would always be together.

Yeah, right.

As if he was looking directly at her, he winked. Too late to tame her reaction, she gasped. Pride demanded that she look away, but she found she couldn't. She broke into a cold sweat and felt as if she was about to be violently ill, and still she couldn't force herself to stop watching.

Noiselessly Clark knelt beside her on the carpet and wrapped his arms around her, hugging her close.

Gripping his upper arms, her nails digging into his flesh, she waged a fierce inner battle between the demands of her pride and the intensity of her pain. She squeezed her eyes closed and trapped the emotion inside her chest until she gasped for air. She was hardly aware of the tightening sensation in her lungs until they felt about to burst.

The release was instantaneous, and with it came a flood of tears. She didn't know which would be worse—letting Clark stay to witness this humiliation, or requesting that he leave, so she could bear her pain alone. She didn't want him with her, and yet she needed him. Needed to be held and reassured. Needed to be comforted.

Whispering soothing words, he gently rocked her, the palm of his hand pressing the back of her head. With nothing left to hide, she slipped her arms around his neck and clung. He was her rock, her stability, her life preserver.

He brushed the hair from her cheek. "It's going to be all right."

She hated to disagree with him, especially now when he was being so kind, but she couldn't help herself. "No, it isn't."

"Carol, trust me. It won't always be this bad."

"Yes, it will. I'll never get over him. I fell in love with a worm, but I never expected this to happen."

"Eddie Shapiro didn't deserve you."

She ran the back of her hand over her tear-streaked cheeks. "I know that, everyone does…but that doesn't make me love him any less."

He spoke into her hair. "Someday you'll look back on this and wonder what you ever saw in him."

"I already do, and it doesn't help."

She felt him smile against her temple. She was the undeserving one. She didn't deserve a friend as wonderful as Clark. That he put up with her was nothing short of amazing.

"Clark," she whispered, lifting her head from his chest and meeting his gaze through tear-filled eyes. "Kiss me."

He blinked as if he wasn't sure he'd heard her correctly. "Kiss you? Now? Why?"

"Because I want to feel something besides this pain. Please…you were eager enough not so long ago." The pain of actually seeing Eddie was bad enough. But that pain was only a small portion of what she felt, and Clark had witnessed it all. She'd bared her soul, unable to hide behind a facade of disinterest. So maybe kissing him wasn't such a good idea, but she certainly hadn't expected an argument from him.

Taking matters into her own hands, she took away his option to choose and kissed *him*. Her palms on either side of his head, she angled her mouth and firmly planted her lips on his. He offered no resistance, giving in fully to the exchange. As before, she was overwhelmed by her own heated response.

He moaned and, pushing his tongue into her mouth, gained control of the exchange.

Even as their bodies moved against each other, she didn't know what had prompted her to ask him to kiss her. Instinct, she suspected. Survival. He was the anesthetic, the drug that would help ease her through this agony. His kiss was the promise that she could, would, feel again. The reassurance her heart demanded and craved.

Again and again he kissed her. But then he pulled back, as if easing away in a slow deliberate process before addiction set in, while she waged a silent war, seeking, wanting, *needing* more of him.

Clark was refusing her. Her pride would have been

badly bruised if she had not been aware of how difficult it was for him to maintain control.

"No more," he gasped between labored breaths, sounding like a man on the rack, crying for mercy. He groaned and lifted his face toward the ceiling, exposing his throat. She kissed him there, pressing her lips to the underside of his jaw, her tongue exploring the taste and feel of his skin.

He rewarded her with a soft moan. He reached behind her, and she didn't know what he was doing until the television abruptly went silent and she realized he held the remote control in his hand.

He set the remote aside, then glanced at his wrist and swore under his breath. "I have to get back to the office."

She barely recognized her own voice. "Now?"

"Yes, now."

This time his rejection *did* hurt, but she pretended otherwise. She dropped her arms and scrambled up from the carpet as though she hadn't a care in the world, as if this little interlude had meant nothing to her.

Clark stood with far less enthusiasm. "Will you be all right?"

"Me?" she asked, as though it was a foolish question. "Of course."

He didn't believe her, and his eyes said as much.

"I've got a million things to do. Groceries, errands…" she said, counting them off on her fingers.

"Carol," he said, stopping her. "I mean it."

"So do I. I feel great. You haven't got a thing to worry about."

He held her gaze for a long time, as if gauging the truth of her words. Good old-fashioned pride saved her. As she had for months, she pretended she was unaffected, unscathed and at peace.

She almost wished she hadn't.

He left soon afterward, and she moved to her window and watched him drive away. Using him as a buffer had been wrong. He deserved better. She liked Clark, always had. Even before they became friends, she'd taken his side. Since working for Softline, she'd discovered she more than liked him. She'd come to appreciate him.

Clark Rusbach was quite possibly the best friend she had.

"Hi, Mom, hi, Dad," Carol said into the telephone. "Happy Thanksgiving."

"Carol, sweetheart. How are you?"

"Wonderful. Great." A small lie, but one she could rattle off without guilt. "I'm subbing at Ballard High School this week, teaching English and PE. I'm loving it."

"What about your job at Softline?"

"I'm working there, too. They've been wonderful, giving me whatever days I need when the school district phones."

"You're spending the day alone? Thanksgiving?"

Her mother made it sound like a fate worse than

death. "I already told you—Clark's family invited me over."

"Clark's your new boyfriend."

Carol had stopped counting the number of times she'd explained otherwise. "We're just friends." And they were. Good friends. She'd never experienced this kind of friendship with anyone else, male or female. While the Door Handle project continued to consume much of his day, he found pockets of time to be with her. He seemed to possess the uncanny ability to know exactly when she needed a friend most.

Following the September Sunday when she'd brazenly thrown herself at him, they both avoided any physical contact. She appreciated the wisdom of keeping their relationship strictly platonic. Nevertheless, she couldn't help wondering...

"I like Clark," her father said.

"You've never met him," Carol said. Her father would champion any man, even Bozo the clown, as long as he wasn't Eddie.

"I don't need to. I'm just grateful you didn't marry that bum."

"Harry," her mother chastised.

"I know, I know, you don't want me to remind her of Eddie," her father muttered. "As far as I'm concerned, she had a lucky escape. I don't care how good a football player he is, Eddie Shapiro is no gentleman."

While Carol agreed with him in principle, she couldn't force herself to admit it outright. Thoughts of Eddie still followed her like dark shadows. Try as she might to not think about him, not a day went by that she didn't think about him. Much of the anger had passed. She wished him well—at least she hoped she did. The only thing she hadn't been able to find was acceptance.

Each time the phone rang, her heart leaped and she prayed against all reason that it was Eddie. She'd stopped counting the times she was convinced she'd seen him on the street, or heard his voice across a crowded room. Each time a small flicker of hope and joy would fire to life, then quickly fade as reality set in.

"Harry, please," said her mother. "Can we not talk about Eddie?"

Her father muttered something Carol couldn't make out. "I'm going to have a wonderful day," she said, forcing enthusiasm into her voice. "So don't worry about me."

"You'll be home for Christmas?"

"I'll be there." By hook or by crook she would find a way to share the holiday with her family. "Give my love to everyone," she said, trying hard to remain cheerful. "And eat extra turkey for me."

The goodbyes were especially difficult. She had missed Thanksgiving with her family before. But this year it was different, and her parents recognized it as keenly as she did herself.

Clark arrived just before noon to pick her up for dinner. He'd trimmed his hair and was dressed casually in an Irish cable-knit sweater and gray slacks.

Carol did a double take, barely recognizing him. He looked good—different, although she couldn't say what it was. She found herself staring, perplexed by what was happening, and when he frowned, she quickly turned away.

"I made an apple pie," she said.

"Wow. I didn't know you baked."

She was pleased to see that she'd impressed him. "My mother insisted I learn two things before I left for college. How to bake an apple pie and the proper way of cutting up a chicken."

"The important things in life," he teased.

"They are!" she said, perhaps a bit too defensively.

"Hey," he said with a smile, and held up both hands. "I'm agreeing with you."

He opened the car door for her and then carefully placed the plastic-covered pie in the back seat. While Carol was grateful for the invitation to Thanksgiving dinner, she couldn't help being curious about his parents. He rarely mentioned them. She suspected they were older versions of him. Successful genius types. Her one fear was that the entire dinner conversation would revolve around things she couldn't even pronounce, much less understand.

She couldn't have been more wrong. His parents were as normal as her own. She might have suspected he was adopted if it wasn't for the physical similarity between him and his father.

Nadine Rusbach zeroed in on Carol's train of thought almost immediately. "I know what you're thinking," she said, as she opened the oven door and tested the turkey.

"You do?" The comment caught Carol unawares, before she could disguise her thoughts.

"Don't worry," Nadine said, closing the oven door. "Everyone wonders how it is that two perfectly ordinary people like Sam and me could have spawned Clark."

Carol was fascinated.

"We knew our son wasn't going to be like other children when he started reading at the age of two."

While Carol had never questioned Clark's brilliance, she hadn't been aware of how intellectually superior he actually was. She thought once again about the fact that, unlike Eddie, he didn't need to boast about his talents to anyone who would listen.

"He didn't fit in with the kids at school, and he could have gone to college when he was thirteen, but we talked it over with him and decided against it. Sam and I wanted him to have as normal a childhood as possible."

Clark stuck his head into the kitchen. "Are you telling tales, Mom?"

Nadine smiled warmly at her son. "Of course. Why don't you take Carol downstairs and show her your first computer?"

"Mom, Carol doesn't want—"

"Of course I do." She loved the idea of getting a look at his childhood firsthand.

"All right," he said. "Just remember, you asked for this."

He led her downstairs into the basement and flipped a switch, bathing the area in warm light. Leading her past the washer and dryer, he escorted her into what might have been a workshop. Only it wasn't tools that lined the walls, but diagrams that resembled hopelessly entangled fishing lines. The workbench held a large, now obsolete computer.

"That's Melba," he said.

"You named your computer?"

"Doesn't everyone?"

She assumed he was serious until she saw the twinkle in his eye. "If I named mine," she said with a smile, "it would be something like Beelzebub."

He chuckled. "Melba took on the personality of a demon more than once. When I built her for my sixth-grade science—"

"You built her, er, it?"

He nodded and went on with his tale. While she listened, her gaze roamed the workroom. Tucked between the diagrams was a small color photograph. There was something vaguely familiar about it.

"What's that?" she asked when he'd finished his story.

"What?"

"That." She pointed.

"Just a picture," he returned nonchalantly.

"Can I see it?"

He hesitated, something she had rarely seen him do. "I guess, although I don't understand why you're so curious."

She didn't understand, either, until he reached

across the bench, unpinned the photograph and handed it to her.

She frowned as she stared into her own smiling face. She was on the football field, pom-poms in her hands. The camera had caught her in midair, arms and legs akimbo, her body like a giant X. The wind had whipped her hair behind her until it looked almost as if she were flying. "That's me," she whispered, completely stumped about when the shot had been taken.

"Yes, I know." He sounded bored, and eager to move on to another topic.

She stared at the photo. It wasn't recent. Not from the last couple of years, of that she was sure. Her freshman year? Sophomore?

"I took it," Clark admitted, as if confessing to a crime.

She raised her gaze to his. "When?"

"The first time I saw you."

Although it was entirely possible that he had attended Queen Anne's football games, she couldn't remember ever seeing him there.

"When was that?" It embarrassed her that she continued to be mesmerized by her own image, but she couldn't stop staring at her own innocence. How happy she'd been, carefree, and full of enthusiasm for life and all that it held in store for her. Her eyes shone brightly; her joy spilled over. She realized now that the photograph had been taken her freshman year before she'd started dating Eddie. Light-years ago.

"Did I really look like this?"

"You still do," he returned, seemingly surprised by her question.

"I do?" She wasn't fishing for compliments, but she no longer viewed herself in the same way. Eddie had robbed her of her happiness, stolen it like a thief in the night. If that wasn't tragic enough, she'd given him permission to do so. Every day she allowed him into her thoughts, allowed herself to hope, to believe, that he wanted her back, he continued to rob her of her appreciation for life.

"You're beautiful, Carol."

Clark wasn't a man who handed out compliments indiscriminately. She couldn't recall his mentioning how she looked one way or another in all the months they'd been friends. And now he tucked his finger beneath her chin and with maddening slowness lowered his lips to hers.

The kiss was gentle, devoid of passion. A friendly exchange. Nevertheless, she felt its impact all the way to her toenails. Her eyes fluttered open when he raised his head. Releasing a deep sigh, she offered him a feeble smile.

"I think you might be the best friend I've ever had," she said.

He smiled. A rare smile that lit up his eyes. "We'd better get back upstairs before my parents decide to eat without us."

She nodded, and when he reached for her hand, their fingers intertwined.

She first heard his parents when she was halfway up the staircase.

"I'm telling you, Nadine, she's the one."

"Sam, please, don't do or say anything to embarrass Clark."

"Me? I'd never do that." A short pause. "Not intentionally."

"Thank you for that."

"We're going to have magnificent grandchildren, sweetheart. With her looks and athletic abilities and Clark's brains—what a combination."

Carol could feel her face growing hotter by the moment.

Clark stopped her on the stairs. "We better let them know we're coming," he said.

Four

When Carol booked her airline tickets to spend Christmas with her parents, her spirits lifted considerably. Spending the holidays with her family and all that was familiar was sure to ease the disappointments and frustrations of the past year. She had been away from those she loved for far too long.

On a Tuesday a couple of weeks before Christmas, she sat in the Softline cafeteria finishing the last of her lunch. But her mind wasn't on her chicken-salad sandwich. It was on her two older brothers and their families. Both Jeff and Jerry were married and had children of their own. She enjoyed being an auntie to her two nieces and her nephew. And although she dearly loved Seattle, it would be good to be home again.

Sipping the last of her tea, she was about to return to work when Mrs. Derby, Clark's secretary, approached her.

The older woman greeted her with a rare display of warmth. Mrs. Derby wasn't the chatty friendly sort. What made her such an excellent assistant was her dedication to duty. And to Clark.

Carol returned her greeting, and for a moment, an irrational fear took hold that somehow Mrs. Derby had unearthed a soy-sauce stain on her desk. She smiled when she realized how ridiculous she was being. Clark would have covered for her.

Her thoughts brightened at the thought of him. They saw each other on a fairly regular basis these days. They'd come to rely on each other, although she recognized that she derived far more from the relationship than he did.

In her own way she'd tried to thank him for being her friend. She'd helped him Christmas-shop for his parents and Mrs. Derby, and he'd done the same for her. They never did make it to the ballroom dancing classes. The one evening he was free to accompany her, he had arrived, looking tired and worn to a frazzle. He'd wanted to know how much it would cost him to get out of it. She had laughed, hugged him, and let him off easy with pizza in front of the television.

It surprised her how often they laughed together. A few months earlier she never would have guessed that he had such a wonderful wry sense of humor. She appreciated his wit and wondered how it was that no one else had recognized it during their four years of college.

Clark helped her in other ways, too. He diverted her from obsessing about Eddie. Thoughts of him didn't plague her as they once had. She was no longer in a state of constant anticipation, metaphorically sitting on the edge of her seat, waiting for him to phone, to knock at her front door. He hadn't and he wouldn't. She knew that now. But her life had ceased to feel so empty without him.

They saw each other once, sometimes twice, a week, but always on a casual basis. She didn't consider their outings dates. They were friends. Good friends. Nothing less, nothing more, nothing else. And she absolutely did *not* let herself think about what they'd heard his parents saying on Thanksgiving.

She looked at Mrs. Derby, who was waiting as if uncertain she was doing the right thing. At last the woman spoke.

"I suppose you've noticed how late Mr. Rusbach sometimes works," she said.

"Yes."

"He's here all hours of the day and night!" Mrs. Derby blurted, and the outer rims of her ears turned crimson.

"I wondered..." Carol admitted, frowning. Clark *had* seemed overly preoccupied of late.

"He needs to take better care of himself." This last part was almost whispered. Mrs. Derby would rather die than be accused of unprofessional behavior. In her mind, discussing her employer's work habits bordered on conduct unbecoming. "He'll listen to you," she went on, glancing over her shoulder to make sure no one could hear.

"So you want me to..." Carol trailed off, uncertain.

"You see, Mr. Rusbach forgets about the time."

That sounded like Clark, all right. The man was a

computer genius, but time seemed to have no meaning for him.

"You'll come, won't you?" the other woman gently pleaded. "I don't mean every night, just some nights." She paused, looking flustered. "Like tonight."

Carol hesitated, still wondering exactly what it was Mrs. Derby wanted. "Are you saying you want me to tell Clark it's quitting time?"

"If you wouldn't mind. I worry about him. The nights he's meeting you, he can't get out of here fast enough. You make him happy, and I can see he makes you happy, too. I don't mind telling you how pleased I am with the way things are developing between you two. Lots of young women these days let their heads be turned by men with more brawn than brains." She pursed her lips, revealing her disapproval.

Apparently now wouldn't be a good time to mention that she and Clark were only friends.

"I've tried talking to him," Mrs. Derby said with resignation. "Some of the other staff members have, as well. He listens, or at least it appears he listens. But he never actually changes his behavior. This morning I arrived for work and discovered Mr. Rusbach hadn't gone home."

"You mean he stayed the entire night?"

Mrs. Derby nodded, then worried her lower lip as if she regretted having said so much.

"I doubt I'll be much help. I—"

"Oh, but you will be," Mrs. Derby insisted.

Carol had trouble believing it, but she said "All

right" anyway. She might not possess an IQ as high as Clark's, but she knew better than to get on the wrong side of Mrs. Derby.

At five-thirty, as promised, Carol arrived at Clark's office. Mrs. Derby, who was cleaning off her desk for the night, glanced up and shared a conspiratorial smile with her.

"Everyone else has left for the night," she whispered.

"Go on home, Mrs. Derby," Carol said. "I'll make sure Clark leaves at a decent hour."

The other woman beamed. "I know you will."

Carol wasn't convinced she had as much influence on Clark as Mrs. Derby believed. He revealed all the signs of a workaholic; even his mother had said so during Thanksgiving dinner two weeks earlier. It would take a lot more than a gentle prod to distract him from his mission.

Right now he was sitting in front of a computer, fully involved with whatever he was doing.

"Clark," she said softly from behind him.

He glanced over his shoulder, and when he saw her, he frowned. "What are you doing here?" Not exactly the warmest of greetings.

It was all she could do to keep from glancing over her own shoulder and asking Mrs. Derby for the answer. As it was, she caught sight of the older woman giving her an I-told-you-so look on her way out the door.

"It's quitting time," she said.

"I know." He returned his attention to the monitor. "Had we planned to meet?"

"No…not really."

He glanced up at her. "Is everything all right?"

She faltered, unsure how to respond. This wasn't going well.

"Carol?"

"Everything's wonderful," she said too quickly. She had his full attention now, when she was least prepared to deal with it.

He studied her, then blinked. In that split second she realized what must have been behind Mrs. Derby's concern. Something must have gone wrong with the software. Without leaking delicate information, the woman had been attempting to tell her that something was wrong without letting on exactly what it was.

In his effort to discover the solution, Clark had driven himself to the point of exhaustion. He desperately needed a break. Then and only then would his mind relax enough to release the solution. And there was one. Carol believed that with all her being. For every negative there was a positive, for every push a pull. She'd seen it happen time and time again.

He undoubtedly knew that, too, but being the intense individual he was, he didn't have the patience to wait for the answer to reveal itself. He wanted a solution, and he wanted it now.

"How about dinner?" she asked, saying the first thing that popped into her head.

"You buying?" he joked.

"No, cooking." She had carefully budgeted every penny over the holidays, and she had no choice. She mentally reviewed the contents of her cupboards, and she groaned inwardly while plastering a smile on her face. She had no clue what she could possibly prepare that didn't come out of a can.

"You cook?"

"I've been known to," she said.

"What's the occasion?"

"Nothing special. I guess I just don't want to be alone tonight." She lowered her eyelashes for fear he would see through her scheme to drag him away from the office.

Perhaps he wanted to believe her. She didn't know, but before she realized it, he'd turned off the computer.

"I'll need to come back," he said.

"Tonight? Here?"

He looked at her as though he had no clue what she was asking.

"You're coming back to work after dinner?" she elaborated.

He didn't hesitate. "Probably."

She restrained herself from chastising him. He wouldn't listen, and she doubted it would do any good. If anything, it might put a strain on their friendship, and she certainly didn't want to do that.

She needn't have worried. When they got to her house, he sat in front of the television while she sorted through her cupboards in a futile attempt to scrounge up an appetizing meal. While deciding between tuna casserole and boxed macaroni-and-cheese, she glanced into the living room. Clark was sound asleep on the couch. Obviously her company was less scintillating than she wanted to believe. If Mrs. Derby hadn't clued her in to his exhaustion, she might have been insulted.

Retrieving the afghan her mother had crocheted for her, she carefully placed it over him. He roused briefly, his eyes fluttering open, when she removed his shoes, but she could see it was too much of a struggle for him to stay awake.

"Rest," she whispered, and smoothed the hair from his brow. The idea of kissing him came out of nowhere. Without stopping to gauge the wisdom of giving in to the impulse, she bent forward and gently pressed her lips to his.

The kiss was sweet, simple and wonderful. Her heart swelled with tenderness. He'd been such a good friend. She smiled, remembering their adventures while Christmas shopping and how they'd laughed over a delicate lacy nightie he claimed he was considering for Mrs. Derby. Then he suggested maybe he should purchase it for her and wiggled his eyebrows suggestively.

She straightened, then dimmed the lights. She couldn't seem to leave him alone and checked to be sure he was comfortable a number of times. She tucked the blanket more securely around his shoulders and ran her hand lightly over his brow. The urge to kiss him again was strong, stronger than it should have been. It worried her a little, though surely the feeling came only from an appreciation of everything he'd done for her. Nothing more.

Suddenly she wasn't so sure of that.

What Mrs. Derby had said disturbed her. She had mentioned how pleased she was with the way things were developing between them. At the time Carol had been tempted to ask *what* things, but she'd stopped herself. Perhaps she'd been afraid of the answer. Then there was that time, ages ago, when she'd challenged Clark to name someone better suited to her than Eddie, and he had suggested himself.

It had been a joke, right? Ego alone had prompted that. But then she thought about how his parents seemed to believe she and Clark were a match. He'd never mentioned what they'd overheard his parents say, and she had assumed that was because he wanted to spare her any embarrassment.

All right, so maybe a case could be built that Clark was at least a little bit in love with her. But she didn't want to believe that, because then she would be forced to confront her own feelings for *him*.

She liked him so much. She didn't know what she would have done without him all these months. He'd helped her through the most difficult time of her life with warmth, understanding, compassion and humor.

She sat down and braced her elbows on her knees as she studied his sleeping face. His features had relaxed, and the shadows under his eyes were gone, along with the worry lines that normally marked his forehead.

Her chin resting in her hands, she mulled over

her feelings for Clark. Did she love him? And if so, why was it so important that she deal with the feeling now? He was by far the best friend she'd ever had, and it was common knowledge that friends often made the best lovers.

What about Eddie? Yes, he was a creep, and he'd hurt her terribly, but she wasn't convinced she knew how *not* to love him. She knew it was over, but he'd been a big part of her life for so long.

The phone pealed, and she leaped to her feet, not wanting Clark to wake up. Grabbing the cordless, she pressed it to her ear. "Hello," she whispered fiercely into the receiver, annoyed with the caller's timing.

"Carol, is that you?"

"Eddie?" His name rushed from her lips. Her knees felt as if they were about to give out. Bracing her back against the wall, she slid to a sitting position on the floor. For months she'd dreamed about this, been consumed by it. And now that he'd phoned, it didn't seem possible. She feared it was a hoax. That someone somewhere was playing a cruel joke on her. But it sounded like Eddie.

"Is it really you?" she asked, afraid to believe what her heart and head were telling her.

"How's it going, sweetheart?" he asked, as cheerful as a five-year-old.

"Good," she responded, without thinking. "How about you?"

"Fabulous. Fabulous."

She yearned to kiss him senseless, and in the same breath, the same heartbeat, she wanted to scratch his eyes out. How narrow the line between love and hate could be. Now that he'd phoned after all these lonely months, how quickly she was willing to forgive him.

Or was she?

The joy she'd experienced when she realized it was Eddie died a quick and sudden death. Eddie, who'd purposely waited until after graduation to cancel the engagement. Eddie, who'd led her to believe they were to be married long after he'd known he wasn't going to go through with it. Eddie, who'd abandoned her without a qualm.

The line, charged with emotion seconds earlier, went strangely quiet.

"So, Carol," he asked, "are you teaching?"

It was all she could do not to tell him she was lucky to be subbing, thanks to him. Even if she had said it, the sarcasm would have flown right over his head. Eddie heard what he wanted to hear and nothing else.

"I know you must be a wonderful teacher," he added. But he couldn't fool her. She knew him much too well. He was worried about whether she was mad at him or not.

"I've been doing some substituting," she explained, keeping her voice calm. "When I'm not working for the school district, I'm doing some work at Softline."

"Softline," Eddie repeated. "Isn't that where… what's-his-name went? Clark the geek?"

Eddie would never think of Clark in any other way. Everyone remained one-dimensional to him because Eddie himself was one-dimensional. "Yes, geek," she echoed, knowing it would do no good to remind him that Clark was brilliant. It would take a dozen Eddies to make one Clark. No, a thousand Eddies.

The stiff silence hummed like a buzz saw between them.

"Does Mark know you're calling?" she asked bluntly.

"No," he admitted reluctantly.

"Then why'd you phone?"

His laugh was forced. "What Mark doesn't know won't hurt him. Anyway, I've only got one more game till the season's over."

The team was paying him megabucks to stand on the sidelines and be prepared to step in if necessary. After being the star player at Queen Anne's for four glorious years, it must have been painful for him to stand idly by and watch someone else collect all the glory.

In a blink of an eye Carol understood. His phone call made sense now, perfect sense. He missed her, all right, because she wasn't there to soothe his ego, to pat his back and tell him how wonderful he was. That was Mark's job now, but Mark wasn't her. He wouldn't have her knack for what had always been her specialty—ego damage control. And his poor ego must have taken quite a beating over the past several months.

He wanted her. He needed her, and despite everything she knew about him, being needed felt awfully good just then.

"Are you glad I phoned?" he asked in a little-boy voice that told her he was craving assurance. Not just anyone's, either. Hers. Only hers.

Poor guy. Poor, pathetic guy.

She delayed answering, wanting him to suffer. "It depends on the reason why you phoned, don't you think?"

He hesitated and lowered his voice slightly. "I thought we could talk about that later."

"Really?" This was proving to be more interesting by the moment. "When?"

"Next weekend."

She held her breath while she debated what to do. She really should give him a piece of her mind right then and there. Tell him exactly what she thought about him—in small words, so he would be sure to understand. It was what he deserved. A swift kick in the butt, and then she would be done with him once and for all.

But she didn't.

"Dinner," he added, his voice dipping to a husky murmur. "Just you and me, the way it used to be."

She wasn't even tempted. Her head snapped up, and she inhaled sharply when she recognized the truth. She was free. Free from Eddie. Free from the endless waiting. Free to move on with her life.

All the weeks, all the months, of mourning her lost love were over once and for all. Her father had insisted she'd made a fortunate escape, and for the first time she acknowledged that he was right.

Eddie was selfish and egotistical. She wanted no part of him. Not now. Not ever.

"What do you say, sweetheart?" he prodded gently.

In the nick of time she bit back the words telling him what he could do with his invitation. He wanted things to be the way they used to be. He wanted her back, and was willing to sweet-talk her if necessary.

Well, by heaven, she would let him. He could talk all he wanted, get down on his knees and grovel, but it would do no good. She would take pleasure in laughing in his face.

"Dinner?" she asked, wanting to make sure they were meeting in a public place with lots of witnesses.

"Sure—anyplace you want. Anyplace. I've missed you, Carol. Tell me you've missed me, too," he murmured.

"Why?"

"I need you to say it. I need you to tell me you've thought about me."

She hesitated, almost choking on the words as they slid past her tongue. "I've missed you," she said, and while it was the truth, it wasn't the whole truth. In the beginning, she'd missed him desperately; her heart had been breaking. Not any longer.

"Wear that blue dress I used to love, will you?" he asked with the same breathless quality he'd used when he'd first seen her in the skintight satin dress.

"All right, I'll wear the blue dress," she said, smiling. She had every intention of doing as he asked. She wanted his mouth to drop open when she walked into the room. Wanted him to know exactly what he was losing.

"Will there be champagne?" she asked softly.

"Anything you want, sweetheart."

"Where are we eating?" Wherever it was, it had to be expensive. Very expensive. Not only would she derive a great deal of delight in flaunting herself, but she wanted to be sure she ordered the priciest meal on the menu before she walked out on him.

He named one of the best restaurants in town. "Is that good enough for my sweetheart?" he asked.

"That's perfect." Lots of people would be there while she made a fool of him.

This was too good to be true. After all these months she was going to have her revenge. She knew that if she were noble and mature, she would be frank but kind and tell him there was no hope of their ever getting back together. She toyed with the idea for perhaps two seconds, then rejected it.

She wanted to see Eddie squirm. It was what he deserved, and she was looking forward to making sure it was talked about around town.

"Saturday, then," he said.

"Saturday."

A moment later she turned off the phone. With her eyes closed, she contemplated the conversation. This was good. Better than good. Though she hadn't known it until now, this was what she'd been waiting for.

She went into the kitchen and threw her arms into the air in silent triumph. Joy all but exploded inside her. She was free, finally, finally free, and it felt good!

She turned and realized that Clark was awake, sitting up and watching her. His face was devoid of emotion, as if he'd only just awoken. She sincerely hoped that was the case.

"Clark," she said, so excited it was all she could do to keep from telling him what had happened. He wouldn't understand her need to see Eddie one last time. "You're awake," she said, hoping her voice didn't betray her.

He nodded, and his eyes seemed to look straight through her. "I thought I heard the phone."

She glanced down at the receiver in her hand as if she'd never seen it before. "Yes…it did ring." Then, attempting to gauge whether he'd heard any part of the conversation, she said, "I hope I didn't disturb you."

He ignored that and asked, "Anyone important?"

She bit the inside of her lip, undecided how to answer. When she did, she spoke the truth. "No."

He didn't say anything for a long moment.

She was grateful, because it gave her time to collect her wits. "Dinner's almost ready," she announced, as though she were serving a culinary masterpiece. "Tuna casserole. I hope you like tuna? I would have asked, but you fell asleep and…" The words tumbled out of her mouth like bowling pins struck by a thirty-pound ball. When she realized she was talking too fast, too excitedly, she shut up.

Rubbing the sleep from his face, Clark sighed heavily. "Who was that on the phone, Carol?"

Five

"Who was that on the phone?" Carol repeated slowly, giving herself time to debate how much she should tell him. Clark deserved the truth, but she was afraid he would think less of her if he knew how she planned to take her revenge on Eddie.

"Carol?"

"A friend," she hedged.

"You seemed to be in a good mood when I woke up," he commented. "I looked up and saw you waving your arms as if you were celebrating something. Whoever it was must have given you good news."

The time to tell him was now, but still she hesitated. Eventually she would explain everything. But all in good time, when they could laugh about it together. She would fill in every detail, and announce that once and for all Eddie Shapiro was out of her life. Then she would look at Clark and suggest that perhaps it was time for them to be more than friends.

The timer dinged and, grateful for the distraction,

she took the tuna casserole out of the oven and set it in the middle of the table. They ate in companionable silence. If Clark was quieter than usual, she didn't notice. Her own thoughts were humming along at high speed as she replayed the phone conversation in her mind again and again, savoring every word.

All at once, for no apparent reason, Clark leaped to his feet, almost toppling his chair.

She gasped. "Clark?"

He said nothing, only stared directly ahead, as if her cupboards contained the answers to the universe's most complex questions.

"What's wrong?" she asked. "What is it?"

"I've got to get back to work."

"Now?"

"Now," he said, and cast her a look so full of joy it was almost blinding. He caught her by the shoulders, half lifting her from the chair, and soundly kissed her. She was certain he'd meant it to end there. Just a happy excited kiss.

But it didn't. Instead, he kissed her a second time, his lips hungry and urgent. She responded in kind, her inhibitions gone. Oh, this was wonderful. More than wonderful. Why had it taken her so long to discover that everything she'd ever wanted was right here within her grasp?

She clung to him, her fingers buried in his thick sweater. She felt as if she were on a carnival ride, ascending higher and higher.

At his unspoken demand, she gave him what he wanted, her tongue mating with his in an endless game of desire. A roaring sound filled her ears, and she realized it was her own blood, her own heart, racing with happiness.

They'd exchanged kisses in the past, but these were different.

She could tell that he felt it, too. He eased his mouth from hers and stared at her, his expression dazed. She herself felt winded, although somehow she continued to breathe normally. This feeling, this sensation, was new, and she reveled in it. Marveled that she could share this wonder, this excitement, with Clark.

She slid her fingers into the hair at the nape of his neck and urged his mouth back to hers. The kiss sent her senses reeling once more. After a few long moments she tore her mouth away and whispered, "Clark?" She wasn't sure what to make of what was happening between them.

He braced his forehead against hers and inhaled sharply, the way a drowning man gasps for air when he breaks the surface.

"That answers my question, doesn't it?" he said softly.

"It does?" Her eyes were still closed.

"Yes. About who was on the phone." He released her, and her eyes flew open. "Eddie Shapiro," he continued, and she felt a sudden chill at his tone. "I know. I heard far more of the conversation than I wanted to hear. You told him you were working at Softline with the geek—who can only be me."

He'd heard that? Oh, no! "Clark, I know what you're thinking, but it wasn't like that."

"I asked, but you weren't exactly forthcoming with information, were you? You'd rather I didn't know you'd talked to Eddie."

"Well, yes, but there's a reason for that, and if you'd give me a chance, I'd—" She wanted to say more, but he cut her off.

"Isn't there always a reason, Carol?"

"Oh, Clark, don't make this difficult. You're right. It was Eddie. He wants to see me and—"

"I know. I heard. He's taking you to dinner, and he wants you to wear your blue dress. And you're happy about it."

She hesitated, then confessed, "Yes, but not for the reason you think."

His laugh was short and devoid of amusement. "Carol, please, I'm not stupid. Be honest—you're thrilled. Don't try to fool me. I saw you dancing around the kitchen as if you'd won the lottery.

"This is what you've been waiting for all these months. Eddie wants you back, and you couldn't be happier. Otherwise you'd never have responded to me the way you did just now. What was that, your swan song, to let me know what I've been missing?"

"No!" She was truly insulted that he'd suggested such a thing.

"Then you weren't pleased to hear from Eddie?"

He was trapping her with logic, using her own responses against her and not allowing her to explain or untangle this mess. "Maybe in the beginning, months ago, I longed to hear from Eddie, but that's all changed."

"When?"

"When did it change? Heavens, I don't know. It was a gradual thing. I'd pined after him for months, and then one day I realized I didn't care anymore. I can't tell you exactly when I stopped, because I don't know."

"That isn't the impression I got. You sounded absolutely delighted when you realized he was on the other end of the line."

She groaned. He was right. If she claimed otherwise, he would know she was lying. "Okay, I'll admit when I first answered, I felt a certain excitement. I'd been hoping he would call me for months, and then it finally happened, but…my delight was more a sense of being right. Knowing that eventually he would need me, then hearing from him."

She paused and held Clark's gaze. "I don't want to talk about him right now," she said. "I want to know what happened just now between us."

"Nothing happened."

"Don't kid yourself. We've got something precious and wonderful, I know it. I don't want to ruin it by dragging Eddie into the middle of it."

A sadness entered his eyes. "Yes, I know. But unfortunately, whatever it is, it's too late. You've got your precious Eddie back." Abruptly he turned away and, without looking back, walked out the door.

Carol followed him outside, her emotions whirling like dry snow whipped by the wind. "Clark!" she called after him. A chill raced up her arms, and she folded them tightly against her abdomen. The cold that struck her had nothing to do with the temperature and everything to do with Clark. "Please listen to me. I'm only planning to see Eddie this one time!" she cried. If Clark would give her a chance to explain, then he wouldn't be in such a hurry to walk out on her.

"Right. One time," he said, as he opened his car door.

"Clearly you don't, or you wouldn't be acting this way. I need closure with Eddie. It has nothing to do with you and me."

He climbed into his car and started the engine.

She couldn't believe he was actually refusing to hear her out.

Her anger carried her for nearly twenty-four hours. This unreasonable side of Clark was one she'd never seen before. The man was both stubborn and irrational. He'd refused to listen. He'd heard one side of her telephone conversation and discounted everything she'd tried to tell him afterward.

For three days she didn't hear from him. Three of the longest days of her life. Finally, deciding that this entire thing was utterly ridiculous, she stopped by his office a few minutes before quitting time on Friday.

When Mrs. Derby saw her, she smiled warmly. "Hello, Carol."

"Hi," Carol said, looking past the woman, hoping to catch a glimpse of Clark. She'd been miserable, and she would be leaving soon to spend the holidays with her parents. She needed to settle things between them before she left.

"I don't suppose Clark's around?" she asked, raising her voice, hoping he would realize she was there and come out to see her.

"Oh, sure, go right in." It surprised her that Mrs. Derby didn't announce her the way she did everyone else.

Carol hesitated. "How's he doing?" Her guess was that he was still working himself to the point of exhaustion and not eating properly. Worrying about him was going to be her excuse to explain this unexpected visit, should Mrs. Derby ask.

"Mr. Rusbach's doing much better," Mrs. Derby surprised her by saying.

"He is?" Carol's ego appeared to be in for a beating, along with everything else. Clark walked out on her, and it seemed he'd never been happier.

Mrs. Derby's smile revealed her approval. "Whatever was bothering him earlier has worked itself out. He's his old self, and I can't credit anyone but you."

Carol wanted to believe it, but she knew otherwise. But it didn't matter. She needed to see him, to talk to him and tell him that she'd received a wonderful job offer—a full-time teaching position. The only problem was, she would need to move to Alaska. Still, the pay was excellent. She couldn't afford to turn it down. She would, though, in a heartbeat, if Clark asked her to stay. And he would, wouldn't he? He'd been tired and had overreacted, and she'd allowed things to escalate. This evening they would laugh about it, then put the problem behind them.

Wearing a smile, she walked toward his office.

The door was open far enough for her to see him sitting at his desk, shuffling paperwork. She was convinced he knew she was there and had opted to ignore her.

This wasn't looking good.

She glanced over her shoulder, and a smiling Mrs. Derby urged her forward with a wave of her hand.

"Hi, Clark," she said.

He glanced up but revealed no emotion. "Hello, Carol."

"I'd like to talk to you, if I could."

"Sure." He gestured toward an empty chair.

She sat on the edge of the seat. "I think we should discuss what happened the other night, don't you?"

"Not particularly."

So he wanted to make this difficult. "We can't let this come between us, Clark. I mean, we're friends, and—"

"I assumed we were friends, yes."

"We are," she insisted. "Good friends." She couldn't have survived the past six months without him. He'd lent her confidence and support. Held her when she'd wept, encouraged her, helped her find a job. The list was endless. "You really are the best friend I've ever had."

He looked bored.

"I know you're upset about me seeing Eddie again, but it isn't what you think." She smiled, convinced that once he understood, he would laugh about how silly their misunderstanding had been.

"I heard everything I needed. Spare me the details. You want to have dinner with your ex-fiancé, that's fine. I don't have any claim on you. I'm just the geeky guy who kept you entertained until Eddie Shapiro wanted you back."

"That's not true!" Knowing how much being called a geek offended him, she wanted more than anything to correct the impression. "And only Eddie called you a geek."

"You agreed with him."

"No, I repeated it, for which I'm very sorry. The only reason was because I didn't want to argue with Eddie. You and I both know he's no rocket scientist. I realize how it must have sounded from your end, but please, Clark, let's put this behind us." She waited for what seemed an eternity before he spoke.

"Apology accepted."

She heaved a giant sigh of relief and planted her hand over her heart. "Thank you. You don't know how badly I've felt about all this. I've got so much to tell you. Has it really only been three days since we talked? It feels like three years." She paused to take a deep breath. "Clark, I was offered a teaching position."

"That's wonderful."

"It's one of those 'good news, bad news' situations. I was offered a job, which is obviously the good news," she said, gesturing freely with her hands. "But the bad news is I'd need to move to Alaska. The second-grade teacher has developed a heart problem and needs to take a medical leave, and you know me and kids—I love that age group. What do you think?"

"Think? What's there to think about? I suggest you take it."

"You do?" The happiness drained out of her like water swirling down a drain.

"This is what you've been waiting for, isn't it?" he asked her, smiling briefly.

"But it means I'll be leaving Seattle." *Leaving you,* she added silently.

"So it seems, but that's progress for you."

She was on her feet but couldn't remember standing. The room felt cold suddenly. "I guess that settles that, doesn't it?" She forced an air of breathless enthusiasm into her voice.

"I guess so."

"You and Eddie are more alike than I realized. Neither one of you has a clue what it means to really love someone. I…I assumed you were different, but I was wrong. Goodbye, Clark." She was too hurt to say anything more. Clutching her purse to her side, she started to walk away.

Then her steps slowed, and with her back to him, she said, "Before I leave, I'd like to thank you. I mean that sincerely."

Her words were followed by a painful silence. She waited a moment with her eyes closed, praying he would say or do something to stop her.

He didn't. She had no choice but to leave.

With her head held high, she walked out of Clark's office and out of his life.

Six

"That's it?" Maddie asked, incredulous. "Clark actually let you leave?"

Carol nodded, and her gaze drifted across the square to the Rusbach Science Building. The bronze plaque outside the building stated that Clark Rusbach had donated the funds for the structure. He'd done well for himself. Very well. His computer company was worth millions. Fifteen years earlier he'd designed software, and these days his computer systems were known worldwide.

"How sad," Gretchen said, and gently squeezed Carol's hand.

Carol hadn't known either Gretchen or Maddie well in her college days, and now she realized that had been her loss. She could have used friends like them, then *and* now.

Even after all this time, the pain of that last confrontation with Clark was fresh and sharp. She'd honestly believed, naive as she'd been back then, that he had loved her. She'd believed he would take whatever measures necessary to keep her in Seattle and in his life. Instead, he'd taught her one of the most valuable lessons she'd ever learned.

"What about Eddie?"

"Yeah, Eddie," Gretchen put in. "Did you have dinner with him after all?"

"Oh, yes," Carol whispered, and laughed at the memory. "Only it didn't turn out the way I'd planned."

"The dress didn't fit?"

"Oh, it fit just fine, but I was so miserable without Clark that it was all I could do to even look at Eddie."

"You fell in love with Clark, didn't you?"

"Oh, yes," she said again. It amazed her how long it had taken her to recognize what should have been apparent. Instead, she'd allowed her experience with Eddie to cloud her judgment, and by the time she realized the truth it was too late.

"Tell me what happened when you met Eddie," Maddie insisted. "Did he want you back?"

"I think so, but actually, I never gave him a chance to ask. The entire evening was a disaster. All I could do was talk about Clark. It was Clark this and Clark that, until Eddie tossed his napkin on the table and claimed he wasn't going to waste his time on a woman who was hung up on another man."

Both Gretchen and Maddie laughed.

"It serves him right," Maddie said. "It feels good when someone who's done you wrong gets his comeuppance."

A silence fell between them. "Are you speaking from experience?" Gretchen asked.

"You could say that," Maddie admitted reluctantly. "You probably remember me as something of a bad girl. I said and did some outrageous things in my college days, but I only did them to attract attention."

Gretchen chuckled. "I seem to recall more than one of your stunts. You were crazy, girl."

"You can say that again," Maddie said, and smiled. "But the craziest trick I ever pulled was falling in love with John Theda."

Gretchen remembered the rumors. It had caused quite a stir—a student capturing the heart of a faculty member!

"Yup. I had one class with him and it was love at first sight. I worked my butt off to gain his attention, and then we started seeing each other on the sly."

"Oh, Maddie."

"I knew it wasn't the smartest thing I've ever done, but I was in love. What can I say? He wanted to marry me—or so he claimed—and like a fool I believed him. After I graduated it was a different story. He couldn't get rid of me fast enough."

"He hurt you, didn't he?"

Pain flashed in Maddie's eyes. "Yes, I won't lie about that. He did hurt me, more than I thought it was possible for any man to hurt me. Eventually I got back at him."

"You did? How?" Maddie had Carol's full attention.

"You sure you want to hear this?"

"I'm sure," Gretchen said.

"Me too." Carol wouldn't miss this for the world. Professor Theda had given her a C on a paper she'd written in order to get out of the final. Eddie had handed in the exact same paper the following quarter—she'd let him copy hers—and had been given an A. She would love hearing how the professor got what he deserved.

Maddie's Story

One

Maddie Coolidge enjoyed her bad-girl image. She thrived on letting others believe she was a sexual tigress on the prowl, changing bed partners as often as she changed her underwear. Her clothes and hair were outrageous. Her thick auburn curls plunged all the way down her back, bouncing against her shapely buttocks. Her skintight pants and thigh-high leather boots attracted plenty of attention, along with her more-than-adequate bustline. That she had ended up at a classy private college was a fluke, a gift from a rich uncle, although she let her classmates assume otherwise.

Maddie was thrilled by her notoriety. Men paid attention to her, women envied her, and she lapped it up, becoming more and more outrageous. That was until she met her Waterloo. Who would have believed that an advanced-mathematics class would change her life? To be accurate, it wasn't the class but the man who taught it. John Theda. For the first time in her life Maddie fell head over heels in love.

Her college career had been marked with average grades. She wasn't stupid, but good grades conflicted with her image; therefore she tended to downplay her brains.

Until she met John.

It hadn't been easy to grab his attention. At first she'd done everything but drape herself naked over the top of his desk. He wasn't like the other professors she'd known. They seemed old and stuffy. Not John. He was only thirty, and handsome as sin. Half the females in class were in love with him, and the ones who weren't were either brain-dead or blind. It was a wonder any of them managed to keep their minds focused on the subject matter.

Because he was outgoing and friendly, John flirted effortlessly with his students, refusing to play favorites. After class the women would flock around his desk like bees seeking nectar. Unlike the others, Maddie realized such obvious tactics wouldn't work, so she bided her time and found far more subtle methods of calling attention to herself. Instead of revealing her interest in John, she cozied up to the subject matter itself. Clearly mathematics was a subject near and dear to his heart. If she was going to have any success with the man himself, she had to play his game. And play she did, as if her very life depended on it.

She studied as she never had before, poring over books, memorizing everything she could. She'd always been good with numbers and mathematical theories and concepts. To her, mathematics was poetry without words. Numbers were precise, rational and real, much easier to understand than people. Numbers she understood. Numbers weren't unreasonable. Numbers were fun.

Before long she had top marks. Still John Theda didn't reveal an iota of interest in her. By the middle of the term, she was convinced nothing she said or did could attract him.

But she was wrong.

Her final plan of action was to dazzle him with how well she did on the midterm exam, the biggest test of the year so far. She studied half the night, falling asleep at her desk in the early-morning hours. To her horror she overslept and then had to race around like a madwoman, arriving late for the test. Breathless, her hair a mass of curls, wearing the same clothes she'd worn the previous day, she crashed into the classroom convinced she'd blown it. Everyone else was sitting at their desks huddled protectively over the exam sheets. Their heads swiveled to her as if she'd purposely disrupted them. She even thought she heard someone whisper about her being up half the night with some guy. Her own fault, she thought, for going out of her way to give people that impression of her behavior.

Standing in the doorway of the classroom, she looked to John for guidance. He smiled sweetly, told her to sit down and handed her a test. The first page was easy. Kid stuff. She whizzed through that, and the second sheet, as well. Then she hit a wall. The last page consisted of one problem.

She read it once. Twice. Three times, and then felt herself starting to panic. Closing her eyes, she cleared her mind and focused all her energy and reasoning abilities on the problem. By the time the period was nearly over, she was the only student left in the room.

With one eye on the clock and another on the empty sheet in front of her, she bit into her lower lip, hating to turn in an incomplete test. The others had gotten it, obviously—and easily, too, apparently.

Then it came to her. The method, the answer, the theory. Scribbling as fast as her fingers would allow, she worked out the problem, then handed the completed test to John with a full thirty seconds to spare.

To her delight and—after that last problem—complete surprise, her plan worked. John sought her out a few days later, complimented her on her impeccable work and on passing the midterm, and invited her to coffee at an out-of-the-way café. They saw each other frequently from that point forward.

Because he wasn't a full professor yet, and because the school would have frowned on any professor dating a student, they kept their growing relationship a secret. He claimed to hate it as much as she did. Meeting on the sly, pretending they meant nothing to each other, was hell for them both, especially once he asked her to marry him. As graduation grew nearer, she found it impossible to hold the news of their engagement inside her any longer. The rumors had been running rampant for weeks, anyway.

She told Janice Hailey, a sorority sister. After that, the news spread like wildfire across campus. People she hadn't spoken to in all four years stopped and asked her if it was true. Maddie refused to lie, so she only smiled mysteriously. Her sorority sisters were less surprised. They had already guessed she was in love; they said she glowed with happiness. And she *was* happy, blissfully so. Although John had never said anything to her about the way she dressed, she knew that as a professor's wife she would need to tone down her flamboyant style. She was willing to do whatever was necessary to be the kind of wife who would make him proud. That knowledge alone told her how much she loved him.

John, however, wasn't pleased when he learned what she'd done. They routinely met at his place when he was finished with his classes for the day. She hurried there and found him pacing the kitchen, waiting for her.

"You couldn't have waited until after graduation?" he demanded, slapping his hand on the table. He hit it hard enough to upset the napkin holder.

She flinched, and then, because she realized she should have talked it over with him first, she apologized. "I'm sorry, but I only told Janice." Of course, she had knowingly chosen the one person in her sorority house who didn't know how to keep a secret. But in her defense, after months of sneaking around on the sly, she was tired of games. Tired of excuses.

"You could get me fired," he said, walking to the kitchen sink and staring out the window.

She wrapped her arms around his waist and pressed the side of her face against his back. "Don't be mad, Honeybun." He loved her nickname for him.

If anything would get him out of his bad mood, it was a little baby talk and some tender loving attention.

"What am I supposed to do if Dean Williams hears about this?"

It didn't sound like much of a problem to Maddie. "Marry me sooner." She wrapped her calf around his thigh and slid her bare foot down the inside of his leg. She felt him tense, and she knew he was fighting the strong physical attraction between them. If past experience was any indication, it wouldn't be long before he forgave her. She decided to make it easy for him to absolve her of her sins. It took some doing, but she managed to get him out of his jacket and unbutton his shirt. Then she spread moist kisses across his naked chest. He smelled of cologne, but tasted salty and sweaty. His hands bit into her shoulders.

He kissed her hard, and she kissed him back, arching against him. This was better, much much better.

Then, without warning, he pushed her up against the wall so hard she could hardly breathe. But she didn't care, giving herself over to his masterful lovemaking. But that, too, had changed. His mouth was hard, angry, painfully so.

"Johnny," she whimpered, twisting her face away from his. "You're hurting me."

"Good."

His response shocked her into stillness. Her arms fell limply at her sides as she attempted to convince herself she'd misunderstood him.

"You're a fool. Did you know that?" He laughed

harshly, the sound echoing in her ear like distant thunder.

"What's wrong?" she pleaded. "Tell me what's wrong!"

"You. That's what's wrong. Get out."

If he'd stunned her before, this last comment paralyzed her with shock and disbelief. This was John, her Honeybun. He'd never talked to her like this, never raised his voice to her, never said or done anything to hurt her.

Backing away, he rammed his fingers through his hair. He surveyed her, and his gaze held undisguised contempt, as if merely having her in his home was more than he could tolerate.

"What is it?" she asked, fighting back tears. "Tell me what I've done that's so wrong."

"Everything," he answered with a sneer. "Now get out."

Pride rescued her. "Fine," she said, reaching for her boots. Before long she was outside. Hardly aware of the fresh sweet air, scented with cherry blossoms and sunshine, she walked back to campus as quickly as she could.

Instead of returning to the sorority house, she found an isolated shady spot under a fir tree and sat, hoping to collect her chaotic thoughts. John's behavior made no sense. Until now, he'd been loving, gentle and good-natured.

True, she'd broken her word by letting Janice know they were engaged, but graduation was less than three days away. It shouldn't matter if anyone knew they were in love. Especially now. For all intents and purposes, classes were over. Graduation was a formality.

She closed her eyes. He had made her feel dirty and ugly. The cool grass and the gentle breeze off Puget Sound helped ease the ache in her heart.

Three seniors strolled past, and she defiantly raised her chin. She knew one of them. Steve Malcom had made numerous attempts to date her. Because she was involved with John, she hadn't been interested. Even if she hadn't been dating John, Steve wouldn't have interested her.

Unfortunately he couldn't take no for an answer. He had a reputation as a ladies' man, and her rejection had tarnished his image. A friend had warned her recently that he had promised to make her his final college conquest.

The last thing she needed just then was to deal with his wounded libido. Despite her lack of welcome, Steve broke away from his friends and headed in her direction.

She groaned inwardly, but rather than lower her gaze, she met his in open defiance. He had an irritating way about him, but, she silently promised herself, she wouldn't allow him to dent her composure, even though she was vulnerable and confused.

His gaze slid over her appreciatively. His look made her uneasy, but she said nothing.

"Sweetie pie, what are you doing here all by yourself?" he asked.

"Enjoying the solitude."

"I've come to help you," he said, leaning against the tree trunk, his hands buried in his pockets. He crossed his ankles in the practiced pose of someone modeling for a catalog.

If she hadn't been so miserable, she might have laughed, but her head and heart ached, and she needed to reason out what had happened with John.

"Is it true?" Steve asked.

She looked at him and blinked, her thoughts racing like a hamster on an exercise wheel. "Is what true?"

"That you and John Theda are engaged?"

In light of what had happened earlier, she wasn't sure how to answer. She neither confirmed nor denied the rumor. "It could be," she returned.

"Either you are or you aren't," he pressed.

"Let's put it in terms you can understand, then," she offered. "It's none of your business."

He laughed sharply. "That's what I thought. A mathematics professor isn't your type. Oh, he might let you think so, seeing the benefits you offer," he added, snickering. "But you're not the marrying kind, and Theda knows it."

That did it. She roared to her feet, knotting her hands into fists at her sides, forgetting her resolve to not allow him to rile her. "I love John, and he loves me. We're going to be married as soon as I graduate."

"Really?" He made it sound like one big joke.

"Really!" Her tone held an equal measure of confidence.

"You and a math professor." He laughed and shook his head.

"I don't need your approval, and neither does John." Anger burned inside her, but she wasn't going to let Steve know that. Her composure was partially back, and she pretended he was nothing more than a pest she was forced to endure. Fortunately he would soon be gone.

He rubbed the side of his jaw as if giving the idea serious consideration. "You know, you've got me curious."

She had no intention of asking him what had piqued his interest. She'd endured quite enough of this mindless conversation, and she turned away.

To her surprise, he captured her arm and pulled her toward him. Her own momentum sent her body colliding against his. Without giving her a chance to recover, he kissed her, rubbing his unpleasantly moist lips against hers.

It required one swiftly delivered jab to the right area to convince Steve Malcom to release her. Unwilling to wait and give him an opportunity to repeat his assault, she reeled away from him and hurried across the campus.

She hadn't gone far, head down and walking as fast as her feet would carry her, when she literally ran into Brent Holliday, another senior. Mumbling an apology, she hurriedly crossed the lawn toward the sorority house. As she walked, she felt his disapproval burning a hole in her back.

Once inside the safety and familiarity of her room, she sat on her bed, her back against the headboard, legs bent, her face buried against her knees.

It didn't take her long to convince herself that she would hear from John that night at the latest. He might even be so anxious to apologize that he would come for her, although he never had before. Until that afternoon he'd always been loving and generous with her. They'd spent as much time together as possible. In fact, because he'd taken up so much of her free time, her grades had slipped since midterms, at least in classes other than math.

When she still hadn't heard from him by the next morning, she mulled over what to do. He had been angry with her, angrier than she'd ever seen him, but when they married, they would face difficult situations again and again. It was important that they learn to resolve their problems. By noon she'd decided that if he wouldn't seek her out, she would confront him.

Her guess was that he was embarrassed by the things he'd said and done. He would appreciate the fact she loved him enough to come to him and settle things once and for all.

As for her part in their disagreement, she wasn't blameless. He was right—she shouldn't have told Janice about the engagement. But John needed to realize that his behavior had been unacceptable. He owed her an apology. Having made the decision to seek him out, Maddie felt worlds better.

Unfortunately, before she could confront him, she was required to attend the graduation rehearsal. As luck would have it, she was paired up with Brent Holliday. He'd never liked her, and judging from their brief encounter the afternoon before, that hadn't changed.

He didn't look pleased to be assigned to be her partner. She wasn't exactly overjoyed, either.

"You can always request a change," she said as they lined up two by two, a male graduate on the left and a female on the right.

"I already tried."

Despite her hard outer edge, Maddie flinched, surprised that his words had the power to hurt her. She didn't know him well and had no desire to. From what she'd heard, his degree was in criminology. He'd already been accepted into the Seattle Police Academy. An interesting occupation for the son of one of Seattle's best-known pastors. The Reverend Earl Holliday faithfully preached fire and brimstone every Sunday morning at eleven. Not that Maddie was interested in attending church services.

"I would expect a preacher's son to have a more charitable heart," Maddie said, favoring him with a saccharine-sweet smile.

He chuckled softly as the processional music blared from the speakers set up on the stage. "Don't make the mistake of confusing me with my father," he warned.

"I don't think there's much to worry about there."

They marched silently up the aisle. With someone else Maddie would have joked and teased. Not with Brent. He'd made no attempt to be friendly, and she couldn't help wondering what she'd ever done to him. He didn't know her any better than she knew him.

As sophomores they'd had a couple of classes together, but her degree was in history, so she'd rarely seen him once she'd declared her major. She'd chosen history for her Uncle Alfie, because it was his passion.

It was because of him that she'd enrolled at Queen Anne University. Although she'd made jokes about her rich uncle, she loved him dearly. Her father had died when she was seven, and she could barely remember him. Alfie was her father's oldest brother, and he'd taken it upon himself to see that his brother's two children were properly cared for and educated.

Although he was getting on in years, Uncle Alfie had insisted on attending her graduation. She wished now that she'd worked harder, earned better grades. Uncle Alfie was a sweetheart, and she owed him more than she could ever repay.

After practice she couldn't escape the school gymnasium fast enough. The last hour had dragged like a dredge scraping the ocean bottom. Sitting through the interminable practice had been pure torture, so great was her need to talk to John. And all the while she'd waited, she'd prayed that he'd cleared up whatever had plagued him the day before.

After rushing across the campus, she found him alone in his classroom, reading a technical journal. When he saw her, he quickly closed the magazine and stuffed it into his briefcase.

She relaxed. All was well.

Then his eyes hardened, and her heart went still. "John?"

"Get out."

"What?" She couldn't believe what she was hearing. This was the man she loved, the man she planned to marry!

He stood, and his face darkened in a scowl. "You heard me. Out."

It was almost comical that he believed he could intimidate her with a few angry words. She'd stood up to bigger men than John Theda. Ignoring his command, she marched into the classroom, then stood her ground, refusing to move until she discovered what was wrong. "You owe me an explanation," she said. "What's going on?"

He stood and snapped his briefcase closed. "I've had a change of heart."

"Just like that?" She snapped her fingers.

"Just like that," he agreed. "I can't trust you."

"But...that's ridiculous!"

"I relied on you to keep our relationship private, and you blew it."

"But surely—"

"That isn't all." He looked as if the mere sight of her was enough to make him sick to his stomach. "Do you seriously think I don't know what's going on between you and Steve Malcom?"

"Steve Malcom!" That was ridiculous.

"I understand the two of you were kissing in full view of the entire student body."

She opened her mouth to defend herself, then promptly closed it. The kissing incident had happened following the ugly confrontation with John, and now he was using it as an excuse to give credibility to his behavior. What nerve!

"It's over," he announced, as if they were talking about something as mundane as a television movie, instead of their lives together.

Her knees felt as if they would no longer support her. "I don't understand," she said, and her voice, faint as a summer breeze, wavered with shock and dismay.

"I don't expect you to. Now leave, and don't try to contact me again. Goodbye." With his spine ramrod stiff, John Theda stalked out of the classroom.

Maddie couldn't remember ever being more hurt in all her life. For almost twenty minutes she sat and waited for the worst of the pain to pass.

Uncle Alfie, so kind and wise, had told her that a person's maturity could be gauged by how quickly they bounced back from disappointment. John's rejection was more than a disappointment. A numbness that refused to go away settled in the area of her heart.

She'd learned her lesson, though, and it would take a long time for her to risk her heart again.

A very long time.

Graduation was a blur. The one thing Maddie remembered was walking across the stage and being required to pose briefly for the camera. Knowing John was sitting somewhere in the front three rows with the other faculty members gave her the necessary incentive to act as though she hadn't a care in the world. She dazzled Dean Williams with the brilliance of her smile, accepted her diploma and walked down the stairs.

Following the ceremony, Uncle Alfie and her

mother met her on the lawn outside. The glorious sunshine made her squint as she stepped out of the gymnasium. Ellie Coolidge hugged her and wiped a tear from the corner of her eye, then turned to speak with a friend.

Uncle Alfie hugged Maddie next. "Your father would have been so proud of you," he whispered close to her ear.

Humbled, she pressed her head to his shoulder. It was then that she saw Brent Holliday with his family. His gaze, dark and full of disapproval, lingered on her. Nuts to him. She refused to allow him or John Theda or anyone else to destroy her enjoyment of this day.

Uncle Alfie insisted on taking her and her mother to dinner at one of his private clubs. They sat at a corner table in an elegant dining room, where the walls were made of dark polished wood and the distinguished gold-framed portraits resembled the waiters in their starched black tie.

"I can't tell you how pleased I am," her mother said as she set aside her menu. The prices were outrageous, but Maddie knew Uncle Alfie wanted them to ignore the cost.

Ellie Coolidge had never remarried. In many ways Maddie felt as if she'd lost both parents the day her father died. Her mother had withdrawn from life, shriveled up and surrendered to her grief. Maddie's world was forever changed.

"I'm pleased you chose Queen Anne University," Uncle Alfie said, breaking into her thoughts.

She smiled, seeing as her sweetheart of an uncle had helped her make that choice. "I am, too," she said, pushing all thoughts of John from her mind and heart. After four years on campus, she would miss the school, miss shaking up a few sensibilities, miss the few friends she'd made.

"It's a good school," her mother inserted.

Maddie agreed with a nod.

"From what I understand, one of your mathematics professors recently made a name for himself in the history books."

"Really." She hadn't heard anything about that. She reached for a dinner roll and a pat of butter shaped like a tiny rosebud.

"John Theda's his name, if I recall correctly," Uncle Alfie continued.

She dropped her butter knife. It hit the edge of the gold-rimmed plate with a clang. Hastily she apologized and stared at her uncle. "Say that again?"

"I read about it in the *Journal of Higher Mathematics*."

She continued to stare at her uncle blankly. "I don't understand."

"The quadratic quandary," Uncle Alfie said. "He solved it. It's gone unsolved for fifty years, maybe longer. It's been years since I wrestled with it myself. Every high-level math student does, you know."

"When did this happen?" she asked. One thing Maddie had learned about John in the months they'd dated was that he was basically lazy. He did exactly what was required of him to teach class and nothing beyond that. If he'd worked on solving the quadratic quandary, it was news to her.

"This April," her uncle explained. "It's big news."

"What *is* the quadratic quandary?" Maddie asked.

Uncle Alfie, an engineer by trade, removed a pad and pen from his inside jacket pocket and wrote out the equation. He stared at it for a couple of moments more, shook his head and scribbled a note, then handed it to her.

She studied the equation and then looked up. "This isn't it."

Uncle Alfie frowned. "It is, as I recall."

She scowled. "I had this problem on a midterm test."

"Yes, that's quite common. I told you that almost every mathematical student is given the opportunity to solve it. So many people trying, but it's never been done. That's why that professor from Queen Anne is making a name for himself."

"But…" The room started to swim, and she gripped the edge of the table.

"Maddie—" her mother gently touched her arm "—is everything all right, sweetheart?"

She couldn't answer, the anger bubbling up inside her until it threatened to explode. John Theda hadn't solved the quadratic quandary. She had. And he was taking the credit.

Two

Maddie hadn't meant to stop in the church. Eaten up with anger and frustration, she had started walking aimlessly, with no real destination in mind. Two months had passed since graduation. She'd found a decent apartment and a good job with an insurance company, and had tried to make a life for herself. Outwardly she was doing well, but inwardly the turmoil brewed like malted beer. Nights were the worst. Try as she might, she couldn't get John out of her mind. The love she felt for him had festered like an infected sore. Bitterness ate at her. Anger. Frustration. She had no peace, no sleep, no comfort.

He had used her, and she'd been too blind and stupid to realize it. Used her, and while he was busy taking credit for her accomplishment, he'd made sure she hadn't a clue what he was doing. No one would believe her if she had the audacity to claim she'd solved the quadratic quandary. And that was exactly what he was counting on her doing. Nothing.

It had taken her almost a week to realize how it had happened. She remembered how she'd arrived for the exam late and therefore hadn't been there to hear him explain that the problem on the final sheet had never been solved, so the students shouldn't make themselves crazy over it. If ever there was a testament to positive thinking, this was it. She'd believed it was just one more problem on an already difficult test, and so she'd raced, full steam ahead, thinking the others had worked out the solution, so she could, too.

Later, when he handed back the tests, he had called her to his desk and apologized for having lost hers, though he'd assured her that he'd graded it first and she'd done well. He'd smiled, and because she'd been so infatuated with him, she'd accepted him at his word. As a means of making it up to her, he'd invited her to have coffee with him. She'd practically fallen all over herself in her eagerness to accept. Thinking about it now made her feel ill.

Everything would have gone smoothly for him if she hadn't blown the whistle and announced their engagement before graduation. His plan was to be long gone before she learned what he'd done and how he'd done it. From what she understood, he would be living in Seattle for what remained of the summer, but he would be leaving in the fall because he'd accepted a position at a prestigious university elsewhere and been granted a full professorship.

The bitterness, anger and frustration made it impossible for her to hold still, and so she walked, often late into the night, until she was too exhausted to do anything but fall into bed and sleep.

This evening she stopped at the church. The door was unlocked, an unexpected surprise. She wasn't sure what had led her to this particular church or why she felt drawn inside. What she sought, she suspected, was peace.

Slipping into the last pew in the darkened sanctuary, she bowed her head and closed her eyes. She hadn't done a whole lot of praying in her life, but she did now, silently pouring out her heart, grateful that the church was deserted. She wasn't sure how long she sat there in solitude. Perhaps she even dozed. The next thing she knew, someone said her name.

"Maddie?" The voice held evident surprise.

Flustered, she glanced up, her heart pounding. Brent Holliday. He was the last person she wanted to see. How amused he must be to find her in a church.

Without waiting for a sarcastic comment, she grabbed her purse and leaped to her feet. She was half out the door when he said, "Don't go."

She stopped midstride, her back to him. She said nothing, didn't turn around, but she didn't start walking again, either. Not sure what had prompted her to obey his command, she closed her eyes, willing this to be over quickly. What John had done to her was humiliating enough.

"Church was the last place I expected to find you." Although the words cut, they lacked his usual biting sarcasm.

"I bet. Well, don't worry, I won't make attendance

a habit. Nice seeing you again, Brent," she said, her tone giving the lie to the words, and then stepped into the night, unwilling to linger. Unwilling to invite his further disapproval.

"Maddie."

She raced down the stairs, her feet bouncing against the concrete steps in her rush to escape.

That he hurried after her, his footsteps echoing hers, was a surprise of its own. Walking swiftly, she buried her hands in her pockets and forged ahead, pretending she hadn't heard him.

"Wait, Maddie. Please."

It was the "please" that did it. She paused beside a streetlight, exhaled sharply and lifted her chin. "What?" she demanded, giving the impression she had places to go, people to see.

Brent was standing about four feet away. He didn't say anything for a long time, but when she shifted her weight from one foot to the next in a silent hint of impatience, he finally spoke. "I owe you an apology."

"Several, I'd say." She wasn't going to make this easy for him, not that she was particularly angry with him. Any irritation with him paled next to what she felt toward John Theda.

"All right, several," he agreed. "I regret the things I said during graduation rehearsal—and other times, too," he added, lumping his offenses together in one fell swoop.

She blinked twice, remembering how his attitude and his words had bitten into her ego and how she'd pretended otherwise. He had never made a secret of his contempt for her.

"Don't worry about it." Her forgiveness came easily. It was unlikely they would meet up again, and she wasn't one to hold grudges. Then again, maybe she was. She would like nothing better than to find a way to hurt John.

Brent hesitated, and she wasn't sure if he wanted to say more. She was about to leave when he asked gently, "Are you okay?"

She bristled, embarrassed by being found praying in a church. By Brent. "Of course I am. Why wouldn't I be?"

"You tell me. You aren't exactly the first person I'd expect to find in a church at night." He sounded edgy himself, irritated, which was exactly what she wanted. If she made him angry enough, maybe he would leave her alone.

Still she didn't look at him. Not directly, anyway, for fear he would notice the shadows beneath her eyes or the weight she'd lost. Afraid he would ask questions she didn't want to answer.

The silence stretched tautly between them. Maddie was eager to be on her way, yet reluctant to leave, which made no sense. But she felt there was something more Brent longed to say and was holding back. Not that she'd encouraged him.

"I...I've got to get home," she blurted, although it was a small lie. No one awaited her return. No one worried if she was home or not.

"Yeah, me too. Do you want a ride?"

"No, but thanks." She stepped away from the light and then hesitated, remembering he'd been a criminology major. It was only polite that she inquire how life was treating him. "Everything going okay at the police academy?"

"Great."

She offered him a brief wobbly smile. "I'm pleased to hear it. Good to see you again, Brent." Surprisingly, she meant that.

"You too, Maddie."

For some inexplicable reason, she thought she heard a hint of sadness in his voice. Well, if he was suffering a few regrets, so was she, but her regrets were bogged down with self-recriminations for allowing herself to be used by someone who didn't deserve or appreciate her love.

"Good night," she added, meaning the words. Brent wasn't so bad, and she wished now that she'd made more of an effort to get to know him when she'd had the chance. She'd gone no more than a few steps when he called out to her once more.

Hands in her pockets, she turned around, poised in the middle of the sidewalk.

"If you ever need someone or something, call me."

"You?" She wasn't sure she'd heard him correctly. Only a few months earlier he'd mocked her. Now he claimed he wanted to help her.

He cocked a smile, one side of his mouth riding up with amusement. "Yes, me. You're not doing my ego any good, you know."

She chuckled softly, and it felt good. The last time

she'd had reason to laugh had been too long ago to remember. She'd buried herself in recrimination, doubts and regrets. It was a tight fit, leaving little room for humor or frivolity.

By the time she'd walked back to her apartment, it was well after midnight and she was exhausted. After a long hot shower, she climbed into bed and slept the night through, something she hadn't done in weeks.

She awoke refreshed and eager for a new day. It took her some time to realize why she felt better. Brent Holliday. What had happened to cause him to apologize she didn't know. It didn't matter. She was grateful to know she had at least one friend in Seattle.

The idea didn't come to her until the following afternoon. While she didn't know Brent Holliday well, she felt strongly that he'd meant what he'd said. If she needed someone or something, all she had to do was give him a call. She wanted to believe his offer of friendship was sincere, so decided to test it.

She hadn't told anyone what John had done. What good would it do? she reasoned. No one was likely to believe her. No one would expect her to be capable of such an achievement. What irked her the most was that she'd done this to herself. She'd played a silly game, dressed and acted like a "bad girl," a brainless twit. An aptitude for numbers didn't fit in with her carefully constructed image.

Her mistake had been that, in assuming the role she had chosen, she'd almost lost her true identity, forgotten who she really was. Well, no more. She'd packed away her thigh-high leather boots, tamed her hair and lengthened her skirts, then stared at the stranger in the mirror. The Maddie who'd been so hungry for attention was forever gone. The one who grieved over the loss of her emotional innocence had laid claim to her soul, and the real Maddie Coolidge had stepped forward.

It'd taken her the better part of the summer to discover who the real Maddie actually was, and she'd learned that she liked this person. The woman without pretensions. The woman who had no need to impress others. The woman willing to take a chance on being herself.

Brent couldn't really have noticed the differences in her in the dark, when she'd been dressed for an evening stroll. But he would. She would make sure of it.

Phoning him, suggesting they meet for coffee, had seemed like a simple plan. All she had to do was get his phone number from his parents—they were in the book, though he wasn't—and place the call. But even that first step required courage.

When she finally managed to dredge up the fortitude, she dialed, closed her eyes and waited. To her surprise and relief, Brent was the one who answered.

"Hello," he grumbled as if picking up the receiver had inconvenienced him greatly. In her surprise she didn't speak right away, and he said hello again in a more pronounced tone of impatience.

"Brent?"

Silence, then, "Maddie."

He'd recognized her voice. "I… Could you meet me for coffee?"

"Sure. When? Where?" he responded with no hesitation.

She decided on the Java Joint, a coffeehouse not far from the Queen Anne campus, and named a time that evening she felt would be convenient for them both.

"Fine, I'll see you then."

His eagerness was a balm that helped ease the ache that had held her heart prisoner all these weeks.

Brent had arrived ahead of her, and he waved when she entered and glanced around. He'd chosen a booth in the back of the room, and she was grateful for the limited privacy it afforded them.

The coffeehouse was a leftover from the early sixties, when beatniks played bongos and recited poetry. Maddie resisted the urge to snap her fingers and say words like "groovy" whenever she stopped by for a latte.

The walls were black, with brightly colored geometric designs in red, orange, yellow and blue. The counter was decorated with polka dots of different colors and sizes, and the room was filled with the pungent aroma of coffee.

"Thank you for coming," she said, scooting onto the wooden bench across from him.

Brent stared at her as if seeing her for the first time. "Maddie?"

"Yes, it's the new me." She beamed at him. Her auburn hair was tied at the base of her neck with a yellow ribbon. She wore loose-fitting jeans and a sleeveless blouse. Cotton, white and plain, with an eyelet collar.

His mouth opened and then slowly closed, as if whatever he'd wanted to say had gotten lost somewhere between his mind and his lips.

"I imagine you're wondering why I suggested we meet," she began after the waiter, a college student, had taken their order.

He nodded. "I'll admit to being curious. About that and...other things." But he appeared patient enough to wait until she explained matters to him in her own time and in her own way.

"I don't know if you heard or not, but I was dating John Theda in the spring." With an effort she managed to keep her voice even and reveal none of her feelings. The waiter returned with their order, and she smiled her thanks.

Brent waited until the waiter left before he responded, "I heard you and Theda were an item, or something to that effect."

"I thought you might have." This was where it grew difficult. If Brent didn't believe her, she didn't know what she would do. "We didn't exactly date," she told him. "We always went to out-of-the-way places. His biggest fear was that someone from the school would see us together."

"I think you should know up front," Brent said, stopping her. "I'm not much of a John Theda fan."

She laughed. "Neither am I."

A heartbeat later he asked, his voice gentle with concern, "Are you pregnant?"

"No!" she cried, angry that he would assume such a thing. After a moment she realized it was a logical conclusion after finding her in a church, clearly troubled. Suddenly his willingness to meet her held greater significance. Even now she wasn't sure she was doing the right thing. She wouldn't be here with him at all if she hadn't been so desperate for a friend.

"Sorry, I shouldn't have asked," he said, gesturing for her to continue. "I won't interrupt again."

"Do... How comfortable are you with math?"

His gaze searched hers. "Comfortable enough to balance my checkbook."

His smile caught her off guard, and for a moment, perhaps longer, she was held captive by it. Men often grinned at her, but generally they were looking for something she wasn't willing to give. Brent's eyes held warmth and genuine concern. Friendship.

"As it happens," she said, forcing herself to look away, "I'm quite good with numbers."

"That doesn't surprise me."

"I'm more than good. I'm competent enough to have solved the quadratic quandary." She waited a moment for that to sink in. Either he believed her or he didn't. She had no way of proving it. No way of supplying irrefutable evidence that would convince him, the school or anyone else.

He frowned, then shook his head as if to clear his thoughts. "Are you saying what I think you're saying?" His left hand tightened around his coffee cup until his knuckles whitened.

"Yes. It was me who figured out the correct answer, not John."

"And he claimed the credit." Brent flexed his right hand as if itching to plow it into the professor's face.

"You believe me?"

"Yes." His emphatic reply removed all doubt.

"Why?"

"Why not?" He met her gaze steadily. "You said it, and that's good enough for me."

If she ever fell in love again, she thought, it would be with a man who cared this deeply that she'd been wronged. A man whose belief in her didn't waver.

"That was the reason he…he asked me to marry him. But it was all a ruse. With my head and my heart preoccupied, I paid no attention to anything else. John knew he couldn't allow a word of 'his' accomplishment to get out until after graduation. He counted on my not knowing what I'd done." She explained the circumstances, how she'd arrived late for the exam and so hadn't understood the significance of the last problem.

"It isn't just that he's taking credit," she said. "It's that he used me, hurt me. I'm convinced he never loved me, never intended to marry me. He played me for a fool." Her voice shook with the fervor of her emotions. "I want him to know what it's like to be embarrassed in front of one's peers. I want him to feel the same humiliation I did."

"And you think I can help?" he asked.

"Yes."

He didn't look convinced. "How?"

"You know people. You have connections. Surely if I talked to a detective, he might be able to do something. If nothing more, I'd like to file a complaint."

"And claim what? That he stole your thought process?"

"He took a lot more than that," she returned heatedly.

"I'm sorry, Maddie." He sounded as frustrated as she felt.

"I know."

"Did you talk to Dean Williams about this?"

"No." It would do no good, for it would be John's word against hers, and it went without saying who the dean would choose to believe. "I want him to suffer," she mused aloud.

"I wish there was something I could do."

Maybe it had been a mistake to tell Brent, but telling someone else what had happened had eased the tension in her stomach considerably. She'd known for a long time that life was unfair. Not only had John Theda hurt her pride and her heart, he'd stolen her work and claimed it as his own. And now he was responsible for what she was sure would end up as a stomach ulcer.

"Well, I appreciate being able to talk to you about it," she said. "So in a way you've already done something."

"Who else have you told?"

"No one."

"No one?" He sounded incredulous. "Why did you choose me?"

The answer to that wasn't as simple as it sounded. "I'm not sure. Because…well, you seemed approachable when we met at the church. Nice."

"Hey, don't sound so shocked."

She laughed softly.

"What made you—" he studied her for a moment "—you know, change…clothes."

"I didn't want to be stupid any longer."

"Stupid?"

"The woman you knew in college was playing a game. I'm through being the bad girl."

His gaze held hers. "You never fit the part."

Oh, but she had, Maddie thought. She'd grown comfortable with the role, high on the attention she received. Daring and bold, wild and fun. That was her, willing to try anything once. Twice if it caused a commotion. Three times if a crowd gathered and someone phoned the police.

"I knew otherwise," he continued, "and that was what troubled me most. I wanted to shake you, demand that you stop and reveal the real you. Let go of the outrageous persona and that hard-edged facade."

She couldn't stop staring at him. He'd believed her when she'd laid claim to the unbelievable, and she could offer him no less than her trust. Which meant that what he said was equally true. He'd known. He'd always known.

"So, what about an attorney?" he said now.

She'd thought of that, too. "I'd need the money to

pay a retainer, money I don't have. Besides, I don't have any proof."

He closed his eyes and exhaled forcefully. "The guy's a slimeball."

"I appreciate you hearing me out, Brent, I really do. It's helped tremendously."

"I'm glad. I know it's going to be difficult for you to let this go."

"Let it go?" She had no intention of doing that.

His gaze narrowed. "You *are* letting this go, aren't you?"

"No way!"

"What do you intend to do?"

"I don't think I should tell you."

"Why not?"

She grinned, hope stirring her senses to life once again. "It's illegal."

Three

"I'd be more comfortable if I knew what you were thinking," Brent said, frowning darkly.

Maddie shook her head. "It's better that you don't."

Despite her protest, he picked up the tab for their coffee and followed her outside. The night was warm, despite the breeze coming off Lake Washington. She had taken the bus to the Java Joint, and now she walked toward the stop to catch one home.

"Maddie!" He was beginning to sound irritated as he caught up with her. "Come on, I'll give you a ride."

She giggled, and oh, how good it felt to laugh again! "You don't know where I live."

"You can tell me. *And* you can explain what you've got up your sleeve."

"Really, Brent, it's best you don't know."

"I'll be the judge of that." Putting her hand in the crook of his elbow, he led her across the street to where he'd parked his car, then unlocked the door and helped her inside. Such a gentlemanly thing to do, Maddie thought. The men she'd dated hadn't been inclined to open the door for her. Not even John.

"Tell me what you're thinking of doing," he demanded once he was in the driver's seat. He put the key in the ignition but didn't turn it.

"I'm going to break into John's house and find my test paper."

His hands folded around the steering wheel, and he glared straight ahead. "You're right, I don't want to hear that."

"I won't involve you."

"Maddie, this is craziness. Pure craziness. You could get thrown in jail for a stunt like that."

"I know." It was incredible how good she felt now that she had a plan of action. It felt as if the heaviest of burdens had been lifted from her shoulders. For weeks she'd wallowed in self-pity, moping around, crying about how she'd been misused and abused. Well, no longer. She would find a way to prove John was a thief and worse. Even if that meant risking jail time.

"Maddie—"

She interrupted him. "Don't try to talk me out of this. I'm serious. I'm going to find that test paper. John must have it somewhere. I know him."

"He'd be a fool to keep it."

"My point exactly. John Theda *is* a fool." Brent didn't understand. The least she could do was try to prove her case. She would never be able to live with herself if she stood by and did nothing, which was what had made her so miserable until now.

"When do you plan to do this?" he asked, heaving a huge sigh of resignation.

"Tonight," she returned, giving no thought to the matter. Why not? She'd waited this long, and now that the decision was made she could see no reason to delay it. As for her odds of locating that test paper, she hadn't a clue. More than likely Brent was right, but she had to discover that for herself.

"How are you going to get there?" he asked, starting the ignition.

"Bus." It was the only means of transportation available to her.

He turned and stared at her. "You're going to take Seattle Transit to commit a felony?"

"That's what I said."

He wiped his hand down his face. "I can't believe I'm hearing this."

She giggled, feeling almost giddy with happiness.

"What if he's home?" Brent asked, as if this hadn't occurred to her.

"On Thursday night? Nope, I know him. He's with his card-playing buddies, unless, of course, it's his turn to host."

Brent pounded his forehead against the steering wheel. "You can't do this."

"I don't have any choice."

He exhaled a deep breath as if he'd reached an important decision. "Then I'm coming with you."

Now it was her turn to be concerned. "Oh, no," she said, and shook her head. "No way."

"You can't stop me any more than *I* can stop *you*." His grin was wide, triumphant and sly. The kind of grin that demanded a response.

"But—"

"Turnabout is fair play," he said. "If you're going to risk your future on something so incredibly—"

"You'll stay in the car?" she demanded, cutting him off. Yes, there were risks, she knew that, but she didn't dare look too closely at them or she would talk herself out of it, which she didn't want to do. Although she put up a fuss, she was pleased that Brent would be there, for moral support if nothing else.

He backed out of his parking space, then finally answered, "Probably."

"Probably? Not good enough. You have to promise. Give me your word that you'll stay completely out of sight. Otherwise I'll do it alone some other time without telling you."

From the intense color his eyes turned and the ferocity with which he pulled out onto the road, she knew he wasn't keen on the alternative. Good. If he was caught with her or anywhere close to her, his career with the police academy would be over. She didn't need that on her conscience.

"All right, I'll stay in the car and wait."

"Give me your word," she prompted.

"On my word," he said. His promise seemed to lack sincerity, and she was tempted to challenge him further, but she had other matters to consider, including whether John Theda was home or not.

She borrowed Brent's cell, on the theory that John wouldn't recognize the number if he was home and checked caller ID, and called his house. The answering machine clicked on after four rings and, without bothering to listen to the message, she replaced the receiver. Smiling triumphantly, she gave Brent a thumbs-up. He looked almost disappointed.

As they approached John's neighborhood, she had second thoughts about involving Brent. She tried to talk him into simply dropping her off. If he drove away now and she was caught and arrested, no one could accuse him of aiding and abetting. Even if he was seen, all he would need to do was claim he was unaware of her intentions. No one would doubt him. He was the son of a preacher, and his word was good as gold.

Brent, however, would have none of it. He was not going to leave her on her own.

He parked half a block up the street from John's rental house, where he could keep it in full view. He kept the engine running.

"John's car is missing," Maddie said. She started to open the car door, but Brent stopped her by grabbing hold of her arm.

"Could it be in the garage?" he asked.

She shook her head. "It could, but I doubt it, seeing that the garage-door opener has needed a new battery from the moment I met him. It isn't likely he's changed it now." Not when he was going to be moving within the next couple of weeks.

He continued to grip her forearm. "How do you plan to get inside?"

That seemed a silly question. "The key."

"You have a key?" he asked incredulously.

"Well, not exactly, but I know where one is."

His eyes widened even more. "You mean to tell me he keeps a spare key tucked under a flowerpot?"

"No, it's hidden in a fake rock in his flower bed." Brent's fingers loosened enough for her to free her arm. She got out, then bent down to look through the window and offer him a reassuring smile. "Wish me luck."

"I wish you weren't doing this."

"Hey, this is gonna be a piece of cake," she said, feeling lighthearted in her eagerness to prove how easy this would be. Why, oh, why hadn't she thought of this sooner? She'd endured weeks of mental turmoil, refusing to seek a solution. Brent's support had empowered her, and she was grateful.

"Come on, wish me luck," she said again.

He offered her an all-too-brief smile. "Good luck."

"Thanks."

From experience she should have realized that the thing that looks the easiest often proves to be the most difficult. She walked up the cement pathway to the house, something she'd done a thousand times before. None of John's neighbors were out or about, and she was grateful. She was sure now that she could nonchalantly slip inside the house without a problem.

It didn't happen.

First she couldn't locate the fake rock. Squatting down in the flower bed, she picked up rock after rock, shaking each one. When she'd checked them all, she made a second go-round, this time placing each stone close to her ear, certain she must have overlooked the obvious.

She glanced up once to discover that Brent had eased down the road and parked much closer to the house than was advisable. Not good. Now he would be watching her every move. No doubt he'd already figured out that she'd run into a hitch.

Okay, so maybe John had done away with his fake rock. There were other ways to get into the house. As she started toward the back, she noted that the lawn needed to be mowed. Perhaps he was out of town, which was all the better. Stopping abruptly, she reconsidered. Before she changed plans, she'd better tell Brent what she was doing; otherwise he might follow her. Bringing along a silent partner was turning out to be a hassle. Muttering under her breath, she trotted back to the car. When she approached the driver's side, he rolled down the window.

"Thank heaven," he breathed.

"Thank heaven for what?"

"You're giving up, aren't you?"

The man obviously didn't know her very well. The phrase "give up" wasn't in her vocabulary. Good grief, how did he think she'd solved that silly math problem? Anyone possessing the qualities of persistence, tenacity and the will to succeed wasn't going to let a little thing like a missing key distract her from her goal.

"No way on earth," she informed him, growing impatient with his attitude.

"Then why'd you want to talk to me?"

"To tell you I was going around the back of the house and—"

"I could see that," he muttered.

"—and to tell you to move the car," she finished. "Why?"

"Because you're too close to the house. People can see you. Go down a block, maybe two. I'll find you when I'm finished."

"Maddie—"

"Please, Brent. You promised, remember?" This wasn't his battle, it was hers, and she didn't want him up to his armpits in trouble because of her.

"All right, all right." She could tell he didn't like it.

She smiled and impulsively leaned into the car and kissed him full on the lips. She hadn't planned that, the action was purely instinctive. Purely natural. A means of thanking him for giving her back a part of herself. A piece of her soul. Her serenity. His immediate response surprised her, delighted her. He took control of the exchange and threaded his fingers into her hair, holding her a willing captive.

Bent over as she was, with her head inside the car, the kiss was awkward. But even that didn't distract from the pleasure of it. She was the one who broke it off. For a long moment she kept her eyes closed and remained silent. His fingers were still in her hair, and he propped his forehead against hers.

"I…I won't be long," she promised when she found her voice.

"Be careful."

"There's nothing to worry about. Knowing John, he won't be home for hours. All I want is to see if he was stupid enough to leave my test paper lying around. I'm not interested in anything else."

"Get in and out as fast as you can."

"OK, partner."

He smiled and kissed the tip of her nose. "Hurry."

Her senses reeling thanks to Brent and the kiss they'd shared, she practically staggered back to the house and went around behind. And then she saw it. The fake rock was sitting on the top step of the back porch. She nearly laughed out loud. Set off by itself, without the camouflage of the other rocks, it looked exactly like what it was. John couldn't have made it any more apparent if he'd tried.

She picked it up and removed the key. The door lock clicked open, and she went inside without a problem. Unwilling to risk any chance of someone walking in on her, she locked the door behind her. She tiptoed two or three steps, then paused and strained to hear any out-of-the-ordinary sounds. Anything that would indicate she wasn't alone.

She heard nothing.

The tension eased from her limbs, and she made herself at home the way she had so many times before. The anxiety of the moment had made her parched; she opened the refrigerator and removed a can of soda. The six-pack she'd bought months earlier was still there. John wasn't much of a soda drinker, so she'd supplied her own.

She took a swallow, then, clutching the soda can, moved into John's office, or what he referred to as his office. Actually it was the formal dining room, but he'd set up his desk and bookcases there.

For someone who routinely worked with numbers and the sense of order that implied, John was incredibly disorganized. She'd tidied his desk a number of times and devised a simple filing system for him. But in the months since she'd been away, it didn't look as if he'd bothered to file a single paper. Clutter obliterated the top of the desk. Unopened mail was stacked in one corner, and it looked as if he'd made only a halfhearted effort to sort through it. Halfhearted and several weeks ago.

She eased herself into his leather chair and leaned back as she had so often. She'd loved his office, loved sitting in it and reading. Loved the smell of leather and old books. She felt a pang of regret, but it was brief. Any genuine regrets she harbored had more to do with her own foolish behavior than missing John, or the man she'd believed him to be.

She opened the bottom desk drawer and leafed through the files she'd taken such time and care to organize until she found one labeled TESTS. Her fingers froze, not because of the subject matter, but because the label was one John had made himself.

He wouldn't keep her test there, she reasoned; that would be much too obvious. Too stupid. But then again, maybe it was exactly what he *would* do.

She reached for the file and held it in her lap, prepared to sort through it, and she would have if she hadn't been distracted by a loud noise coming from the direction of the bathroom.

Was John home after all? Had he slipped and fallen in the shower? Her mind and heart raced at the speed of light. Should she investigate, or get out of the house and leave him to his fate? Should she—

"Maddie!" She recognized Brent's voice. "Theda's coming."

Her heart, which was already beating at double time, nearly exploded out of her chest. John must be about to walk through the door at any second, otherwise Brent wouldn't have risked everything to warn her.

She dropped the file on the desk and nearly fell off the chair in her rush to escape. She took three steps in the direction of the back door and then abruptly changed course, afraid John would come in that way. Her heart was jammed in her throat, and she was halfway to the front door when she heard movement on the front porch.

Oh, no. John was going to walk in and catch her red-handed.

"In here," Brent whispered urgently. He appeared out of nowhere, grabbed her hand and jerked her toward the narrow hallway that led to the bathroom and two bedrooms.

"Wait," she whispered, spying the file on the desktop. She refused to leave that behind, not when she'd come this far.

"There isn't time," he warned. "He'll be inside any second."

"I won't leave it." She raced across the living room toward the office and realized Brent was right—there wasn't time. She turned back and made it into the hallway and out of sight just as the front door burst open.

Brent pulled her into the bathroom and stepped with her into the tub behind the shower curtain. She prayed that the thick floral print would conceal them. She'd noted that the window was open and realized that this was how Brent had gotten into the house in time to warn her. He'd risked everything for her. The chance he was taking left her trembling.

She heard John speak, and then a second voice followed. So he wasn't alone. That didn't surprise her. Neither did the fact that the other voice was a woman's. The words were too low for her to understand, but she didn't need to. The woman's sultry tone told her everything. It was the tone that belonged to a woman who knows what she wants and is convinced she's about to get it.

While Maddie wasn't especially shocked, she did experience a stab of pain. She bowed her head and covered her mouth with her hand. She'd been so foolish, so incredibly foolish, to believe John had ever loved her.

Hardly breathing for fear of being discovered, she instinctively leaned toward Brent. He stood behind her and braced his hands on her shoulders, urging her closer, lending her his strength.

She felt him stiffen, and a heartbeat later realized why. John and his friend were in the hallway outside the bathroom. She couldn't see what was happening, but judging from the sounds, it was clear the two were heavily involved with each other. Kissing, groaning, whispering, panting. The sound of their sexual eagerness rang as loud as church bells. It was abundantly clear where they were headed, and it wasn't the bathroom. Too bad, because she would have loved shoving aside the shower curtain and giving them both the shock of their lives. But common sense and the fact that Brent was with her kept her still.

The sounds of their foreplay continued.

Maddie's stomach churned. Unable to stop herself, she turned around and buried her face against Brent's chest. His arms closed protectively around her, and he placed his chin on top of her head. How gentle he was, how caring.

The sounds moved into the bedroom, and she flinched when she heard the mattress springs squeak.

Brent pulled the shower curtain aside and motioned toward the window, gesturing for her to go first.

She shook her head vehemently. She wasn't leaving without that file, and she let him know that with hand gestures and pleading looks.

His eyes widened and he shook his head furiously as they continued their silent but impassioned argument.

She realized she needed to change tactics. Forcing herself to relax, she smiled sweetly and attempted to assure him, charade-style, that he didn't have anything to worry about. John and his friend were so wrapped up in each other, they would never hear a thing.

Brent rolled his eyes to the ceiling in a display of frustration.

Her mind made up, and not wanting to waste any more precious moments on this fruitless "discussion," Maddie carefully climbed out of the tub and moved through the bathroom, her footsteps muffled by the thick bath mat. Brent was right behind her. Although she knew she never could have convinced him, it would have been best if he'd left the same way he'd entered.

The sounds coming from the bedroom were more distinct now. She peeked down the hallway and was greatly relieved to find the bedroom door half-closed. Holding her breath, she shot into the living room, her steps muffled by the broadloom—not that John was likely to hear, as preoccupied as he was. The intensity of her anger at his treachery was enough to make her want to throw something, knock over furniture. But once again common sense prevailed. There was nothing to be gained by such an action and everything to lose.

Brent's hand reached for hers, and he silently led the way into the office. She grabbed the file off the top of the desk and grinned triumphantly.

They tiptoed to the back door, and when Brent opened it, the hinges squeaked. They both froze, held their breath and waited, though for what she wasn't sure. Retribution. To be discovered and arrested. Fear kept her immobile until Brent urged her forward. Then he closed the door with great care.

Once outside, she removed the key from her pocket and locked the door, then carefully replaced it in the fake rock. The sun had long set, and the lack of light was a welcome cover. The moon afforded them enough illumination to find their way out to the street.

"I'm parked down here," he said, pointing the way with his free hand. His other continued to grip hers.

"You never should have come," she said as they hurried along.

His face was softened by the moonlight. "If I hadn't, he would have found you. I couldn't let that happen."

She sobered, deeply moved. She would be forever in his debt for the terrible risk he'd taken on her behalf. What would have happened had she been caught didn't bear thinking about.

"I was an idiot, though," he went on, "to allow you to do this in the first place."

"Do you honestly think you could have stopped me?"

"Yes! If I'd had my wits about me, I could have. Should have. I need to have my head examined."

They were nearly at the car, and she said, "I guess all's well that ends well."

"You mean to say Theda actually saved your test?" he asked, glancing at the file she held.

"I don't know," she told him. "I didn't have time to look."

They reached the car. He opened the door and helped her inside. She waited until he'd joined her to open the file. She didn't have far to look. Her midterm was right on top.

Her gaze found Brent's.

"That's it?" he asked.

She nodded. John *had* saved it.

"Great!" The excitement in Brent's voice said everything they'd gone through was worth it.

As they drove away, she continued to stare at the test paper. It seemed unreal. She'd actually done it. And now, here was the proof of John's treachery and fraud.

Suddenly she cried, "Stop!" and grabbed his arm.

He slammed on the brakes and stared at her.

She cast him a panic-stricken look. "We have to go back."

Four

"Go back?" Brent stared at Maddie as if she'd just escaped a mental institution. "Back where?"

"To John's house." The man was being purposely obtuse. "I left my soda behind."

"Your soda?" Each word was said slowly and distinctly.

"Yes." Clearly he didn't understand the significance of what she was saying, and if he would stop asking her silly questions, she would explain.

"Where in the name of heaven did you get a soda?"

"Where else?" she cried, growing more frustrated by the moment. "Out of John's fridge!"

"You were thirsty and so you helped yourself?" His mouth fell open in disbelief.

"Yes, but—"

"I'll buy you another," he offered carefully, as though speaking to an unreasonable child.

"You don't understand!" she all but shouted.

"I'll admit there appears to be a missing piece of information."

"Of course there is. Did you honestly believe I'd risk everything because I was thirsty?"

"To be honest, the thought *had* entered my mind."

"John doesn't drink soda. He prefers bottled water or white wine. He considers soda unhealthy. I can't tell you the number of times he lectured me about its evils."

"And?" Brent prompted.

"And…well, I really didn't care what he said. The decision was mine, and I like soda. So I bought my own and kept a supply at his house. This evening, after I got inside, I realized I was thirsty. I looked in the fridge, and sure enough, there was my six-pack."

"If he hates the stuff so much, why didn't he throw it out?"

"Because he's basically lazy."

"Okay, okay, continue," he said, urging her to explain further.

"I took the can to John's desk, and in my panic, I left it behind. The minute he sees it there, he'll know something's not right. He'll guess it was me, and he'll know why I'd been there. My fingerprints are all over that can."

Brent groaned.

"We have to go back," she insisted, furious with herself for being so careless. "I can't believe I did something so stupid."

"You honestly think he'll notice?"

"Yes. But probably not until morning." Not while he was wrapped up in his current preoccupation, which from the sound of things, would keep him engaged well into the night.

"Maddie, I know what you're saying, but we can't risk returning. Not now."

Part of her realized he was right, but another part was chomping at the bit to remove the one piece of evidence that would clue John in that she had been in his house. "Maybe he won't contact the police," she suggested hopefully. All she'd removed from the house was something that belonged to her. But he would. Deep down, she knew it. This wasn't something he would be willing to overlook. Not when she held the one piece of evidence that would show him for the fraud he was.

They drove out of the neighborhood in silence. All at once she was exhausted, both mentally and physically.

"You okay?" he asked when he stopped at a red light.

She smiled weakly. "A little tired." Thoughts of the soda can drifted away. There was nothing she could do about that now.

"Close your eyes and put your head on my shoulder," he said.

She did as he advised and was comforted by his solid strength. "When I was a little girl, my dad used to sing to me when he carried me up to bed."

"What song?"

"Just an old lullabye. My dad loved to sing. I do, too, sometimes." She wasn't sure why she felt the need to chatter. Rarely did she mention her father.

After his death, she'd learned not to, because it upset her mother. Later, it seemed more important to hold the memories close to her own heart, as though exposing them would water them down, weaken them in her own mind. She'd been secretly engaged to John for almost two months, and except to say that her father was dead, she had never mentioned him. Never told John how she grieved for her father to this very day.

She didn't want to examine her reasons for sharing this favorite of all memories with Brent. If she stopped to think about it, she was sure to find some profound significance, but she was too tired. Too tired and perhaps a little afraid.

Brent started to hum, the sound low and melodic. Tears formed in the corner of her eyes at his kindness.

Rather than let him see her tears, she closed her eyes and pretended to be asleep. Pretended she was once more protected by someone she loved and who loved her. The fantasy worked far too well, because the next thing she knew they were parked outside her apartment building and Brent was whispering her name.

"Maddie." His voice seemed to come from a great distance. "You're home. Don't you want to go inside?"

She made a soft protesting sound, too warm and comfortable to move.

"If you want, I'll walk in with you and check behind the shower curtain to be sure no one's hiding there."

"Okay." She didn't hesitate to accept—and not

because she was afraid of a robber taking up residence in her apartment. Truth was, she wasn't ready to be separated from Brent. It was too soon, and she didn't want him to leave. She suspected he felt the same way about leaving *her*. In the short hours since they'd met at the Java Joint, they'd bonded. He had risked everything for her. His reputation, his career, his future. No one had ever cared that much for her. No one had ever put so much on the line for her. She snuggled closer to his warmth, and he stroked his chin across the top of her head.

After a moment or two his shoulder rose and fell with a deep breath. "Maddie, look at me." His words were little more than a wisp of sound.

Slowly she lifted her head, and their eyes met. He wanted to kiss her. She wanted it, too, and when his mouth swooped down on hers, she felt as if she were being lifted up, transported to another sphere. After the initial contact, he kissed her again, slowly, carefully, as though he feared his need would frighten her. His teeth tugged at her trembling lower lip and then he introduced his tongue, delicately tasting her mouth.

It didn't take her long to respond and kiss him back, catching his lower lip with her own teeth, nibbling, and then teasing him with the tip of her tongue. Kissing had never been this good. Not with anyone.

At one time she had considered herself an expert in the art of kissing. She'd been tutored by some of the best, but what she'd learned was technique. What she experienced with Brent was a tenderness, a purity of emotion, that pierced her soul.

He broke off the kiss and, after claiming a moment to compose himself, he escorted her to the door of her apartment. She discovered that her hand was shaking too badly for her to insert the key into the lock.

He did it for her, though his hands didn't appear much steadier. He turned the knob and opened the door for her to enter. She walked in, clutching John's file to her breast. When she realized Brent hadn't followed, she turned around.

"Are you coming in?" she asked, mildly surprised that he remained in the hallway.

He shook his head.

She frowned. "Why not?"

He hesitated, as if weighing his response. "Because if I do, I won't be leaving until morning."

Hot color roasted her cheeks, and she lowered her gaze. He reached out and brushed the soft skin of her face with the back of his hand. She closed her eyes and covered his fingers with her own. She yearned to thank him, to tell him that his honesty, his restraint, his generosity in refusing to use her, had renewed her faith in men. She'd known him four years, and yet she had never really known him, the same as he'd never completely known her. But then no one at college had. She hadn't allowed anyone close enough to see her as she actually was.

Until now.

Brent's kindness when he'd found her in church had deeply affected her. Less than forty-eight hours later he'd jeopardized everything for her. No one had ever cared that much. That alone had rejuvenated her belief in human goodness and kindness. Now he was admitting a desire to make love to her, but because he was an honorable man, he wouldn't place either of them in the path of temptation.

Moisture filled her eyes.

He seemed to think she was asking him to explain himself, because he said, "You trust me, Maddie. I'm not willing to destroy that."

She did trust him and always would. Completely. Utterly. With everything in her. Again and again he'd proved himself. In the past two days he'd revealed the true depth of his character. By contrast, John, whom she'd dated and loved and trusted, had used her, belittled her and broken her heart.

"I'll call you in the morning," Brent promised.

She smiled and nodded, reluctant for him to leave.

He turned to walk away, then abruptly turned back and hugged her fiercely. "Don't ever sell yourself short again, understand?"

"Never," she promised.

His hold relaxed. "Good night, Maddie."

"Good night."

Maddie awoke feeling refreshed and alive. The sun shone through her bedroom window, glorious and bright. She rolled her head to one side and groaned when she realized the time. She'd forgotten to set her alarm. If she didn't rush, she would be late for work.

Tossing aside the covers, she hurried into the bathroom, showered and dressed. Breakfast consisted of an English muffin, which popped up from the toaster at the precise moment the phone rang.

Brent. It had to be.

She almost tripped in her eagerness to get to the phone. "Morning," she answered cheerfully.

Cold silence slapped her in the face.

"Hello," she tried again, and a chill scooted down her spine.

"You were in my house."

John.

A breath jammed in Maddie's throat before her defenses snapped into place. "I don't know what you're talking about," she returned indignantly. "As I recall, you asked me not to contact you again, which I haven't. I expect the same courtesy from you." With that she replaced the receiver in its cradle. Hanging up on him might have been childish, but it sure felt good. Besides, she had nothing more she wanted to say to him unless it was in a court of law, and she would let an attorney do the talking for her there.

The phone rang again, and she jumped as if she'd received an electrical shock. Fearing it might be John again, she allowed the answering machine to pick up the call.

"Maddie?" Brent asked. "Are you awake?"

"Brent." She leaped for the phone, saying his name even as she brought the receiver to her mouth. "Good morning."

"Morning." He sounded groggy and relaxed, as if he'd just awoken.

"Did you sleep well?"

"As well as can be expected," he murmured, and she could hear the smile in his voice.

"Me too."

He yawned. "Are you doing anything special this evening?"

"I...no, nothing." If she was, she would cancel it.

"No bank robberies or any other crimes plotted?"

"No," she said, and laughed, giddy with happiness. John could call and say whatever ugly things he wanted, but he couldn't destroy the joy she felt being with Brent.

"Do you think you could pencil me in for dinner?"

"I'll have to check my day planner, but I believe it could be arranged." Her feet floated several inches above the ground.

"Six o'clock?"

"Perfect." That gave her enough time to arrive home, change and freshen up.

"My parents want to meet you."

His parents! She nearly dropped the phone. He was joking. He had to be. He was playing a trick on her. A silly prank to pay her back for the craziness she'd subjected him to last night.

"You're not serious, right?"

"As a matter of fact, I am."

In all the years she'd been dating, no man had taken her to meet his parents. And Brent's father was a minister, and his mother...well, she was a minister's wife.

"Uh...why?" She wanted to suggest it was a bit early for her to meet his parents but stopped herself.

That would have implied Brent was serious about her, and it was much too soon for them to be serious. Wasn't it?

"Why?" he said. "A number of reasons. I mentioned you earlier in the week and—"

"You mentioned me?" Oh, no. "What did you say?"

When he didn't answer right away, she was sorry she'd asked. She said quickly, "That's all right. You don't need to tell me." He must have done what she feared most—relayed the stories about her that had circulated around campus. The men she'd supposedly known, slept with, entertained. Her wildness, her antics, her pranks.

"I told Mom I'd run into you recently," he explained, "and I mentioned that I'd never really known you and was sorry I hadn't made the effort while we were in college, because I find myself completely enthralled with you now."

"Oh, Brent." She closed her eyes and pressed the phone hard against her ear.

"Mom seemed to think I've been given a second chance and should make the most of it."

"We've both been given a second chance, don't you think?" she asked.

"Yeah, I guess I do. Now, are you coming to dinner or not?"

She needed time to mull over this invitation to his parents' home. It was such an important step....

"Maddie?" he asked when she remained silent. "It's my parents. They won't bite, I promise. Well, not unless provoked." He paused. "There's no need to be nervous."

"Oh, all right," she said, tossing out her acceptance to hide how deeply affected she was. "I mean... tell your mother I'd be honored to join her and your father for dinner."

"If it'll make you feel better, I'll hold your hand the entire evening."

"I don't need anyone to hold my hand," she assured him, though his offer filled her with pleasure.

He responded with a hearty laugh. "OK, we're on. I've got to get going, or I'll be late for the academy. I'll see you tonight at six."

"I'll look forward to it." Not so much the dinner, because she knew she was going to be poked and prodded with questions, but being with Brent.

The workday was over before Maddie knew it. She was never quite sure why the large downtown insurance agency had hired a history major. She suspected Uncle Alfie had something to do with it. He had his connections and didn't hesitate to use them. But she was happy to have the job and worked hard to prove herself.

At five o'clock, spirits high, she breezed out of the office and was back at her apartment in plenty of time to be ready when Brent arrived.

He was prompt. When she opened her door to him, he took one look at her and his eyes widened with appreciation. "Hi," he said, and whistled softly. She had chosen to wear a short-sleeve ankle-length summer dress in a pastel floral print. It was one of the most demure outfits she owned.

"Hi." She had never been shy around men, but she felt shy now. Her eyelashes fell, fanning her cheekbones.

"Have you thought about me as much as I have you?" he asked, his words low and raw.

She wouldn't have admitted it if he hadn't spoken first. All day Brent had been on her mind and in her heart. Earlier, too. From the moment he'd found her in the church, he'd dominated almost her every waking thought and ventured into her dreams, as well.

"I've thought about you, too," she admitted, afraid to let him know how much and so saying too little. She didn't want to discount their attraction, nor did she want to build it out of proportion. This was all happening so fast.

He slowly expelled his breath, reached for her and pulled her into his arms. It didn't take him long to claim her mouth with his own. The kiss was infinitely tender and prolonged, as if this was a reward he'd been waiting to collect all day and he refused to be cheated by his own impatience.

Her heart was spilling over with joy. Once more she experienced that incredible urge to weep, but she fought it. Tears made you weak. Tears made you vulnerable and were to be avoided at all costs.

"Mom and Dad are eager to get to know you," he said as he escorted her outside.

"If you're telling me this to make me feel less nervous, try something else, all right?"

He chuckled. "It's the first time I've ever brought a woman to meet my parents."

"Knowing that doesn't help, either, Brent," she told him, her teeth clenched.

He chuckled again. "At one time you infuriated me more than any woman I've ever known," he said as he eased the car into the heavy flow of traffic.

"That I can deal with," she announced, then relaxed and smiled at him. "I'm accustomed to irritating others. I guess that's why I'm so good at it."

"Mom found your picture in the yearbook."

Her spine went ramrod straight. Not the yearbook! Anything but the yearbook! She'd dressed in the most outrageous way possible when she'd posed for her senior photo. And then there were the candids....

Remembering, she groaned. "Please don't tell me your mother found the picture of me streaking at the football game last October."

"That's the one she liked best."

She groaned more loudly.

"You had on flesh-colored underwear beneath the trench coat." It was true, despite the rumors that she'd been in the buff.

"Take me home. Just turn around and take me home." No one needed to tell her how this evening would go. No mother would want her son to date someone like her—the someone she'd once been.

Her demand appeared to amuse him.

"Brent, I'm serious."

"I know you are," he returned calmly. "But there's no reason to worry."

She didn't believe that for a moment.

"My mother looked at the photo, and after her initial shock, she told me…" He paused.

"Told you you're a fool to so much as talk to me."

"No," he returned forcefully. "She laughed and confessed to appreciating your individuality and grit. She knew about the incident."

"So you told her about me way back last fall."

"Just what you'd done. As I recall, I was rather put out about it myself. I thought it was just plain stupid."

"It was." She would be the first one to admit that now.

"My mother said anyone who would do something that bold is…"

"Nuts," Maddie supplied.

"Brave, I believe was her word."

"But not the type of girl a mother is anxious to have her son date."

He reached for her hand and squeezed it. "On the contrary. My mother is a very special woman. It didn't take her long to see past that bad-girl act of yours."

"Brent, I'm nervous." The woman who'd raced across a football field in front of the marching band wearing little more than a trench coat was afraid of meeting a preacher's wife.

"Don't be."

As it turned out, he was right. The dinner, the evening, everything was perfect. Brent's parents were gracious and warm. In retrospect, it made sense that they would be. They were the ones who'd shaped him into the person he was, weren't they? Brent Holliday was by far the most amazing man she'd ever known. Honorable, kind and good.

After dinner he took her to his apartment, which was above the garage. They sat at the kitchen table while their coffee was brewing, and at his insistence she worked through the quadratic quandary on a piece of paper. He watched and declared her brilliant. Then they sat side by side on the sofa, drinking espresso and listening to a Beatles CD, holding hands and frequently kissing. She couldn't remember spending a more enjoyable evening.

"Are you free tomorrow night?" he asked when he dropped her off at her apartment. Before she could tell him she was available *every* night, he kissed her, and then kissed her again.

"I'm free," she whispered, her eyes closed, her lips moist and slightly swollen from his kisses.

"What about the night after that?"

"Free."

"Good." He eased away from her with a reluctance that made her heart sing. "I'll call you in the morning."

"Please." She smiled and leaned against her open apartment door as he walked backward, taking small unwilling steps.

She blew him a kiss, and he grinned and did the same. She didn't close the door until he was completely out of sight. Then she raced to the window and stared down on the street, watching till his car turned the corner and was gone. Never had she felt so giddy or so young. Like being fifteen all over again. In love, truly in love, for the first time in her life.

She walked around her apartment as if in a dream. None of this seemed possible. Only a few days earlier she'd been in a pit of despair, certain life had done her wrong. Now she was so happy it was almost frightening.

The test that proved she'd solved the quadratic quandary didn't seem important any longer. John Theda was a fraud, and sooner or later others would learn that, too. Still, she fully intended on setting the record straight. If he got away with doing this to her, he might try it again with another student. He might use another unsuspecting female student the way he had her, and she couldn't allow that to happen.

First thing in the morning she would contact Dean Williams. Brent had talked it over with her that evening and was in full agreement. He felt strongly that now that she had the proof she needed, she should use it.

She smiled as she recalled his reaction to her showing him the solution to the quandratic quandary. Not only had he claimed she was brilliant, but he'd talked about her future and all the things she could do, growing more excited and animated by the moment. She had laughed off his praise, embarrassed by it. The only way to stop him had been to kiss him, and so she had, again and again, loving him for believing in her, for encouraging her to be all she could be.

The phone rang, and she looked at it, hesitating. It couldn't be Brent—he wouldn't be home yet. She hadn't told him about John's call earlier in the day. It would have alarmed him, and anyway, she could handle John.

"Hello," she said, her voice cool and even.

"That was a touching little scene."

She squared her shoulders, though it made her shudder to think that he'd been out there watching her with Brent. "What do you want, John?"

"You mean you haven't figured it out?"

"I told you this morning and I'll say it again— don't contact me. It won't do you any good. I'm having my phone number changed first thing in the morning."

He laughed, and the sound was cold and heartless, sending chills down her spine. "You're a fool. Don't try to play games with me, Maddie. I'm the master, and you'll only end up getting hurt."

"Goodbye, John." She wasn't waiting to listen to any more of his threats. She had the test in a safe place, and she wasn't going to allow him to intimidate her.

Almost as soon as she replaced the receiver, the phone rang again. This time she let the answering machine take it.

"You didn't give me a chance to mention something important," John said. "Something you should know." A pause. "I talked with Mrs. Johnson this morning. You remember Mrs. Johnson, don't you? She lives next door." He paused again, as if to give his words time to sink in.

"It seems that Mrs. Johnson saw something rather unusual the other night. It's actually rather humorous." He chuckled. "Apparently I was just pulling into the driveway when a young man—a former student of mine, she guessed—launched himself over her fence and all but broke the land-speed record in an effort to get into my home. When the back door turned out to be locked, he hauled himself through my bathroom window. No easy task, I would guess.

"Being the concerned neighbor she is, Mrs. Johnson went out to the street and wrote down his license-plate number."

Maddie's blood went cold.

"I had a friend run the number, and it seems the car belongs to Brent Holliday. He's a good friend of yours, I've noticed. A very good friend. I imagine the police academy would be interested in knowing about young Holliday's nighttime activities, don't you?"

"No!" Maddie cried, although there was no one to hear her.

"Pick up the receiver, Maddie," John ordered. "We have something important to discuss."

She hesitated.

"Now!" he shouted, then, more calmly, "Before you force me to do something you and your boy-friend would find very…uncomfortable."

She flinched and with a trembling hand did as he requested.

Five

"I don't understand," Brent said, studying her. "I thought we'd already talked this out." They were sitting at the kitchen table in his apartment drinking tall glasses of iced tea. All Maddie had wanted to do was explain that she'd changed her mind about reporting John to Dean Williams and then be on her way, but he had refused to let her leave.

She felt his disappointment as keenly as her own. This wasn't what she wanted, but she had no choice. John hadn't given her any alternative. But Brent didn't know that and never would.

"I've changed my mind," she said in what she hoped was a convincing tone. She downed the last of her tea and set the empty glass on the tabletop, signaling that now she really had to go. "I've already canceled my appointment with Dean Williams."

"Why?" His eyes narrowed.

She had known it wouldn't be easy to fool him with this apparent change of heart, but she'd hoped she could pull it off and leave him thinking she'd come to a decision that was best for everyone involved. A nearly impossible task when she had trouble believing it herself.

"Why'd you cancel the appointment?" he pressed a second time.

"Dean Williams won't believe me." She tried to make it sound as simple as that. "The date on the top of the test is May sixth. Unfortunately I write dates in the European style—the day first—so it could just as easily be read as June fifth."

"But it was a midterm test, and it says so. Dean Williams knows when midterms were given. You shouldn't have to prove a thing. It's all there in black and white for him to read. That sounds like a convenient excuse to me. Come on, Maddie, what's up?"

She'd been afraid of this. Afraid that Brent would use logic against her. In reality she had no reason for canceling the appointment other than to keep John from reporting the burglary. He had more than enough evidence to have Brent and her arrested. If she'd acted alone, she would have willingly called his bluff, but she refused to drag Brent's name through the mud. Nor would she allow John to destroy Brent's future. Not when it was within her power to prevent it.

"Nothing's up," she insisted. "I thought everything over and decided it didn't matter what John claimed. I know who solved the quadratic quandary, and that's all that really matters. Setting the record straight, embarrassing him…well, it isn't worth the hassle."

Brent's eyes told her that he didn't believe her. He went very still. "What happened?"

"What makes you think something happened?"

"You." His face tightened until his mouth formed a pinched line. "You're different."

"How could I be different?" she said, attempting to make a joke of it. "I'm the same person I was a couple of days ago. Just remember, what you see is what you get."

"That wasn't the way it always was."

His words suggested something she didn't like. "What do you mean by that?"

"Just what I said. You wore a facade for years. It's back, Maddie, and something's happened that you're not telling me about. I know you, and I want to know you better, but I can't do that when you put up a steel gate locking me out."

"You're being ridiculous."

"Am I?"

She needed something, anything, to distract him. "Is this what you're going to say every time we have a disagreement?" she demanded. "Accuse me of blocking you out? Dredge up the past and throw it in my face?"

"I want the truth."

"You got it." She stood and walked over to the kitchen sink with her glass. She'd downed the cold drink so fast she'd developed a headache. Dear heaven, how she hated deception. But she had no choice.

"I have to go," she whispered.

"Where are you headed?" he asked with more than a hint of accusation.

"You think a few kisses give you the right to demand my whereabouts twenty-four hours a day?"

Looking ashamed, Brent buried his hands in his pockets. "I apologize. I had no right to ask you that."

"True, but I'll tell you anyway. I'm meeting a friend."

The question all but burned from his eyes, but he wouldn't ask, and because she wanted them to part on good terms, Maddie sighed and hugged him. "OK, if you must know, I'm having lunch with Susan Cabot. We grew up together. Now stop, please. What I do or don't do about that test paper is my decision."

He said nothing, but she felt his disapproval as keenly as if he'd spoken. He followed her outside to where she'd parked her bicycle in the driveway. "The person you're cheating is yourself, Maddie. That's what bothers me most."

"It's my decision, Brent," she reminded him again.

"You're giving Theda a license to hurt someone else. By not reporting him, you're giving him the impression he can get away with fraud."

"He won't need me to prove anything. John will do it to himself. His type always does. Haven't you ever heard the expression 'Time wounds all heels'? John's a first-class heel, and in time it will catch up with him." When it did, she would love to be around to witness it. The man was a major jerk and deserved everything he had coming to him.

"Fine," Brent said resignedly. "If that's what you want."

"It is." The words nearly stuck in her throat. As

hard as she'd argued, as hard as she'd worked to convince him this was the best way, she didn't believe it for a minute. But she couldn't, wouldn't, hurt Brent, not when all she really wanted was revenge. The trade-off was fair. In exchange for serenity, she would give the file back to John and nothing would be said either way.

Brent kissed her lightly and stepped back while she climbed on her bike.

"You'll call me?" she asked, needing to know he wouldn't allow this to stand between them.

He hesitated, smiled briefly and then nodded. "Sure. You want to catch a movie later?"

Her relief was palpable and she smiled back, loving him so much it was all she could do not to throw her arms around him and explain everything. Instead, she said calmly, "That'd be great." Her heart swelled with emotion. He was disappointed in her, but he would work his way through it. By inviting her to a movie, he was telling her that, despite this, the two of them would continue as a couple. He hadn't liked what she'd had to say, but he'd accepted it.

Early in her dating career Maddie had discovered that a man's pride was often wrapped around his advice, and if she refused to do as he suggested, it deflated his fragile ego. Brent's sense of self was strong.

"I've got to return a book to the library this afternoon," he said, "and I'll give you a call when I'm back. How does that sound?"

"Come here," she instructed, holding on to the bike's handlebars.

"Come here?" he questioned as he advanced.

She looped her arms around his neck and, standing on tiptoe, the bike balanced between her legs, kissed him. When she pulled away, his breathing was ragged and so was hers.

"Thank you," she whispered.

"For what?" He seemed to have a problem finding his tongue.

"Just because."

He grinned, his look almost boyish. "You can thank me again later, all right?"

"Anytime you want."

He chuckled, then watched her ride down the driveway, waving when she entered the street. She smiled and waved back. But her smile faded as she rounded the corner. She had never really hated John Theda. He'd hurt and disappointed her, broken her heart and used her, but she'd never hated him. She was close to doing so now, however. How she could have been so blind before, she didn't know.

Maddie hadn't lied to Brent about her appointment. She was having lunch with Susan Cabot, all right, but afterward she was meeting John. It wasn't a confrontation she looked forward to, but it was necessary. One last meeting, and then it would be over once and for all.

Her lunch with her childhood friend went well. "You've changed," Susan said almost immediately. "What happened to my friend the rebel?"

"I fell in love with a man who turned out to be a

rat," Maddie explained sheepishly. "And the rebel in me died. I discovered I didn't like the woman I'd become and decided it was in my power to change that."

"You look terrific." Susan's enthusiastic smile revealed her approval. "Now tell me about Uncle Alfie. Is he still a darling?"

They spent the better part of two hours reminiscing, and the dark cloud that had hung over Maddie's head seemed less threatening by the time they finished lunch.

After she left the restaurant, Maddie checked her watch. Her meeting with John was scheduled for three-thirty at the fountain in the center of the Queen Anne campus. In exchange for the file—including her test paper, of course—John had promised to forget the entire incident and not report the break-in to the police.

She thought of how long and often Brent had spoken of working in law enforcement. He loved his work, loved the challenge, and the mental and physical demands. He would be a good police officer and touch many lives for the better. It helped to remember that as she biked toward campus.

Her sacrifice was small compared to what she had to gain, she decided. John could accept all the credit he wanted; she didn't care, as long as he stayed out of Brent's life and, for that matter, hers.

She arrived on time and was left twiddling her thumbs and worrying. It was just like John to let her stew before he bothered to show. Fifteen minutes after their agreed time, she saw him walking toward her.

Perspective being what it was, she took one look at him and wondered how she could have been attracted to such a man. At the time she'd thought of him as a modern-day Adonis. Now she could see he wasn't anywhere near as handsome.

"Hello, Maddie," he said when he joined her. He eyed her with undisguised approval. "You're looking good, real good."

"Sorry I can't say the same for you."

He laughed. "That's what I always liked about you. A smart comeback for everything."

"Let's get this over with," she suggested, eager to be on her way.

"Fine." He held out his hand, expecting her to surrender the file.

"Not so fast," she said, and snickered softly. Could he really believe that she would be so naive? He'd taught her well about mistrust, and she wasn't about to give him anything without a signed assurance. "I'll need your signature to our agreement."

"You mean you don't trust me?" His hurt-little-boy look was almost laughable.

"Exactly."

He scowled. "All right, all right. What exactly do you want?"

"Other than your signature, I'd settle for a quart of your blood."

He laughed. "I do miss that wit of yours. You'll always be the same ol' Maddie, won't you?"

She didn't bother to answer. Knowing John had changed her. A part of her innocence had been forever destroyed. His treachery had tarnished a piece of her soul. It had taken her a long time to fight back, but she'd won that battle, thanks in part to Brent. For that she owed him far more than she could ever repay.

From her backpack she removed the agreement she'd written up. It was in an envelope, and she handed it to him to open and read. Since he refused to admit in writing that she'd been the one to solve the quadratic quandary, she'd listed some rather unsavory details about his personal life, and his signature gave her permission to use these facts against him if he made trouble for either Brent or her.

John set his briefcase on the cement rim of the fountain. He read and signed the agreement grudgingly, then placed it back in the envelope and gave it to Maddie. In exchange she handed him the test file.

"I won't say it's been a pleasure," she said, reaching for her bike. "I hope I never see you again, John."

"Let me assure you, the feeling is mutual," he said, and turned away.

She climbed on her bike and rode off, eager to make her escape. She biked down the narrow cement pathway toward the parking lot. Only a few cars were there; when classes started up in a couple of weeks, it would be full again.

Not until she was close to the street did she spy Brent's car, or at least she thought it was his. Her feet went slack on the pedals, and she coasted several feet as she took a closer look.

It *was* Brent's car, and he was sitting inside. When he glanced up and saw her, he climbed out.

"Brent," she said, shocked to see him, "what are you doing here?"

"The library book, remember?" His words were charged with anger.

He hadn't told her he was returning the book to the *college* library, and now she wondered how much he'd seen and how she could explain.

"You sold out, didn't you?" he demanded.

"Sold out?"

"You sold Theda that test file. Blackmailed him. How much did you get, Maddie? Forget justice, forget what's right. Forget anyone else he'll cheat and hurt in the future, right? I hope he made it worth your while."

The words to explain and defend herself stuck in her throat. "Matters aren't always what they seem."

"Yeah, right. I saw the exchange. He handed you an envelope and you gave him the file. I saw everything I needed to."

She considered showing Brent the contents of the envelope, but didn't, because then he would know she'd surrendered the test file to protect him.

"I'm asking you to trust me, Brent," she said.

He stared at her for a long moment. "Show me the envelope."

Briefly she closed her eyes. "I...I can't."

His look hardened, and she knew he was steeling himself against her. "That says it all, doesn't it?" He climbed back into the car. "I don't think it would be a good idea if we saw each other again, Maddie."

"Brent—" She broke off before she could add "please."

"I knew something had happened when I saw you earlier at my place. Now it all makes sense. Goodbye, Maddie. I wish you well."

Six

"You told Brent, didn't you?" Gretchen asked. "You didn't let it end there. That would have been so unfair to you."

"I didn't have a choice," Maddie whispered. Even after fifteen years, it still hurt to remember their confrontation that day. "I could never let Brent know what I'd done."

Gretchen, Carol and Maddie sat on the rim of the fountain, and Maddie realized they'd drawn close to one another in the past couple of hours. Fifteen years. Who would have believed time could evaporate that easily? Like an eraser wiping a blackboard clean, the years had faded away. Some things had changed and others had remained the same. Maddie wasn't the girl she'd been back then—the one desperately seeking to be noticed, no matter what the price. She'd paid dearly for those mistakes. The steepest price of all was the afternoon she'd lost Brent Holliday.

"You must have loved him very much to have sacrificed so much," Carol Furness said softly.

Yes, Maddie had loved him, heart and soul. "John taught me some valuable lessons, but Brent taught me even more."

"Can you tell us what happened after that day?" Carol asked, and placed her hand over Maddie's.

"I lost him," Maddie said. "I had a hard time accepting it in the beginning, but eventually I realized it was probably for the best. He'd come into my life like a knight in shining armor and then he was gone. I had no regrets."

"But you weren't any better off than before you met him," Gretchen said.

"Oh, but I was," Maddie hurried to explain. "Brent gave me a tremendous gift. He helped me find myself, taught me to take control. My level of self-esteem rose the moment I discovered that I could do something about the situation with John. In the end, allowing John to accept the credit was a small price to pay for what Brent had given me in return. He gave me back my soul."

"Were you ever able to let him know that?"

Maddie shook her head sadly. "In the beginning I tried to fix things between us, but I soon realized Brent meant what he said."

"That was pretty narrow-minded of him, wasn't it?" Gretchen asked.

"I know now that he was as idealistic as I was. It's easy to look back and judge him from the perspective of time, but that would be wrong. Gradually the pain of losing him lessened. I refused to mourn, when what he'd given me had been a tremendous gift. It was because of him that I made the smartest decision of my life."

"Which was?" Carol pressed.

Maddie smiled, knowing her friends would be amused. "I went back to school."

"Queen Anne?"

"Oh, no." Maddie shook her head. "I was paying my own way, and I couldn't afford a private college. I started out working days and taking night courses. It took me nearly five years to earn my master's, but I did it, one course at a time."

"In mathematics," Gretchen guessed.

"In mathematics," Maddie confirmed.

"Oh, my," Carol said, checking her wrist. "Look at the time."

"Good grief!" Maddie cried, leaping to her feet. "We've got less than an hour before the dinner. I've got to shower and feed the kids and…" She paused, knowing her friends were equally rushed. "I'll see you there, right?"

"Of course," Gretchen promised. "And my husband. I'd like you to meet him."

"Me too," Carol added. "With my husband. Let's find a table and sit together?"

Maddie and Gretchen both agreed.

Together they rushed to the parking lot, chatting excitedly as they walked. Maddie smiled to herself. She was anxious for her friends to meet *her* husband, too. She'd almost given up on love when she met and married him a mere five years ago. That was when life had tossed her a second curveball, only this time she'd stepped up to bat and been ready to swing.

Epilogue

Japanese lanterns swayed gently in the breeze, their lights flickering, telegraphing secretly coded messages around the lush garden patio. Gretchen stepped away from the pre-dinner reception and stood in the doorway, looked around, then sighed when she saw him. So this was where her husband had taken off to.

The festive noise of the reunion faded as she stepped from the gaily lit hall to the peace and quiet of the flowering patio.

"I thought I'd find you out here," she said, moving to her husband's side.

Josh Morrow slipped his arm around her trim waist and smiled down at her, his eyes filled with love. No matter how many years they'd been married, Gretchen had never tired of seeing him smile. Her heart was full to overflowing with the love they shared. They would celebrate their thirteenth wedding anniversary this year, and it seemed like yesterday when he'd roared up to her family home, his

Harley spewing dust and fumes. Two years he'd kept her waiting. Two years, and he'd actually expected to find her waiting.

The irony was…she *had* been. She'd never been able to believe he wouldn't be back.

As long as she lived, Gretchen would never forget the day he came for her. Defiant as ever, he'd parked the Harley, rung the doorbell and nearly given her mother heart failure.

She had been home visiting her parents. When she realized it was Josh at the door, she'd stepped outside. He'd looked at her and smiled, and she'd smiled back.

"Do you still want to ride off into the sunset with me?" he'd asked.

"That depends." He'd kept her waiting all this time. She wasn't about to make it easy for him.

"Would a wedding band and life with a starving law student be inducement enough?"

"Plenty. Oh, Josh, what took you so long?" Simultaneously laughing and crying, she'd hurled herself into his arms. He had locked his arms around her waist and swung her around. By that time both her parents had come out to the front porch, not knowing what to think. Josh had glanced at them, kissed her as if he'd dreamed of it every day for the two years they'd been apart, and then asked to speak privately with her father.

Gretchen had paced outside the den until they were finished. When they appeared, she'd stepped to Josh's side and grabbed hold of his hand. Then her father had grinned and announced that he felt Josh would make her a fine husband.

He had. Thirteen years, and she hadn't regretted a single day. They had three children, a beautiful home, a good life. The children—a twelve-year-old boy and twin ten-year-old girls—and her charity work kept her more than busy. Josh needed her, too. He'd recently been elected as a Supreme Court judge in Orange County, and his position on the bench was almost as demanding on her as it was him.

"Where'd you go this afternoon?" he asked, sipping his drink.

"To take a look around campus."

"The fountain?"

How well he knew her. "I met up with some old friends."

"I don't suppose you ran into Roger Lockheart?"

"No." She pressed her head to his shoulder. "Don't tell me you're worried about my seeing Roger again."

"Well, you once loved him."

"Oh, Josh, be serious. Roger was a rat. You couldn't possibly believe I'd want anything to do with him." She ran her hand over Josh's back, never tiring of the special closeness they shared. "I will admit I'm curious about him. From what I understand, he's here."

"I saw him," Josh admitted.

"You saw him?" She couldn't believe he'd kept this information from her. "What's he look like?"

"Hah! So I was right!"

"Josh." She punched his arm playfully.

"He looks fine. He introduced me to his friend, and—"

"Friend? You mean he isn't married?"

"Three times, from what I understand."

"You're joking!"

He chuckled. "It's the truth, I swear. He apparently didn't join Daddy's law firm, either, because he's selling cars."

"Roger is selling cars. I love it!"

Josh pulled her into his arms, his eyes dark and serious. "I love you. I don't think I tell you that often enough. You're in my blood, Gretch, in my heart, and so much a part of me I couldn't make it one day without you." He held her close for a moment. "I tried to live without you all those years ago and couldn't. That was when I realized I had to make myself worthy of your faith in me. Every day of those two years we were apart I prayed you still loved me."

"Not a minute went by that I didn't long for you."

He kissed her softly. "It looks like they're ready to serve dinner."

"Great." She slipped her arm around his waist. "Remember those old friends I mentioned? Well, I want you to meet them."

He grumbled something about preferring to have his wife to himself, but followed her inside.

Carol was sitting in the hotel suite talking on the phone when her husband wandered out of the bedroom, unsuccessfully attempting to fasten the top button of his dress shirt.

He was a fine figure of a man. She loved him more than she'd thought it possible to love another human being.

"Who are you talking to?" he asked.

"Your mother," she whispered, covering the mouthpiece. "OK, Mom, yes, I'll wait." She looked back at him. "The kids are giving her problems. Timmy and Adam are fighting over the laptop again. Erica refused to eat her vegetables, and Clark, Jr., has disappeared, but she thinks he's hiding in the library. Your father's searching for him now." Her mother-in-law came back on the line, and Carol nodded, relieved. "They found Junior."

Clark sank into a chair. "Does she want us to come home?"

"No, no. I asked her that myself and she insists we enjoy the reunion. She can always call Frieda if matters get out of hand." The nanny had her own quarters, but was available any time Clark's parents felt they needed help.

She finished the conversation and hung up the phone. "It's a good thing we don't escape often."

Clark chuckled. "Every time we *do* manage to get away, you end up pregnant."

She climbed onto her husband's lap and brushed his hands away from his throat. "I'll do it," she promised, and quickly secured the button. "Four children isn't so many, is it?" she whispered, and nuzzled his neck, licking the skin with her tongue. She loved the taste and feel of him.

"Carol—" his voice was low and full of suspicion "—I know that tone."

"You do?" she asked, playing dumb.

"You want another baby."

"Would it be so terrible?" she asked, her lips nibbling his ear.

He shivered with awareness, and if he'd intended to remove her from his lap, he changed his mind.

"I love being a mother, and you love getting me pregnant," she reminded him. She'd always enjoyed children, and with Clark's software company so profitable, there wasn't any reason they couldn't have as many kids as they liked.

He sighed and rested his head against the back of the cushion. "I never could refuse you anything, you know that."

"That's not the way I remember it," she whispered, unbuttoning the very shirt she'd just spent time fastening. "You let me take off for Alaska without you."

"What brings that up?" he asked.

"I met a couple of women from my old sorority at the fountain this afternoon."

"And they thought you were married to Eddie Shapiro."

"At first, but I was quick to tell them I fell head over heels in love with you. We agreed to meet for dinner later—you don't mind, do you?" Gretchen and Maddie would be surprised and delighted when they saw she'd married Clark after all.

"No...we can have dinner with whomever you want," he whispered, and closed his eyes as she continued to kiss the underside of his jaw.

"You were a big disappointment to my friends when I told them you let me leave for Alaska."

"But technically you didn't make it there."

"No, but that's beside the point." She eased the open shirt from his shoulders.

"I flew out to your parents' house instead."

He'd arrived Christmas Eve, and his timing couldn't have been better. "You were the best Christmas present I ever received."

"You could have married Eddie," he reminded her.

That was true. Two years into his pro career, Eddie Shapiro had torn a ligament in his knee that had ended his days on the football field. He'd called Carol from the hospital bed and asked her to marry him. It had given her great delight to inform him that not only was she married to Clark Rusbach, but she was eight months pregnant with their first child.

"I wonder if he'll come to the reunion."

"I doubt it," Clark said, and reached for the zipper in the back of her dress.

"Clark," she teased, "we'll be late for the dinner."

"So?"

She couldn't think of a single reason why it was so all-fired important that they be on time. She'd never been keen on eating her salad first, anyway. "I'd like another little boy this time," she said, before directing her husband's mouth to hers.

He stood, lifting her with him and carrying her into the bedroom. "I'll do my best," he promised.

Maddie admitted to being nervous. Gretchen and Carol hadn't recognized her earlier at the fountain, and she doubted that anyone else at the reunion would, either.

Her husband placed his hand at the small of her back and steered her into the rented hall, festively decorated for the class reunion with banners and ribbons.

"I don't recognize anyone, do you?" she asked Brent.

"Not a soul." He glanced at her and chuckled. "You're actually nervous. I can't believe it. My wife, the woman who revolutionized the way mathematics is taught across the United States, is actually nervous."

"Brent, don't tease."

"The woman who's dined with the president."

"Brent!"

"And the queen of England."

"Brent, don't tell anyone about that, all right?"

"You'd rather I told them you wore falsies?"

"I did not." He always knew how to rile her.

"Yeah, but everyone would believe it."

Although she knew he was teasing, she glared at her husband. "Sometimes I wonder why I married you."

"You loved me."

"For fifteen long years, I've loved you." But for ten of those years they'd had no contact with each other. Maddie had left Seattle almost immediately after they broke up. For several years she worked at a day job while attending night school to obtain her master's degree. Her life was consumed with math. It was while she was working on her doctorate that she devised a new method of grasping basic mathematical concepts. Soon she was working with the Department of Education in Washington, D.C.

Out of the blue one afternoon she ran into Brent Holliday on the White House lawn. He'd come to Washington to receive a hero's award from the president, along with forty-nine other law-enforcement officers. She'd given him her phone number, though she really didn't expect him to call. But he had.

They met for dinner the next night, closed down the restaurant and then walked to the Lincoln Memorial. Along the way she'd finally told him the truth about the deal she'd made with John. They'd talked there until the sun rose, and by then Maddie knew she'd never stopped loving Brent. He felt the same way about her.

They were married a month later, and she was pregnant almost immediately. Their second child was born the following year. Brent had recently become the assistant chief of police in Seattle. They were happy, exceptionally so, and very much in love.

He reached for her hand and their fingers entwined. "There's Gretchen now," Maddie said, waving to her friend. "She married Josh."

"Josh Morrow?"

"Do you remember him?"

"Sure do. The class troublemaker. Wow. So Gretchen Wise married him."

"Hey, troublemakers can be tamed. You should know."

"Indeed I do. Did you tell her about John Theda

ending up in prison for fraud?" John wasn't due to be released for another ten years.

"No." She shook her head. "It's all rather sad, don't you think? I never wished him ill. Not really."

"But you were right—he ended up doing it to himself."

"Come on," she said, "I want you to meet my friends." She waved to Gretchen, who smiled and waved back.

Maddie stood on tiptoe and scanned the crowd for Carol. She wondered what could be keeping her.

* * * * *

AN ALASKAN WEDDING

Jennifer Snow

Also available from Jennifer Snow

One

This venue could not have been Leah's idea.

The Wild River Resort Hotel was posh and chic, and her best friend was more… Urban woodsy. Aurora Klein had once heard Leah say that if she could get married anywhere in the world, it would be on the top of Snowcrest Peak with two witnesses and a justice of the peace. Maybe a photographer to capture the special moment. Leah believed that weddings were about the bride and groom and should be intimate and personal.

Somehow, Leah must have been outvoted.

Aurora would guess it was the combined efforts of the mothers of the newly engaged couple that had convinced the bride that she wanted the elaborate wedding with two hundred guests, a sit-down catered menu, lavish flowers, an expensive dress she'd only wear once, a DJ that was stuck in the eighties and a four-layer cake that she wouldn't get a chance to eat.

Unless her best friend had suddenly developed

a flair for over-the-top and overdone, Aurora suspected that Leah was absolutely miserable by now.

Being so far away at university in Stanford, Aurora hadn't had much to do with her best friend's wedding planning. Leah had told her she was getting married five months ago, the same day she asked/assumed Aurora would be her maid of honor. She'd been dating Rick less than three months at that point, and Aurora thought they were moving crazy fast. But how could she be honest with her friend when she was so obviously head over heels in love?

She might not have been feeling as queasy about the whole thing if Leah wasn't marrying the brother of the man who broke Aurora's own heart years before.

And just her luck, the best man at this wedding.

"Best man, right," she scoffed. "More like *mediocre* man." Aurora straightened her skirt and entered the dining room at the resort for the rehearsal dinner.

"Are you referring to me?"

Aurora whipped around at the sound of Tyler Forrester's voice. Dressed in a charcoal suit with a light blue button-down shirt opened at the collar, his hair spiked in his usual fauxhawk and his five o'clock stubble adding to his casual sexiness, the sight of him had her pulse going crazy, as usual. Would she ever see her ex-boyfriend and not want to fall straight into the arms that had pushed her away? Why did he still have this effect on her? Although they had dated for most of their teenage life, it had been almost six years since he dumped her—right after her high school graduation.

She'd tried to move on when she left weeks later for university to pursue her degree in Engineering, but despite time and distance and every last ounce of effort, Tyler still held her heart.

"Um, no?"

"Are you asking *me* whether or not you were just insulting me?" His grin was too much.

"Well, if you see yourself in the comment…" Her voice trailed off.

Change. Subject. Now.

"Have you seen Leah?" She looked around—at everything but him. She couldn't breathe all of a sudden, like someone had a vise around her airways, squeezing tight. The large dining room seemed to shrink, the walls closing around the two of them.

"I think she's with her mother and my mother. They were in the kitchen making sure everything was under control with the dinner arrangements," Tyler said, staring straight at her.

Her cheeks burned under his intense gaze.

How the hell could he act so calm and unfazed? They'd only seen one another three or four times since they split up. Mostly when Aurora was home for the holidays or summer break, and usually it was at The Drunk Tank surrounded by hundreds of locals and tourists, so they never really had time to talk.

Correction: She avoided any opportunity to talk. It was a self-preservation thing.

But now, being the only two to show up so far for the rehearsal dinner put them in the super uncomfortable position of being alone.

Super uncomfortable for Aurora at least.

Tyler seemed completely at ease as he shoved his hands into his pants pockets and rocked back and forth on his heels. "Should we take our seats?" he asked. "Get into the wine a little early?"

Seats? Oh no. Of course they'd be seated at the same table. She'd been trying to get up the nerve to make it through the next day glued to Tyler for the walk down the aisle and the countless photos and the dinner and the dancing. Now she had to make it through *that* evening with him close by as well. At least until the engaged couple parted ways for their prewedding bachelor and bachelorette parties.

But the wine part sounded good. She'd be needing more than one glass to survive the next two days. "Sure," she said.

He motioned for her to walk ahead, and she tensed feeling his hand on her lower back. So natural. So familiar. *Too* familiar. The smallest touch from him brought back unwelcome memories of soft caresses, lingering kisses, days and nights spent together camping and hiking in the Alaskan wilderness, connecting on a deeper level than just friendship. She knew their love had been the real thing.

Yet, he'd tossed those years away like they'd meant absolutely nothing to him.

Tossed *her* away.

She walked faster, breaking the too-intimate contact. How was she going to survive the next forty-eight hours?

At the table, he held out a chair for her and she reluctantly sat.

He removed his sports coat and draped it over the back of his own chair, then rolled the sleeves of his dress shirt before reaching for the bottle of wine on the table. His shirt lifted over his sculpted forearms, and the sight of his aurora borealis watercolor tattoo made her chest tighten even more.

The tattoo had been for her.

She'd been named after the breathtaking northern lights, and Tyler had gotten the tat the minute he'd turned eighteen. It had meant everything to her. She'd believed the tattoo signified that *she'd* meant everything to him. How wrong she'd been.

Did he regret the tattoo now?

Unfortunately, no matter how much his rejection had hurt, she couldn't regret their time together.

All Aurora regretted was that it had ended.

Tyler had known Aurora was coming to the wedding. He'd known he would be paired with her in the wedding party. He'd also known that there would be pictures and dancing and dinners together. What he hadn't known was that the sight of her would stop his heart. Six years should be plenty of time for a heartache to heal, so why the hell was his taking its sweet time?

He took a bigger sip of wine than he intended and nearly choked on the dry flavor on his tongue. Since she'd left for California, he'd only seen Aurora a few times when she returned on school breaks, and each time had been torture. He'd been able to avoid her as much as possible on those previous visits, but there would be no avoiding her now.

Obviously, she was just as uncomfortable as he was. At least *she* only had to deal with the close proximity issue for the next two days. Tyler was uncomfortable with everything about this wedding. As much as he hoped his brother was making the right decision, he couldn't completely get on board with the whole marriage thing and he was surprised that Rick could.

Their parents had divorced when he was four and Rick was six. Both of their parents had remarried twice since then. It was hard to believe in an institution when both of his parents hadn't been able to make any of their relationships work.

He wasn't sure he believed in forever.

Since Aurora, he'd been living the single bachelor lifestyle here in the ski resort town of Wild River. Tourists made for the perfect casual flings. They were here for a short time, and Tyler was the guy who helped make their vacation more exciting. He didn't sleep with them, but he had fun, distracted himself from how lonely he actually was for a little while. Then they left.

Like Aurora had.

"What time is this supposed to start?" Aurora asked, lifting her dark hair away from her neck. It cascaded like silk down her back, stealing his focus, and Tyler fought the urge to tangle his fingers in it. The smell of her familiar lavender-scented shampoo hit him like a wave of nostalgia. So many hours spent, holding her, breathing her in…

"Tyler?" She waved a hand in front of his face.

"Oh…um, I was told five o'clock," he said checking his watch. It was already five fifteen and no one else had shown up yet.

"Me too," she mumbled.

"Think we were set up?"

She sighed. "Looks that way."

And she didn't seem all that impressed by it. Obviously spending time alone with him wasn't something she was eager to do. His brother was getting an earful when he saw him. He didn't know what Rick was trying to achieve, but whatever it was, it was failing miserably. This was just awkward and tense.

Still, he'd try to make the best of it. He cleared his throat. "So, how's school?"

She stared into her wineglass. "Good…busy."

So busy that the minute she'd left Wild River, she'd forgotten all about him. No calls or texts…hell, he was still waiting for her to accept his Facebook friend request. Seemed when she left him behind, it was for good. "Your mom said you made the dean's list—impressive," he said.

She swung toward him. Her dark chocolate–colored eyes with the fire-orange starburst around the center burned into his. "You talked to my mom?"

He fought to hide his embarrassment. Truth was, he kept in contact with her entire family—her mom, her dad, her brother—he'd basically grown up at their house. In the years that they'd dated, Tyler had adopted Aurora's family as his own. As the one he *wished* he had. Her parents were still married, and their relationship had been something Tyler only saw on television sitcoms. Her mother stayed at home and baked cookies as an after-school treat, drove the kids to all their sports and extracurricular activities and had dinner on the table by six when Aurora's father got home from work. Old-fashioned maybe, but Tyler had craved that kind of security and routine.

His home life couldn't have been more different. Switching back and forth between his parents' separate homes with their current spouses each week, he'd never felt settled. The only place that had truly felt like home was Aurora's house, and he hadn't been willing to let go of that even after he'd been forced to let go of her.

"I see her around town all the time," he said, noncommittal. And he was regularly invited to dinner. He'd assumed Aurora knew that, but obviously not. She must think he'd completely forgotten about her the moment she boarded that plane to California. Nothing could be further from the truth. He thought about her all the time, especially when the northern lights lit up the sky or he caught a glimpse of his forearm tattoo.

Basically all the time.

"How's the search for a firefighter opportunity?" she asked.

At least she remembered that passion of his. "Slow. There aren't too many opportunities here in Alaska. I'm still volunteering with S & R and working with Dad's construction company." He didn't admit to her that he also searched for firefighting opportunities in Stanford and L.A. and a dozen other Californian cities closer to her. He always stopped himself before he could apply. Alaska was his home. He might be a snowboarding playboy here in the snowcapped mountain region, but he'd be useless on a surfboard, trying to survive the sweltering heat and humidity and city traffic. "I imagine life on campus is exciting," he said.

Translation: Was there a hot, blond, tanned surfer boy distracting her from her studies?

He knew from Rick that she hadn't RSVP'd a plus-one for the wedding… So neither had he. But that didn't mean she wasn't seeing someone.

Unfortunately, she revealed nothing. "It's definitely not boring," she said, checking her cell phone.

He nodded and a long silence followed.

Right. Six years was a long time not to communicate. They barely knew one another well enough now to hold a conversation. How had they gone from being best friends, so crazy in love, to barely more than strangers?

Unfortunately, that wasn't true—not on his end at least. His heart still felt their connection as strong as ever. He had to say something. But what could he say? That he thought about her all the time? That he was sorry for the way things ended? For hurting her?

He took a deep breath, but she spoke first. "I'm going to text Leah and see what time this dinner actually starts."

Wow. She really did not want to be alone with him. Any courage he was summoning to be honest with her, to tell her how he still cared about her—more than anything—vanished. "Yeah, good idea," he said, as casually as possible.

While she texted the bride, Tyler scanned the rehearsal dinner setup. The following day the same room would be used for the wedding ceremony, then pictures, then the reception. The entire event was stressing him out, but pictures were probably what was terrifying him the most. How was he supposed to smile and stand next to Aurora without looking either heartbroken or still in love with a woman he couldn't have?

Two

"Oh my God, get me out of this thing, quick!" The minute they were alone in her bridal suite after the rehearsal dinner, Leah turned and lifted her long dark hair so Aurora could quickly unzip the tight-bodice-corset-thing she wore with a ballerina-style tutu skirt. Leah immediately released a deep exhale as though she'd been holding her breath all evening.

Aurora knew the feeling. She'd been holding her own breath but for completely different reasons. The familiar scent of Tyler's cologne had plagued her the entire evening. And his handsome smile had her stomach fluttering so badly, it had been impossible to eat the fifty-dollar-a-plate dinner. "I should have left you trapped in there after that setup," she said.

Leah's fake look of innocence almost made her laugh, but her friend wasn't off the hook that easily. "It was a simple mix-up with the time," she said with a shrug, reaching for her plaid button-down and ripped jeans.

Aurora raised an eyebrow. "That somehow only Tyler and I received?"

Leah sighed. "Look, Rick and I thought that maybe if you two had some time alone together before the actual wedding stuff started, you'd have time to…"

"To what?" Kiss and make up? There had been countless opportunities for that over the years. When she'd been home before, Tyler basically ignored her. And he'd completely dismissed the idea of a long-distance relationship years before when she'd tearfully suggested one. She still cringed when she thought about the day they'd ended things and the way she'd practically begged him to reconsider.

No, Aurora, I'm not interested in having a girlfriend thousands of miles away.

His words had stung. They still did when she remembered them. And the crazy part was that she'd almost reconsidered going away for university until he'd also made it clear that he didn't see things working out between them even if she stayed.

She'd been devastated and torn, but her parents had forced her to see reason. If things were meant to be, they'd be… In time, at the right time, they'd said.

Apparently, they weren't meant to be.

"You two can deny it all you want, but you're both still crazy about one another," Leah said, picking up the hotel phone and dialing room service.

Since kindergarten, Aurora could never successfully lie to her best friend, so she didn't even try to deny her feelings. "Don't eat too much. You still have to squeeze into a dress tomorrow." At least they'd both feel sick the next day, for different reasons.

Leah picked up a pillow and threw it at her as she ordered chicken fingers, fries and a burger.

While her friend ordered, Aurora took the opportunity to stare out the large bridal suite window at the breathtaking view of the mountains all around them. She loved her hometown of Wild River, nestled between the Chugach Mountains and Denali National Park. The ski resort town was the best combination of excitement during tourist seasons and quiet tranquility in the off-seasons. With its picturesque Main Street and outback experiences for all levels of adventure seekers, it really was the best place to live or visit. She hadn't loved the idea of going away for university. She would have been happy to attend the university in Anchorage, a short one-hour train ride away, but her parents had insisted that she should not waste a full scholarship or her amazing brain by turning down the opportunity to study at one of the best engineering schools in the world. She'd worked hard to ensure she could go anywhere she wanted.

And her parents were right.

Letting a guy stand between her and her future goals would have been a dumb idea. Especially when that guy was Tyler. He was a Forrester after all, and while it was unfair to judge the kids by their parents, it wasn't rocket science figuring out where Tyler's fear of commitment and anti-marriage opinions came from.

She'd have expected Rick to have the same affliction.

It took all her energy not to confess her fears to Leah. The last thing she wanted was for her best friend to be heartbroken ex-wife number one if Rick turned out to have the same wandering eye as his father.

Unfortunately, her friend was head over heels in love, even if this elaborate wedding wasn't exactly what she wanted.

Aurora just had to be supportive and then pick up the pieces of her friend's heart if and when it all fell apart the way she predicted it would.

"This resort is too much, isn't it?" Leah asked, hanging up the phone and joining Aurora at the window.

Aurora could hear the apprehension and nerves in her friend's voice. Despite her efforts to hide it all evening, Leah was second-guessing her wedding choices. "No. It's wonderful. The wedding will be absolutely gorgeous." In twenty hours, Leah was planning to walk down the aisle. Now was not the time to freak her out about the fact that she was marrying into a family that struggled with commitment.

"You are a terrible liar," Leah said.

"Okay, well, maybe it's not exactly the wedding I'd ever thought you'd have," Aurora said carefully. A spooked bride was not what she needed that evening, but she wanted to be as honest as possible.

"You're my best friend. You know this was the complete opposite of my idea of the perfect wedding."

"So why did you agree to all of this?"

"That's such a complicated question..." The bride-to-be looked at her hands.

"Yet, the answer is simple, isn't it?"

Leah sighed, collapsing into the chair near the window. "The truth is, a part of me believes that if we go through all of this, all of this effort, Rick will be happier and the marriage will last."

Aurora secretly thought it would take more than a fancy, overpriced party for Rick to stay loyal to his vows, but she kept that level of honesty to herself.

If there was ever a time to be convincing, it was now.

She sat on the edge of the ottoman in front of her friend's chair and took Leah's hands in hers. "Hey, listen to me. Rick will be happy and this marriage will last," she said.

Leah studied her. "I really want to hear you right now, but your face speaks so loudly."

Damn. Would she ever learn how to hide her real thoughts and emotions? "What does it say?"

"That I'm making a mistake. That I'm going to end up heartbroken like…" Leah's lips pressed together.

"Like me?"

"I wasn't going to say that."

Aurora forced a smile. "Yeah, well, your face is pretty loud too." She took a deep breath. "Look, Rick is not Tyler, or his father, or his mother. Everything will be fine."

"Will it?"

Her friend was looking for honesty, and unfortunately, Aurora was torn between giving it to her or giving her the reassurance she needed.

Unfortunately, both answers weren't the same.

* * *

Bachelor party or just another Friday night—it was hard to tell inside The Drunk Tank, Wild River's most popular nighttime hot spot. It was low tourist season, being late March, so the bar was bustling with locals. Being a small town, everyone in the bar knew everyone else...and their business.

If one more person asked him how he was handling Aurora being home, Tyler was going to lose it. He was handling it the same way he always did—by not handling it at all. He just needed to get through the next twenty hours without doing something dumb like confess he still had feelings for her.

If the awkwardness earlier that day had been any indication, a confession of feelings would not be well received.

Tyler lined up a shot at the pool table, going for the win with a clear image of the eight ball rolling right into the corner pocket, but unfortunately, a memory of Aurora's cold shoulder that evening at the rehearsal dinner threw him off as he struck the cue ball. It went sailing in the opposite direction and straight into a side pocket.

Rick and Wade—the opposing team—high-fived and Tyler's father, Mitch, looked at him in disbelief. "What just happened?"

Tyler shrugged. "I don't know. Off night, I guess."

His father sent him a knowing look. "Awww, that's right. Aurora's in town. I thought I'd felt the earth shift off balance around you."

"I don't know what you're talking about." Only he

knew exactly what his father meant. When she was away, his feelings weren't out of sight, out of mind, but it was definitely easier to leave the past in the past. Whenever she was back in Wild River, it was impossible not to think about all the what-ifs. What if he hadn't ended things? What if they'd at least tried to make the long-distance thing work? What if he'd gone with her?

"Have you spoken to her yet?"

"We spoke at the rehearsal dinner. You were there," Tyler said.

"All I saw was two people trying desperately to ignore one another, but sneaking glances whenever the other wasn't looking," Mitch said, taking a swig of his beer.

Tyler shrugged, hanging up his pool stick on the wall. "We really don't have much to say." That was a lie. They had so much to say. At least he did, but he got the impression that she didn't want to hear it.

"You could tell her you still have feelings for her," Mitch said, emptying the pockets and racking the balls.

"I don't know what you're talking about." He didn't need or want relationship advice from the man who would have three of his ex-wives at the wedding the next day. His mother and two of his former stepmothers all wanted to be there to support Rick. How his father wasn't sweating this event more, Tyler didn't know. Spending the day with his one and only ex had Tyler hoping for a search and rescue call to avoid the event.

"Oh come on, you haven't been serious about a woman in years...since Aurora," Mitch said.

"Maybe I'm not the settling down type." Keeping the hint of bitterness from his voice was a challenge. He loved his father. Despite his inability to stay in a marriage, Mitch had been a good father. But Tyler couldn't help but blame him a little for his own hesitation regarding relationships and love and commitment.

Mitch shrugged. "Okay. That I can understand."

Tyler reached for his beer.

Empty. Wonderful. Probably for the best though. The next day was going to be challenge enough without being hungover.

Hours later, after they shut down the bar for the evening, Tyler and Rick walked along Main Street back to the hotel. "So, last twelve hours of freedom," he said to his brother.

Rick laughed. "I'm so ready to be chained up."

Tyler shot a look at him. He really didn't seem nervous about the wedding at all. "Really?"

"One hundred percent."

"But the two of you haven't been dating that long." It was less than a year. That was fast.

"But we've known one another for years."

"And yet you two only got together last year... Doesn't that worry you?"

"Nope. We were both in other relationships. The timing was never right before," Rick said, zipping his coat higher as a cold breeze blew past.

Timing. Tyler understood that, but he needed to

ask. "How are you so sure Leah is the one?" Maybe it was the alcohol or the emotions swirling around inside of him for the last twenty-four hours, but he had to know how his brother could be so sure about this. They'd both been raised in the same house, with the same parents and stepparents. They'd both attended all of the weddings, then felt the pain of the divorces. So, how could his brother have such a different outlook on relationships?

Rick stopped as they reached the front lobby doors of the hotel. "Because I love her, man."

Right... "But is that enough?" He'd loved Aurora for as long as he could remember, but he was hesitant to believe that things could last forever.

"No. A marriage also takes mutual respect and honesty and compromise..."

"And you can do all those things?"

Rick nodded. "Yeah, bro. I can, and so could you, because neither of us are Dad."

Tyler breathed in the cool mountain air as he processed his brother's words. He was right. They weren't their father, but until Tyler could be sure he hadn't inherited Mitch's happy-for-now approach to relationships, how could he take another chance with the woman he loved?

Three

That couldn't be the right time.

Aurora sat straight up in her king-size bed in the resort hotel room and reached for her cell phone. Nine eighteen. She'd overslept.

Or rather, after four hours of tossing and turning, she'd finally fallen asleep just after 4:00 a.m. The makeup artist would have her work cut out for her that day.

She jumped out of bed, threw on a pair of yoga pants and a tank top, and grabbed her maid of honor dress and shoes from the closet. Then she left her room and hurried down the hall toward the bridal suite.

She raised her hand to knock on the door, just as it swung open and Leah's mother, Candace, stood there looking frantic. "Oh thank God, Aurora—where's Leah? Is she with you?"

Her stomach plummeted. "No. I left her here around midnight," she said. "What's going on?"

Inside the room, Tyler's mother paced, her cell phone to her ear. Three bridesmaids—hair in curlers, makeup already done—were chatting amongst themselves.

Leah's wedding dress was gone, off the hanger where it had been the night before, but she couldn't see the bride in the room.

"She's not here," Candace said, moving aside to allow Aurora to enter. "How was she when you left her last night?"

Aurora bit her lip. Leah had been fine. It was Aurora who'd been on edge about the wedding that day. Oh no... Had Leah sensed her unease? Had it caused her to have her own doubts? "She was okay, I think. Has anyone been able to reach her?"

"No," Candace said, redialing Leah's number on her phone.

Tyler's mother disconnected her call and turned to Aurora. "Hi, darling... Nice to see you," she said, but the concern on her face couldn't mask the slight look of suspicion.

Since the breakup, Aurora hadn't really spoken much to the other members of the Forrester family. It still felt slightly weird to be around them, especially under the circumstances.

Damn, had she expressed her unease about that to Leah the night before? Had her tension with Tyler given Leah second thoughts somehow?

She had to find her and talk to her.

"I'll be back," she said, leaving the room and heading down the hall toward the room where the men were getting ready. She took a deep breath before knocking.

Tyler answered, and it was hard to concentrate on the reason she was there as she took in his disheveled hair and sleepy-looking expression. She loved the way he looked in the morning: slightly grumpy until he had his coffee. Wearing only his tuxedo pants, his sculpted chest and abs and shoulders had her momentarily distracted.

But when her gaze returned to his face, he looked as exhausted and stressed as she felt.

Well, it was about to get worse.

"Hey…" he said. "What are you doing here?"

"Have any of you seen Leah this morning? Or last night?" Maybe the bride had broken the rule about staying away from the groom. Maybe Rick was gone too. Maybe they'd eloped and gone ahead with the wedding they really wanted.

But, unfortunately, Tyler's panicked expression was all the answer she needed. "Isn't she getting ready?"

From behind him, Aurora could see the other groomsmen and Rick getting dressed. She grabbed Tyler's arm and dragged him out into the hall. "We can't find her."

"What do you mean? Wasn't she with you last night?"

"Yes. We went to the spa with the other bridesmaids and then had a few drinks in the lobby bar. Then I left her safely in her room. But she's not there now. No one's heard from her. Her mother's in a panic," she said. Aurora was close to an anxiety attack as well. If she was somehow responsible for ruining her best friend's wedding day, she'd never be able to live with herself. What had she said the night before? Why hadn't she tried harder to be more supportive and encouraging of this wedding?

"Where could she have gone?" Tyler asked.

"I don't know."

"Well, did she say anything last night about having cold feet? Doubts?"

She hesitated.

He placed his hands on his hips. "What did you say to her?"

Annoyance rose in her chest. "Me? Why do you naturally assume this is my fault somehow?"

"Because you were the last one to see her, and I know your opinion of me and my family isn't exactly the best."

"And that's my fault?"

Tyler sighed, running a hand through his hair. Messy, spiky hair that, despite her irritation, tempted her to reach up and run her own hands through it. "Look, arguing isn't going to help. What are we going to do?" As maid of honor and best man, making sure there was a bride at the wedding ceremony definitely fell into the category of their responsibilities.

"Well obviously we need to find her," he said over a yawn.

She cocked her head to the side and gave him an exasperated look. "You think?"

"What's going on?" Rick asked, appearing in the doorway behind Tyler.

Tyler's panicked expression was a mirror image of her own. "Um…nothing."

Rick looked back and forth between them and zeroed in on her. "Aurora, do you want to try lying to me?"

She sighed. The problem with having known the Forrester family for most of her life was that everyone could tell when she was trying to bend the truth. "We can't find Leah," she said, reluctantly.

"But we're going to find her," Tyler said, reassuringly. "Just keep getting ready and—"

Rick wasn't listening. He went back inside the room, grabbed his keys, wallet and coat and appeared in the hall. "I know where she is."

He did?

"Well, tell us and we'll go get her," Tyler said.

"Yeah, Rick," Aurora said. "Tyler and I can totally handle it." She glanced at him as she said it. As long as he put a shirt on…

Rick shook his head. "I appreciate the offer, but if anyone's getting my fiancée back, it's me."

"Well at least tell us where *you're* going," Tyler called after him down the hall.

"Snowcrest Peak," Rick said, disappearing inside the elevator.

This freak snowstorm had come out of nowhere. The weather forecast for that weekend had been sunny and mild. The blizzard suddenly hitting Wild River wasn't ideal.

The unpredictable terrain on the trails leading to the top of Snowcrest Peak, combined with the low visibility of the bride in this winter wonderland had resulted in Rick needing their help after all and calling in assistance from several other members of the Wild River Search and Rescue team as well.

It didn't escape Tyler that he'd been secretly hoping a mission would call him away from the wedding. But he hadn't meant a search for the bride.

"Let's split up and take both trails—the north and south—up to the peak. She could be trying to make her way back down on either one." Reed, his friend and the head of the crew, directed the group as they met at the base of the mountain.

Tyler nodded. "Four with Reed, four with me." His gaze settled on Aurora. Would she pick his team? Or would she want to avoid spending time with him and pick Reed's? What did he want her to do? Having her with him could be a distraction, but he'd worry about her if she went with the others. She'd always been a volunteer member, but being away, she hadn't gone on many missions. She hadn't trained in a while... "Tank, Riley and Aurora—you three are with me," he said, making the decision for her.

She opened her mouth to protest maybe, but Reed quickly nodded and gathered his own team together.

"Guess I don't have a choice," Aurora said through clenched teeth as he huddled his team together for a quick debrief on strategy. Not that there was much of one.

"Okay here's the plan. We hike along the south trail. Look for anything white," he said.

Aurora scoffed. "It's snowing. Seeing Leah's dress will be nearly impossible. Look for her long dark hair and her red high-top runners," she told the others.

Tyler nodded begrudgingly. "Yes. Right. Look for her hair and runners. Let's go."

As they trudged along the deep snow quickly accumulating on the trail, Tyler fell into step next to her. He cleared his throat. Then cleared his throat again.

"Something you want to say?" Aurora asked.

"Yes… I apologize for blaming you for Leah running off."

She glanced at him, her expression slightly sheepish. "You may not have been completely wrong."

He knew it. Wow. Did she really have that low of an opinion of him that she'd warn Leah against marrying his brother? He wanted to be irritated, but he couldn't deny the part he played in her assessment. Or his family's history of breaking their share of hearts. "So…graduation is in three months?" he asked instead.

"Mmm-hmm," she said, reaching into her pocket and pulling out a hat. She tugged it on over her dark hair.

"Any thoughts on what you plan to do afterward, jobwise?" She'd completed her bachelor's degree in three years and had opted into the three-year master's from the university. She'd have no trouble finding work.

"I have a few offers from different companies already," she said, sounding almost embarrassed about it.

Of course she had offers. She was as brilliant as she was beautiful. "That's incredible, Aurora. Where are they?" Did that sound casual? He'd meant it to sound casual, but it was difficult to sound nonchalant when she could be planning on taking a job thousands of miles away.

"One is in California." She paused. "And one is in Fairbanks."

He nearly tripped over a fallen branch on the snow-covered trail. Fairbanks. His heart soared. Not Wild River, but closer. Like a quick two-hour drive every day to see her closer. Like someplace he might find a firefighting position closer. He cleared his throat. "Well, obviously the California one would be better, right?" He was testing her. Did she want the job in California? Did she enjoy her life there? Did she plan to make a life in the sunny, beachside city?

But his intentions backfired as she shook her head and her expression darkened with a look of hurt. "Unbelievable. Even Fairbanks is too close for you."

He stopped walking.

She continued on.

He reached out for her arm as she moved several feet ahead. "Wait. That's what you think? That I don't want you here?"

She folded her arms across her chest as she turned around to face him. "Yes."

"Well, that's not true."

"Isn't it? You certainly seemed eager to get me out of Wild River six years ago."

Wow, she really had things wrong. "I didn't want you to leave," he said quietly. Riley and Tank had stopped farther ahead on the trail and turned back to see why they'd stopped. Tyler waved them on ahead.

Aurora was staring at him in disbelief. "You broke up with me three weeks after I graduated high school and practically bought my plane ticket to California yourself."

"Because I knew you wanted to go…" He'd been trying to be supportive. He'd been trying not to be selfish and ask her to stay when he knew what she really wanted.

"I had other options. I could have gone to university in Anchorage," she said.

"But the one in California had the better program. You'd gone on about it for a year, and then when you qualified for the scholarship and your application was approved, it seemed like the choice was made." He hadn't felt like he'd had a say in it. Not that he should have. They were high school sweethearts and everyone knew those relationships rarely lasted. Whether Aurora went to university in Anchorage or California, he hadn't been certain of a future with her. She was going out on her own for the first time. Leaving their small town and moving to a bigger city. She would be meeting other like-minded people who shared her passion and intellect.

Smart guys. Smarter than him. More interesting than him.

So, if there was a chance of losing her anyway, he hadn't wanted her to stay in Alaska and wish she'd accepted the other school's offer once their relationship naturally dissolved.

"I would have stayed if you'd wanted me to." The pain in her voice held layers of regret.

He knew what those layers felt like. How many times had he rethought his actions over the years? How many times had he wanted to reach out to her and try to undo them? "Exactly. You would have stayed and then resented me for it in time."

Her eyes widened, and big, fluffy snowflakes gathered on her eyelashes. "Resented you?"

He nodded. "For holding you back." Unfortunately, now she resented him for letting her go.

Seemed there was no right thing when it came to loving Aurora.

She shook her head. "Don't you think I should have at least had a say in that? You could have told me how you really felt and we could have discussed things. Figured them out together. Instead you just threw our relationship away as though it didn't matter to you anymore."

It killed him that she actually believed that. "It did matter." It still mattered. She still mattered... If only he could tell her that. He ran a hand through his wet, snow-covered hair, frustration getting the better of his emotions. "Damn, I'm so tired of doing the wrong thing, thinking it's the right thing."

"Well stop thinking then!" Her fiery expression

and lack of patience with him simmered on the air, hot enough to melt the frozen ground beneath them.

He stepped forward and wrapped one arm around her waist, pulling her in tight and close to his body.

She willingly moved even closer, wrapping her arms around his neck.

His gaze burned into hers, searching, waiting for any sign that she wanted him to stop, but her eyes closed and she leaned her head a little to the left, the way she always had in anticipation of his kiss.

He swallowed hard, his heart pounding in his chest so hard she had to feel it through the thick layers of their clothing. "Aurora…" he whispered against her mouth. Last chance for her to stop this before waves of repressed emotions would be impossible to keep away anymore. Once he kissed her, he was afraid there would be no going back to pretending he could live without her.

"Stop thinking. Stop talking," she whispered back.

He could do that. He lowered his head and cupped the back of her neck as his lips grazed hers. Slowly, cautiously… Terrified of what this kiss could mean. What it meant to him. How many times over the years had he thought about kissing her again? Now she was here in his arms. His mouth met hers and her sigh had him abandoning all hesitation as he deepened the kiss, savoring the familiar taste of her.

She clutched the front of his jacket as her body fell into his. She returned the kiss with all the same passion and longing he'd been holding back for so long.

Six years of missing her, loving her, regretting

letting go of her came out in his kiss, and when she reluctantly pulled away a moment later and her gaze met his again, the questioning he saw in it mirrored his own conflicted thoughts.

What now? He had no idea, so he remained silent.

What had the kiss meant for her? Where did they go from here?

If she expected him to speak first, they'd be standing there in silence until Christmas. He had no answers and she'd just told him he needed to stop thinking and stop talking.

Unfortunately, his silence *now* apparently wasn't what she wanted. Her disappointed expression only deepened as the seconds ticked by. Women were a mystery he'd never understand—Aurora in particular.

And before he could figure out what to do or say, she backed away and cleared her throat. "We should keep moving." She turned quickly on her heel and started hiking up the trail.

Tyler stood there staring after her. The moment was over and, once again, he'd messed things up.

Aurora unzipped her search and rescue jacket as she jogged along the trail to catch up with Riley and Tank. She needed distance and more people between her and Tyler before she either fell back into his arms and kissed him again or pummeled him with snowballs until he woke up and found the right words for once.

Aurora, I still love you.

Five simple words that he just couldn't string together, despite the kiss, despite her obvious feelings for him.

Sure, she hadn't told him that she still loved him either, but he'd been the one to end things, so he should know that she still had feelings for him.

She sighed.

Would they ever get this right? She was only in Wild River for another twenty-four hours... Didn't seem like enough time to sort anything out when six years hadn't been enough.

And right now, she needed to put aside her own troubled heart and find her best friend.

The feeling of Tyler's eyes on her back as they continued up the trail toward the peak made the climb that much harder and longer. What was he thinking? Did he regret the kiss? Did she? No. But it definitely slid her backward a few notches from any progress she'd made trying to heal her heart, from trying to move on and forget him.

"I see red," Riley said, pointing toward the peak as it came into view.

Oh thank God. She was there, in her wedding dress and red running shoes. Aurora's heart swelled at the sight. She knew this feeling of conflicted emotions, and her friend had an even bigger decision to make than Aurora did.

"Let me talk to her alone, okay?" she said to the group.

Tyler nodded, leading the rest of the team away to radio Reed and let them know they found Leah and she was safe.

Aurora walked toward her friend, the snow crunching beneath her boots. "Hey...you look a little overdressed for hiking," she said.

Leah turned, looking panicked and scared. Aurora wasn't sure it was completely because she'd gotten stuck out here in this unexpected weather either. "I can't do it," she said, pacing, rubbing her bare arms. "I thought I could. But I can't. I don't know if I can trust Rick to be my forever."

"Of course you—"

Leah wasn't listening. She was obviously talking to herself. Almost unaware that Aurora was even there. "I mean, he says he's committed, but they all say that in the beginning, right? And we haven't been together long. Most couples date for years before they get married. They live together first..."

"When you know, you know," Aurora said, feeling the truth of it more than ever before. All these years, despite his rejection, her heart had belonged to Tyler. She'd known. The kiss had only confirmed that it was possible to know, when you know. Leah knew it too; she just needed to be reminded.

The bride-to-be stopped pacing and turned to look at her. "Aurora, what if it's a mistake?"

Normally she'd say, if it was a mistake, then together they'd fix it. Like they always did. But in this case, she knew in her heart that it wasn't. She'd been wrong about Rick... And Tyler. Wrong to assume that just because their parents hadn't been able to find "the one" that neither of them would or could either.

Aurora moved closer to her friend and, removing

her search and rescue jacket, she wrapped it around Leah's bare shoulders. Then wrapping her arms around her friend's waist, she said, "Leah, listen to me. This is the right thing. Marrying Rick is the right thing. You love him and he loves you."

"I don't know..." Leah bit her lower lip, looking torn.

"Shhh... I do know."

Leah frowned. "But last night you were worried too."

"But I shouldn't have been. Rick knew exactly where to find you," she said, tucking a strand of Leah's wild, snow-covered, dark hair behind her ear. "When he found out you were gone, he was desperate to get your butt back to that wedding today. He's out here looking for you. Does that sound like a man who might eventually change his mind...change his heart?"

Leah looked emotional, tears in her eyes as she swallowed hard. "Really? Do you really believe Rick and I are forever?"

"Absolutely," she said honestly. "And more importantly, so do you."

Voices behind them made her turn. Rick came hurrying up the trail toward them. Leah looked remorseful as she turned toward Aurora. "He's not supposed to see me in my dress before the wedding."

"I'm pretty sure the bride running away is the worst thing that will happen today. I think you're safe," she said with a gentle laugh.

Leah nodded, wiping the tears from her cheeks. "You're probably right. So, what do I do?"

Aurora smiled at her best friend. "Follow your heart," she whispered before moving away to let the groom take over.

Unfortunately, her gaze met Tyler's as she rejoined the others, and her own advice had never sounded so loud, echoing in her ears.

Four

Standing at the front of the room a few hours later, staring across at Aurora, the tug in Tyler's chest was stronger than ever before. He'd always thought they would be standing together at the top of the aisle someday. But he'd told himself that teen romances weren't forever romances. He'd told himself he wasn't good enough for her. He'd told himself a lot of things to try to ease the pain of heartache over the years.

He realized now none of it was true and no matter how many lies he told himself, nothing would stop the feelings he had for her—he didn't want them to stop. It was liberating to finally stop holding himself back from what he wanted.

But now he had to try to convince Aurora that his feelings were just as real and strong as they'd ever been. He couldn't lose her again, and he refused to be the one to push her away this time.

The impulsive kiss they'd shared on the mountain wasn't just fueled by their passionate argument or intense adrenaline. It was long overdue, and he wanted her to know he'd meant every emotion he'd poured into it.

Her gaze met his, and despite the lovely decorations and the hundreds of people in the room, all he could see was her. Beautiful, dressed in her lilac-colored, floor-length gown, her hair piled high on top of her head with loose curls spiraling down to graze her exposed shoulders, the look of happiness and support on her face as her best friend married his brother. Tyler could barely breathe.

He couldn't keep hiding behind the mistakes of the past. If he wanted to be with Aurora, he needed to tell her. Let her decide if her feelings for him were worth making her own sacrifices.

As the officiant pronounced the couple husband and wife, Aurora smiled at Tyler, and in that moment, he knew he'd give up anything she asked him to in order to be with her.

The bride and groom's first dance was quickly coming to an end. Too quickly.

Aurora's mouth was dry and her palms were sweating like crazy. The wedding party dance was next and that meant, for three and a half minutes, she'd be back in Tyler's arms.

Just breathe. In and out.

Nope. There was no air in this ballroom.

After the rescue mission to find the bride, the day had zoomed by, and they hadn't really had any time to talk about the kiss or what it meant… Or if it might happen again. Standing across from one an-other at the ceremony had been the first time Aurora had really had a chance to look at him. And damn, if the sight of him in the tuxedo—his hair gelled back, the stubborn stubble on his chin the perfect length—hadn't had her heart racing and her mind reeling.

And the way he hadn't taken his eyes off her hadn't helped.

She'd felt the connection between them just as strong and real as ever. As though the six years apart had never happened.

She swallowed hard as the song ended, applause for the couple erupted and the next song started to play. Aurora could barely hear the slow, familiar rhythm of a popular love song over the pounding of her heart.

Tyler was walking straight for her.

Should she run away or dive straight into his open arms?

He stopped in front of her, and she forced what she hoped was a nonterrified expression as she ac-cepted his outstretched hand and they joined the oth-ers on the dance floor.

Leah sent her a wink, and Rick's grin said *there's no avoiding each other now.*

Tyler spun her into his arms and held her close as they started to sway to the music. The smell of his cologne and the feel of his stubble against her cheek had so many memories of being held like this com-ing back, making it difficult to steady her thunder-ing pulse. One of her hands on his back, the other wrapped tightly in his, Aurora looked everywhere but directly into his gaze. Tyler would know the truth if she let him catch her eye, and until she knew where his heart was, she was determined to guard her own.

Or try at least.

She cleared her throat. "This is weird, right…everyone watching us dance?"

Tyler leaned closer to her ear. "All I see is you."

He was getting better with words. Definitely making it harder for her not to give in to the feelings threatening to overwhelm her. This whole environment was conducive to thoughts of love, forever and happily ever after; with the heartwarming vows, the elegant decor and the blissful bride and groom, she needed to keep her head on straight.

"The ceremony was nice," she said.

"It was. And in case I didn't mention it earlier— you look beautiful," Tyler said, the attraction in his eyes pulling her in.

All afternoon she'd thought of little else besides the kiss on the mountain and now, standing there in his arms, she longed to taste his lips again, feel his mouth against hers. "Thank you," she said, her voice wavering slightly. "So do you."

"When do you fly back to California?" he asked, suddenly sounding slightly anxious.

She knew the feeling. "Tomorrow morning." She'd booked the whirlwind trip on purpose, knowing being there with him those few days would be tough. Now, leaving so soon didn't appeal to her.

Obviously, it didn't appeal to Tyler either as his

smile faded a little and his grip on her tightened. "Want to get out of here?"

She did. Desperately. But they were part of the wedding party. "Won't we be missed?"

Tyler nodded toward Leah and Rick, so wrapped up in one another in the middle of the dance floor, they were completely oblivious that there were two hundred people staring at them. Aurora laughed. "Okay, so, probably not." Still, they couldn't just bail, could they?

"Come on, what do you say? My shotgun seat is waiting."

She swallowed hard at the familiar words. The same ones he'd used years before to ask her out on their first date.

"It has always belonged to you," he said as he tucked a strand of her hair behind her ear. Another too-familiar gesture that had her entire body tingling. She wanted to be alone with him, but she was leaving the next day. Her heart was already back in the palm of his hand, and just the memory of the kiss on the mountain had her mentally stocking up on Ben & Jerry's ice cream back home in California.

"I don't know, Tyler. I mean, all of this…is magical, but tomorrow morning it will be over, and things won't be any less complicated," she said.

He nodded slowly. "You're probably right…"

Her heart fell.

"But…"

Oh thank God there was a but.

"If tonight is all we have, I'd prefer not to waste it worrying about tomorrow and what happens next."

She stared at him, barely breathing, torn. But then she nodded quickly. "Okay, let's get out of here."

Her heart was already a mess—how much worse could it get?

Five

He knew exactly where to go.

Fifteen minutes later, Tyler parked his truck in the empty lot at the base of Snowcrest Peak and cut the engine.

"If you've brought me here to make out, you're going to be disappointed. That kiss on the mountain was a onetime thing," Aurora said with a shaky laugh.

He grinned as he reached into the back seat for a sleeping bag. "That's not why we're here." Though he hoped she was wrong about that kiss being the last one he'd get before she left to go back to California. "Come on," he said, opening the truck door and climbing out.

At the back of the truck, he lowered the tailgate and unzipped the sleeping bag, spreading it out. Then he climbed up and extended a hand to her.

She smiled as she took it, but he could feel her tremble, sense her nervousness. She had nothing to worry about. The day had made everything so much clearer for him. He knew what he wanted and refused to let his own fear stop him from going after it.

He lay on the sleeping bag and opened his arms to her.

She only hesitated a fraction of a second before lying next to him and cuddling close, resting her head on his chest. "Do you think we'll see them?" she asked.

"It's the perfect conditions for it. Overcast, just below zero... I saw them two nights ago," he said, pulling the edges of the sleeping bag around them.

He stared up at the sky, willing the northern lights to appear.

"I've definitely missed seeing them," Aurora said, shivering.

He held her tighter. "Every time I've seen them over the years, I've thought of you. Wished you were here with me," he said, his voice slightly hoarse with emotion. All this time trying to fight his feelings or push down the emotions whenever they resurfaced hadn't worked at all. He still loved her. He always would love her.

"Why didn't you ever...?"

"Reach out and tell you?"

"Yeah."

"Too afraid, I guess," he said.

"And you're not afraid now?"

"Absolutely terrified," he said, kissing the top of her head.

They lay in silence for a long time until the first flashes of green-yellow light danced across the sky.

Purple, red, blue—the lights lit up the cloudy night, and Tyler could feel the effect deep in his heart. This felt right. It was the only thing that did. Without her in his life, it had felt like a part of him was missing. She was here now and he didn't want to let her go.

"So beautiful," Aurora whispered.

Propping himself up on his elbow, Tyler stared down into the face of the woman he loved. "You're beautiful," he said, lowering his head toward hers. He paused a fraction of an inch away from her lips, waiting.

Aurora lifted her head, bringing her lips the rest of the way and kissing him with all the passion and love he'd never realized he'd needed so badly.

A long time later, once the lights disappeared from the sky, he reluctantly stood and helped her to her feet. "Guess we better call it a night."

She nodded, looking as disappointed to end the night as he was.

"Can I drive you to the train station tomorrow morning?" He hated to let her go at all, but maybe they could spend a few more minutes together.

She looked down and shook her head. "I don't think that's a great idea. Tonight was…perfect."

"Right, so—"

She silenced him with a quick kiss. "Tomorrow you might feel differently, and I'm not sure I can say goodbye to you, so let's just have tonight. In our memory and in our hearts."

What was she saying? That she thought he was just having a good time right now? That these emotions threatening to drown him were just the magic of the last twenty-four hours? The wedding, the lights, the kiss? "Aurora, I…"

"Please, Tyler. Just kiss me again and let me have tonight."

He hesitated, swallowing hard. He desperately wanted to explain to her that he wanted this, him and her, forever. Whatever that meant. Whatever that looked like.

But he understood that her heart was conflicted, slow to trust, and she deserved to have that night, so he kissed her and hoped she could feel everything she wouldn't let him say.

Leaving Wild River never got easier. And this time was probably the hardest of all. The night before with Tyler had been a dream, but maybe it really was just a dream—the two of them together, able to make things work, both on the same page at the same time.

Aurora rested her head against the seat of Leah's car and watched the scenery fly by. Main Street, the mountains, the sights of home—where her heart belonged. She knew she wanted to come back to Alaska after graduation. And that decision hadn't been based on Tyler—at least not completely.

"You should have let him bring you to the train station," Leah said. "And not just because I'd rather be curled up in bed with my husband right now."

Aurora sighed. "Sorry to drag you away, but I couldn't do it. Last night was…"

"Everything you've ever wanted? Everything you'd been missing for the last six years? Everything you're terrified to let yourself have?"

She swallowed hard, unable to answer. She had to leave the night before in the past with all the other memories of her and Tyler. Despite what he'd said, she knew not to expect anything from him, or herself. What they'd had clearly wasn't over, but she was reluctant to trust that they could keep it going either.

"We've had years to try again and we never did before now. If it was meant to be, wouldn't we have tried sooner?" she asked.

"Maybe…but maybe not. You're three months away from graduation, so maybe Tyler's finally feeling like there's no risk of you giving up on your dreams like there was before."

Aurora hated that everyone assumed that she would have thrown it all away years ago for Tyler, but maybe they were all right to have been nervous. She'd loved him enough back then… She still did.

Leah pulled in front of the train station, and Aurora's heart stopped, seeing Tyler's truck parked in the drop-off lane. He was sitting on the lowered tailgate. Jeans, hoodie, baseball hat and hiking boots, he looked like the boy she'd fallen for years before… And all over again the night before. "Oh God, what's he doing here?" Was the air suddenly thinner in this hemisphere?

Leah smiled. "He wanted to say goodbye, I guess," she said.

Aurora turned to look at her best friend. "You knew."

She shrugged. "Maybe…"

"Leah! I specifically said I didn't want to see him. Saying goodbye to him will be torture," she said.

"Look, you're miserable without him anyway, right?"

She nodded. No sense lying about it.

"Well then, what's the harm in taking a chance? Trying to make this work? Here, or in California, or long-distance, or whatever way the universe allows…it can't be any worse than living without him at all, right?"

Aurora wanted to believe that her best friend was right, but what if it *could* get worse? What if the pain of his rejection years before was even harder to recover from this time, if he decided he didn't want this again once she was gone? What if time and distance put a wedge between them? "I don't know," she said honestly.

"Either way, you have to get out of my car because my husband is waiting."

Aurora slapped her friend playfully and couldn't help but smile, despite her own tumultuous heart. She was happy for her friend—so obviously in love and looking forward to her future with the man of her dreams.

Would Aurora have that someday?

Her gaze drifted out the windshield toward Tyler. With him?

"Seriously, Aurora, get out."

She huffed in mock annoyance as she climbed out of Leah's car and Tyler met her at the passenger's side door. He took her bag from her. "Hey…"

"Hi."

"Love you! Bye!" Leah yelled before reaching across to shut the door and speed away.

Leaving her abandoned with Tyler.

The cool breeze did nothing to stop her sweating beneath her bulky winter coat. A nervous energy made her want to escape. Fast. If she could hop on the train and drive it away herself right now, she would. "I…uh…thought we agreed that we said goodbye last night," she said to Tyler.

She was so happy he was there. But also very terrified. Was he there to say he'd already had a change of heart? That he didn't want to let her go only to disappoint her by ghosting her? Letting her down face-to-face again was less cruel. But only slightly.

"I know," he said. "And I wasn't going to come… But I kinda got the feeling that you didn't quite believe me when I said I want to make this work this time."

So he'd read her correctly then. "I just don't want to put pressure on you…on us. If things work, then they work." Aurora tried to sound casual, nonchalant—even though she certainly didn't feel that way. She wanted things to work but would be devastated if they didn't.

Tyler took a step closer and set her bag on the train platform as he took her face between his hands. "This is going to work."

She swallowed hard. He sounded so sure. So confident. She desperately wanted to believe him. Believe in him. Believe in them. "Tyler…"

"I love you, Aurora. I always have and I refuse to let you leave this time feeling unsure. I'll be waiting here for you when you come back," he said, lowering his mouth to hers.

Her sigh was muffled by his kiss. Deep, long, passionate… Revealing all the emotions in his heart and hers. He'd said he loved her and she felt it in the connection between them in that moment.

He slowly pulled back as the train whistle blew. "I love you," he repeated.

She closed her eyes, savoring the moment, the sound of the words she could hear him say over and over again and never tire of. "I love you," she whispered.

She did love him, and she understood now why he'd let her go before… So that she could come back to him, and their love would be stronger than ever. And in three months, she would be back and they could finally take that second chance at forever.

* * * * *